Chris Frost grew up in Northern Ireland and now lives in the appropriately-named Marple. He is the author of ten crime books, including the Erika Piper trilogy and The Stonebridge Mysteries. He is a scriptwriter, and a regular voice on The Blood Brothers Podcast and Friends Of The North. He is a fan of football, heavy metal and dogs.

THE KILLER'S CHRISTMAS LIST

THE KILLER'S CHRISTMAS LIST

CHRIS FROST

Harper
North

HarperNorth
Windmill Green
24 Mount Street
Manchester M2 3NX

A division of
HarperCollins*Publishers*
1 London Bridge Street
London SE1 9GF

www.harpercollins.co.uk

HarperCollins*Publishers*
Macken House, 39/40 Mayor Street Upper
Dublin 1, D01 C9W8, Ireland

First published by HarperNorth in 2023

3 5 7 9 10 8 6 4 2

Copyright © HarperCollins*Publishers* Ltd

Chris Frost asserts the moral right to
be identified as the author of this work

A catalogue record for this book
is available from the British Library

PB ISBN: 978-0-00-861629-8

Printed and bound in Great Britain by
CPI Group (UK) Ltd, Croydon

MIX
Paper | Supporting
responsible forestry
FSC™ C007454

This book is produced from independently certified FSC™ paper
to ensure responsible forest management.

For more information visit: www.harpercollins.co.uk/green

For Sean Coleman,
for getting me to this point.

Memories are wild animals,
hard to tame and impossible to order,
They'll creep and they'll lurch,
they'll bite your ankles too,
Then they will turn on you
when you least expect them to.

Benjamin Amos, 'Foreigners'

Prologue

I HAD NEVER KILLED anyone before, but that was about to change.

I stepped out from my hiding place and walked towards the man in the chair. The warehouse was dark, aside from a thin shaft of moonlight spilling through a skylight, where the glass had shattered long ago. Snow tumbled in through the hole, the man positioned just under it. It might've looked like a scene from a music video, were it not for the blood oozing from a deep wound on the back of my captive's head.

The bound man looked up when he heard my echoing footsteps, but only saw me when I was close, judging by the way he flinched. Long black robes concealed my body, and a rubber Grinch mask obscured my face.

'Please—' the man started, but I cut off his words with a sudden shove, tipping the chair backwards onto the hard concrete floor. I was on him then, the weight of my body pinning him down, my hands tightening around his neck.

The man tried to fight back, but his hands and feet were secured tight. Still, he tried to buck his hips and pull away. I felt his pulse quicken beneath my fingertips as the realisation of what was happening spread through his body. He couldn't do anything to prevent his fate. He kept thrashing, though his movements became less frantic as he slipped out of consciousness. But I did not let go. I had researched strangulation, and knew it took a lot longer than it seemed. Unconsciousness was simply the body's self-preservation state; like playing dead.

Well, I had not come here to play.

With one hand still around the man's throat, I used the other to pull a knife from my robe. For a moment, I marvelled at the simplicity of it; at the damage this sharpened piece of metal could impart. And then, casting all thought aside, I thrust it into the man's stomach.

The skin gave way more easily than I was expecting, and I found my gloved hand immediately soaked in blood. I pulled the knife out and pushed it in a couple more times, adjusting the pressure.

An old joke sprang into my head:

'How do you get to Carnegie Hall?'

'Practice.'

* * *

Afterwards, once I'd lifted the body into the boot of the car and deposited my own blood-smeared clothes and mask into the river, I reflected on my experiment. If forced to choose between strangulation and stabbing, I'd favour the knife. In many ways, it was a statement: there is nothing ambiguous about a stab wound. I knew I should probably get rid of the weapon, but I was growing fond of it. I couldn't just toss it away like a piece of rubbish.

As I cruised down the winding, snow-lined A roads and onto the motorway, listening to The Ronettes sing about Mommy kissing Santa Claus, I couldn't help but feel elated. The first one had been easy, and I'd already started thinking about who would be next.

Of course, I didn't want to lose sight of my first victim – the first would always hold a special place in my heart. I'd picked him specially, as he would no doubt make headlines around the country. I allowed myself a little chuckle at the thought of the broken, punctured body in the boot; at the chain of events I had just started. My plan was now in motion.

The next week was going to be a lot of fun.

1

Tom Stonem sat back in his seat and stifled a moan.

The comedy club he was currently trapped in was standard fare. The room was small and the owners had managed to make it seem even smaller by squeezing in around twenty circular tables, only half of which were currently occupied. The walls were painted a deep crimson and covered in framed posters of comics who had graced the stage in their formative years as performers. Tom spotted some he recognised: Rob Beckett, Sarah Millican and a couple more whose names he couldn't remember. He had been to several comedy gigs before and loved them, but this one… Not so much.

There was something about up-and-coming comics that he found hard to stomach. Maybe it was the fact that most of them tried so hard to be edgy that they fell off the edge and onto his last nerve.

In tonight's case, the first comic's jokes sounded like they'd been lifted straight from *Mock the Week*, and the second was so young, Tom didn't understand her pop culture references. Which left him feeling old, bored and, frankly, up past his bedtime. The group of people he was here with, his girlfriend's friends, seemed to be loving every minute of it, though.

'You enjoying it?' Anna asked.

'Yep,' Tom lied. 'Loads.'

'Are you sure you don't want a drink?' she whispered, nodding at his glass of water.

'Better not. I want to be fresh for tomorrow.'

She nodded and turned back to the performance.

Tom had met Anna a month previously when he had travelled to Newcastle for a job interview. It had gone well and, keen to celebrate his promotion, he and a friend went out on the town. Tom was quite shy and wasn't much of a drinker. Never really had been. In one of the bars, he and Anna had locked eyes. Fuelled by this rare dalliance with alcohol, he'd made his way over, confidently told her he'd thrash her at a game of pool, and that had been that.

During the following month, Anna had come to Manchester to visit, and to help him pack before his move to the North East. He had been staying with her in Whitley Bay over the weekend, which was a nice arrangement, if a little intense. He liked his own space and, as none of his previous relationships had progressed to the point of co-habiting, he wasn't used to how all-consuming it could be. So, although he was grateful for her hospitality, he was looking forward to moving into his own place the next day. He figured that the thirty-minute drive between her house and his new place in Kibblesworth would be the perfect buffer for his foibles, moving forward.

A shrill wail from his phone interrupted his thoughts (and, regrettably, the performance). As he dug about for it in his jacket pocket, the small audience booed, and the third comedian of the evening rounded on him. 'Is that your mum calling to make sure the nasty comedians aren't picking on you?' he taunted in his thick Scouse accent.

'My mum's dead, pal,' Tom replied.

It was a retort straight from the playground, but it stopped the comedian in his tracks. While he tried to get back to his set, Tom worked his way through the humble crowd, squeezing through the narrow gaps afforded by the proximity of the tables. He pushed through the double doors at the back of the room and crossed the small foyer, where a couple of bored employees were playing cards at one of the tables near the bar. Through the glass doors, the snow was falling so fast he could barely see a couple of feet in front of him.

'Tom Stonem,' he answered when he was outside.

'Detective Inspector Stonem, this is DCI Freeman.'

His new boss. He wasn't due to start work for a few days yet. Was everything okay?

'Ma'am,' he said, adjusting his voice to sound deeper and more professional. A strange feeling was rising in his stomach. Was she calling to tell him there'd been a mix-up with his paperwork? That they'd hired the wrong person by accident, and had only realised it now?

What she said instead made him feel better, strangely.

'We need you to start early. Some poor bastard has been stabbed to death.'

2

WHEN TOM SNEAKED BACK inside (to more booing and another snarky comment from the stage) and told Anna why he had to go, she didn't seem annoyed. Instead, she seemed proud of him, rushing off into the night like a knight in shining armour. She kissed him quickly on the cheek, whispering that she'd be fine with her friends, and that she'd see him at home.

Still, he couldn't help thinking he was already letting her see behind the curtain. His contract technically hadn't even begun yet, and here he was, abandoning her and rushing off into the blackest of nights towards a corpse. He was thirty-three years old, and she was five years younger. Was this the kind of life she would want – him at the beck and call of the world's murderers and rapists?

Or was this his old self-sabotaging nature creeping in, sneaking in the excuses for the inescapable break-up? Anna was well aware of what she had signed up for. He had laid out the information for her as clearly as he could, about his working hours and the risks he'd inevitably have to take as a detective. She'd nodded and assured him that she could handle it.

Thoughts of Anna and any sort of relationship were pushed from his mind as he raced down the Durham Road. On a normal day, the Angel of the North looked somewhat demonic. Now, with the pulsing blue lights of a fleet of police cars and a solitary ambulance bouncing off its rusted skin, it looked positively other-worldly; like an alien overlord freshly arrived on Earth, surveying all that lay before it.

The car park was cordoned off by a fluttering length of blue and white police tape, so Tom put his hazards on and pulled into the side of the road. He put his window down to talk to the uniformed officer stationed at the entrance.

'ID?' he said to Tom.

'I don't technically start until later this week, so I don't have ID,' Tom said. 'But Natalie called me. My name is Tom Stonem.'

The officer looked dubious. 'I can't let you in without ID.'

'Call Natalie.'

The officer gave him one more disapproving look, and then turned his back. He pulled a walkie-talkie from his pocket and mumbled into it. A blast of noise answered him, the crackly voice barely discernible through the blight of static. Whatever was said seemed to make sense to him, for he turned back to Tom and nodded, before lifting the tape high enough for him to drive underneath. He parked in one of the last remaining spaces, grabbed his thick North Face coat from the back seat and got out. From the boot, he pulled out a pair of heavy walking boots and exchanged them for his Adidas trainers, which were already soaked through just from stepping outside.

Tom walked up the path from the carpark towards the monument. Though snow was still falling, here it had become a thin slush on the ground, due to the foot traffic that had been up and down in the past hour. At the end of the path was a white tent, and standing outside it was a tall man, probably in his mid-forties, wearing a white protective coverall suit. Snow had gathered on top of his hood, and he looked frozen out of his skin.

'Can I help you, sir?' he said as Tom approached. His accent showed him to be a displaced Cockney.

'I'm here for the murder,' Tom said.

'I'm afraid you're a bit late, my friend. It's already happened.'

Tom smiled. 'I'm the new DI.'

'You're the new detective inspector?' He smiled back at Tom. 'Well, it's nice to meet you, boss. I'm DC Barnes. Alan.' He extended a hand, which Tom took in his own.

'Tom. Nice to meet you, Alan. You look freezing. Want me to see if I can get someone to swap? Give you a go in the tent?'

'All good, boss,' he said, shaking his head. 'I'm a Buddhist. As the great man himself said: "Pain is inevitable. Suffering is optional".'

Tom could tell he was going to like DC Alan Barnes. Suffering was unavoidable in their line of work – the sleepless nights, the frustrations of a case – maybe some of Alan's positivity would rub off on him.

'How is it, in there?' he asked.

'Grisly,' Alan said, making a face. 'You can see for yourself, boss. Log book is inside, and some suits. Help yourself.'

'Thanks, Alan. But, do me a favour. Call me Tom, not boss.'

'I can't promise anything.' Alan chuckled. 'I've never had a boss who didn't want to be called *sir*. It might take time to break the habit.' He grabbed a tent flap and hoisted it high enough for Tom to sneak under. Another suited officer was inside, watching over the log book. Tom signed his name and his time of entry, and fought to pull one of the coveralls over his bulky coat. He snapped blue foot coverings over the soles of his shoes, pushed his hands into a thin pair of neoprene gloves, and left the tent.

Ahead of him, on the hill leading up to the monolithic monument, was another tent. This one was bigger, with high-powered forensic lights dotted around it. The dull fabric of the tent flashed brighter every couple of seconds, and Tom knew a crime scene photographer would be inside, recording every detail they could before the area was taken apart by the forensic team.

Illuminated by the camera flashes was a woman Tom had met when he came for his interview – DS Lauren Rea. His new partner. She was busy talking to one of the forensic team. Her eyes were lined with mascara and her lips were painted a shocking red. Tom wondered if she had been out on the town, too, before receiving her own call from the DCI. She noticed him, and raised a hand in acknowledgement.

'Tom,' she said, and walked over to greet him. 'Aren't you supposed to be starting later this week?'

'Yeah, but it seems that crime waits for no man.' He motioned to the forensic tent. 'Have you been inside?'

'Not yet,' she said. 'Iain, the pathologist, has pronounced the victim deceased. Not that it took a brainiac to work that out, to be fair, from what I've heard. Henry has his team working the scene now, and when he's happy, we can go and have a look.'

'Who's Henry?'

'Henry Pearson. Head of the crime scene investigation team. He's in the tent at the minute, but he'll no doubt want a word with you when he's done.'

'Who found the victim?'

'A couple. They're down there,' she pointed in the direction of the car park, 'if you want to have a word, in the back of an ambulance. Might be a nice excuse to get out of the snow.'

They set off together in the direction Lauren had indicated, passing Alan who was now jogging on the spot, his exhalations fogging the air. Tom repeated his offer of finding someone to stand in for him, but Alan declined again, a smile resolutely fixed on his face.

When they reached the ambulance, its lights were still flashing, but mercifully its siren was silent. The paramedics who were sitting on the benches in the back gave up their places as Tom and Lauren climbed aboard, retreating to the seats in the front of the vehicle.

Tom took in the couple in front of them. They looked broken – literally and figuratively. A man in his mid-thirties was lying on the gurney, one of his long legs strapped to a rigid board. His clothes were soaked through and muddy, his jaw set against the pain. A red beanie that looked a bit like a Santa hat was pulled low over his glassy eyes, though some strands of long blond hair spilled from the sides. Judging from the faraway look, Tom presumed he had been given something to help with his discomfort.

The woman didn't look much better, though at least she was uninjured. She was sitting with her head in her hands, her dark hair falling over her face like a waterfall. When she looked up, Tom saw that her eyes were red and puffy. He tried to offer a reassuring smile, but was unsure if it made any difference. He introduced himself and pulled out his notebook.

'Can I take your names?' he asked.

'I'm Rebecca Jenns, and this is my husband, Teddy. Short for Edward.' Her voice cracked as she spoke, and it seemed like a seismic undertaking to persuade each fragmented syllable to leave her mouth. Tom noted a hint of a Yorkshire accent.

'How did Teddy hurt himself?' Tom asked.

'He fell in a big hole up at the Angel. Fell on top of the body of the man. In a big bloody pit in the middle of the field,' Rebecca said. 'Can you believe it?'

'Can you tell us why you were up here so late at night?' Tom asked.

'We wanted to have a winter picnic,' she said. 'Next to the Angel.'

'Your accent doesn't sound like you're from around here,' Tom noted.

'We drove up from Leeds,' she said.

'In the snow?'

She shook her head. 'We came up yesterday. We've been staying in a hotel in the city centre.'

'Which hotel?' Tom asked.

'The County. By the station.'

Tom wrote the name in his notebook. It would have to be checked. 'You drove for two hours to have a picnic?' he said.

'No. Teddy's mum lives in South Shields, and we're up visiting. I've always loved the Angel, and thought it would be nice to sit by it with a flask of tea and a pork pie when no one else was around.'

Tears left thin tracks as they flowed down her face. Tom gave her a moment.

'Have you been here before?' he asked.

'Only once. This afternoon, but it was busy so we left. That's why I wanted to come back when it was quiet.'

'I'm assuming there wasn't a body here this afternoon?'

'Definitely not. The pits were empty then, except for the snow.'

'Pits?'

'Yes,' said Rebecca. 'There were two big rectangular holes in the ground, on either side of the Angel. I don't know what they're for. But there was nobody in either of them, until we came back.'

Tom noted this down. 'And did you see anyone else around here when you returned to the site?'

'No,' Rebecca replied, stroking her husband's good leg. 'There were no other cars in the car park when we arrived. We were the only crazies around here tonight.'

'Teddy, sorry to have to ask you this, but did you touch anything when you fell in the pit?'

'I landed on the fella's legs,' Teddy managed, 'but I didn't go poking around or owt.'

With nothing else to learn for now, Tom told the couple they would need to come to the police station the following day to give a proper statement, and thanked them for their time.

As he and Lauren walked back up the path, her radio burst into life.

It was almost time to see the body.

3

With the few spare minutes he had before meeting the dead man, Tom took the opportunity to walk around the site and take it all in.

The Angel naturally drew the eye, positioned as it was on top of the hill. Tom approached it, shining his torch. At just over six feet, he was tall, but he only came up to its ankle. He sat on the bulge that was the Angel's feet, and looked out over the scene. A swathe of suited figures were spread out around the tents, ready to spring into action as soon as the green light was given. Some stood in groups; others, like Tom, seemed keen for a moment alone before the investigation properly began. Once it did, free time would be a luxury.

Tom stood up again and circled the statue. The back of the Angel's body was covered in graffiti: colourful proclamations of love and lust from over the years. Tom wondered if any of the couples commemorated were still together. Probably not, he decided – defacing a work of art on your first date probably wasn't the most solid foundation to build a relationship upon. Would the artist, Antony Gormley, be annoyed to learn his magnificent sculpture had been daubed over? Or was that simply an occupational hazard for twenty-first-century public art? Nothing was sacred anymore – not even life – although Tom supposed that statement had rung true since time immemorial.

He gave the Angel two taps on its base and made his way slowly down the bank. The ground, hidden by a thick layer of snow, was muddy and uneven. Twice, he nearly fell on his backside, but managed to regain his balance in the nick of time. The last thing he needed was a nickname like Grassy Arse on his first day. He had once seen a new DC hand a DI his coffee, with one sugar more than he'd asked for. The new DC had immediately been christened Two Sugars. It was childish, but it had stuck; case in point, Tom had never known his actual name.

He crept along the boundary of the site, interested in the laminated photographs of children and young adults that hung from the bare tree branches. He'd seen bunches of flowers taped to lampposts before – a way to remember the dead – but never anything on this scale. These shrines to the fallen were on another level. There were painted shells with messages of remembrance and plush teddies. Brass name plaques illuminated by fairy lights had been nailed into the ground nearby. Tom wiped the snow from them with a gloved hand and read some of the names and details of the departed. He didn't know why families and friends had chosen this location. On a normal day, the A1 that ran parallel to the area would surely provide a soundtrack of revving engines and blaring horns, and the nearby council estates were hardly picturesque. But, perhaps the 208-tonne Angel behind him was enough of a heavenly symbol to mark the place as religious – and Tom knew grief struck families in different ways. Tom had known loss, and on seeing how young some of these kids were when they passed on, he felt a sadness bloom in his stomach.

He wondered if anyone would be putting up a memorial for the poor soul in the tent when they heard the news.

'DI Stonem?' someone called.

He turned around to see a man's head poking out of the tent.

'I'm ready for you,' the head said, before disappearing again.

It reminded Tom of a fairground attraction from his youth. A black tent decorated with clumsily cut fabric stars and moons. An old woman stood with her head poking out from between the curtains, proclaiming to passers-by that she could see into their future. When a punter foolish enough to entertain her nonsense stuck a fifty-pence piece in her palm, her head disappeared and the curtain opened. Tom and his mate had been captivated by it. Not by the woman, per se, but by the process of trying to work out who would be idiotic enough to be the next to part with their hard-earned cash.

Here and now, Tom reached the crime scene tent, pulled a flap back and ducked under it. Inside, two men dressed in matching paper suits were looking down into a rectangular hole in the ground. They turned to him and extended their hands at the same time, and Tom was put in mind of a double-act. He shook both as they made their introductions.

Iain Duncan, the pathologist, was short, with wire-rimmed glasses and a drinker's nose. His hair was receding, but what was left was still a fiery red. He spoke in a brisk Scottish accent softened somewhat by time spent on this side of the border.

Henry Pearson, head of the crime scene investigation team, was around the same height as Iain, but his body looked lean and well-exercised. He too wore glasses, though he'd gone for thick tortoiseshell frames. A thin layer of dark stubble coated quite a prominent chin.

'What do we have?' Tom asked.

'Take a look for yourself,' Iain said, motioning to the hole.

Tom moved to the edge of the hollow and looked down. Death was inevitable in this job, but the sight of it never failed to stir something deep within him.

A man's lifeless eyes greeted his own. He was wearing an expensive-looking navy suit, a once-white shirt and light blue tie – all of which were mud- and blood-stained and soaked through. His chest was stained crimson, with three deeper puddles dotting over his stomach. Thin ribbons of red and shadows of blue and black had bloomed on his face, his features distorted and bulbous. His feet were together, and his arms outstretched, like the Angel in whose shadow he lay.

'Stabbed,' Tom said, motioning at the puncture marks on his abdomen.

'Oh, they said he was good,' Henry said.

'Aye.' Iain nodded. 'Criminals of the North East, beware. The new detective inspector knows a stab wound when he sees one!'

'Jesus, do I get to choose who I work with, or am I stuck with you two halfwits?'

'Stuck with us, I'm afraid,' Iain joked. 'At least for a couple more years until I retire.'

Gallows humour was essential in police work, and these two had it down pat. It was how you coped with crime scenes and the horrors that humans can inflict on one another. Laughter, even in the presence of a body, was how you got through the blackest of nights. Keen to bring back some sort of profession-alism, though, Tom asked:

'Is that how he died?'

'It's a good question,' Iain replied, 'but not one I'm prepared to answer right now. A betting man would say yes, but you and I both know that the most obvious answer doesn't necessarily mean the correct one. I've done my routine bits and bobs, but I want to get him on the slab before I give you definites.'

'How soon?' Tom asked.

'First thing tomorrow morning.'

Tom rounded on him.

'Tomorrow morning? Jesus, that's quick. Is that usual up here? In Manchester, it can take over a week sometimes.'

'Not usual at all,' Iain replied. 'We're full to bursting, actually. The mortuary looks like a deleted scene from *Night of the Living Dead*, but the DCI has put an urgent stamp on him.'

'Why?' Tom asked.

'It's hard to be sure,' Henry said, 'what with the bruising and all, but we think it might be Richard Handsworth.'

Tom's face was blank.

'Not into your politics, eh?' Henry said. 'He's the MP for Gateshead.'

'Oh fuck,' Tom whispered.

'Oh fuck, indeed,' Iain said. 'And if rumours are to be believed, three-quarters of the town could be behind it. He was a hateful so-and-so. You've got your work cut out, young Stonem. Call round to the hospital at ten or so in the morning and I'll see if I can be of any use to you.'

Iain left to call his team and arrange for the body to be taken to the hospital. Tom and Henry were alone.

'Do you think he was killed here?' Tom asked.

'No.' Henry shook his head. 'There's not enough blood. We think he was killed somewhere else and deposited here. It's a very deliberate act, bringing him to the Angel and posing him like that. I'd hazard a guess that it's some sort of message.'

Tom nodded. It certainly seemed like a message, but what could it mean? MPs were not usually known for their angelic qualities – maybe the killer had chosen this place with a sense of dramatic irony.

Tom pointed at the hole. 'The witnesses said there are two pits at the scene, dug before the body was dumped. Did the killer dig them?'

'No. There's building work going on here. I think they're installing lights around the Angel, or at least the electrical infrastructure for them. A local building firm has a banner up on the metal fencing at the back of the site. Might be worth giving them a call to see when the work began, and if it's still ongoing.'

'Good idea,' Tom said. 'Anything else?'

'Not for now, no. Whoever did this knew what they were doing. As soon as Iain lets us work the scene, I'll get back in touch.'

Tom took a few minutes at the edge of the pit, staring down at the body, trying to commit as much to memory as possible. Every murder was barbaric – taking a life was a heinous act – and Tom felt the fire that stoked an investigation begin to burn in his belly. He silently promised the body in the hole that he would see justice done.

Tom thanked Henry and left the tent. If the victim was indeed Richard Handsworth, the investigation was going to be under a lot of media scrutiny. Tom needed to make sure his team was well prepared for an intense couple of days. The nation would expect them to deliver results – and deliver them fast.

4

THE NIGHT PASSED IN a blur of activity.

The clouds parted, exposing a canvas of black, embellished by only a couple of faraway, twinkling diamonds and a thin sliver of moon. The main roads weren't great, but the country lanes that led to Richard Handsworth's house were dreadful. From time to time, Tom felt the wheels take on a mind of their own as the ice on the roads lured them towards ditches on either side of the narrow track, like sirens beckoning drunken sailors to their destruction.

He was almost surprised when he made it to the MP's house in one piece. The crunch of the tyres on the driveway's gravel seemed deafening in the remote countryside. The blackness here was almost absolute, save for a lone Victorian-style lamp hanging beside the front door. Tom killed the engine, and the cooling ticks and rattles coming from under the bonnet sounded like gunfire.

Lauren pulled up behind him, and they got out of their respective cars, closing their doors as quietly as they could. They walked up to the front door of the house, and Tom knocked, imagining all the things a person might expect when they hear a rap on their door in the middle of the night: that their partner had forgotten their key? That he or she was too pissed to find the keyhole?

But he reckoned, for the majority of the population, their overriding feeling would be one of primal fear.

After a minute there was still no answer, so Tom knocked again, this time with a little more force. In one of the upstairs rooms, a light bloomed and the net curtains swayed. A woman's face flashed in the window, and Tom glimpsed the panic in her eyes before she retreated from view.

Then there was the thud of footsteps on the stairs, and another light flicked on in the frosted-glass window beside the door. Footsteps again, louder now, as the woman hurried down the hall. The door opened a crack. A blue eye appeared in the space.

'Is it about Dicky?' she asked, a tremor in her voice.

Tom nodded, and she opened the door a little further. She was wearing a fleece dressing gown, the ties pulled tight around her slim midriff. Baggy silk pyjama bottoms hung in folds around her bare feet, which she rubbed absent-mindedly on the bristles of the welcome mat. Metallic blue toenails glinted in the moonlight.

'What has the silly bugger done now then?' she said.

* * *

Tom hated this bit.

Seeing a body being taken apart, medically, was no picnic. But once you were in the mortuary, it was simply part of the job. You became desensitised to it, knowing that the corpse, in all likelihood, held clues that could help the case along; clues that often led to the killer.

What he hated was the waiting.

Before the pathologist summoned you, the time spent outside a mortuary was akin to sitting in a dentist's waiting room, listening to the drill whirring through someone else's enamel in the next room. Knowing that it was your turn next. Running your tongue over your teeth, feeling a day's accumulation of fur, wishing you had brushed for a couple of minutes longer in the hope of outrunning the dentist's tools.

To take his mind off it, he pulled his notebook out and sketched a timeline for the evening.

At just after three in the morning, he had followed Lauren (who was driving Sarah) to the very room Tom was waiting outside now. Sarah had taken one look at the battered body on the metal gurney and confirmed it was her husband with the smallest of nods. Tom had thanked her and pulled the white sheet back over the man's bruised face. Sarah had stood where she was, unwilling or perhaps unable to move. Tom had felt a little bad when he ushered her from the room.

There was always a slim chance that the body was not who the police thought it was. That the person called in to identify them would discover that *their* loved one had been given a reprieve from the mortician's tools. But when the body *did* turn out to be their husband, wife, brother, sister… it didn't matter who… the response was the same.

Tom had seen it in the eyes of hundreds of people. Their apprehension on leaving the mortuary room was fundamentally different from the kind they entered with.

Married. Safe. Secure. Financially supported. And now not.

All of that gone, acknowledged in one brief nod of recognition.

Tom had been told by the first DI he had worked under to get the relative out as soon as possible. He'd seen cases destroyed as mourners threw themselves on the dead body, shedding tears and skin cells and all sorts of other DNA, contaminating the evidence. Best to guide them away. Let them mourn elsewhere. Be cruel to be kind.

These words of wisdom had been shared in some dowdy police station canteen, under strip lights that flickered and with a background cacophony of droning coffee machines and clinking cutlery. The words may have come easy, but the actions they alluded to usually did not. Being cruel to be kind often didn't feel right.

Outside, in the crisp fresh air, Sarah's tears had come. Tom had watched, feeling he was intruding on a very private moment, as she turned her face skywards and uttered a wretched sound. Something animalistic and primeval.

It had chilled him to the bone.

Lauren had driven her back to the station, with Tom once again following. At the station, he had left the grieving widow in the care of his new partner, who was arranging a family liaison officer for Mrs Handsworth. The idea was that Lauren and the FLO would accompany Sarah back home, and Tom would follow later, to ask some questions once he had been to see the pathologist.

He'd had a quick catch-up with his new boss, Natalie, who was acting as the senior investigating officer on the case. She had made it clear, as if it wasn't already buzzing in neon within his central cortex, that as soon as the details got out about who the victim was, they would be expected to get a quick result.

The spotlight would be on them, and it would be blinding.

With the snappy little pep talk fresh in his mind, he had left her office and trooped back to the hospital for his ten o'clock appointment, which brought the timeline up to the present.

'Tom, I'm ready for you,' Iain called from the mortuary door.

Tom nodded, put his notebook away, and followed Iain inside. The door closed behind him of its own accord.

The mortuary was like every one Tom had ever been in.

A metal table was the star attraction, standing in the centre of the tiled floor, with Richard Handsworth's body laid upon it. The perimeter of the room was taken up by four granite work-benches, each punctuated by a stainless-steel sink, beside which sat a bin stencilled with the biohazard sign. The whole place had been scrubbed to within an inch of its life, and the air was heavy with the stench of disinfectant, mingled with notes of inner body parts. It wouldn't make a very pleasant perfume.

Tom noticed one thing that was not in keeping with other mortu-aries he had been in. Classical music emanated from a speaker in the corner. Tom wasn't sure why, but the playful violin part put him in mind of a scene from *The Simpsons*, where most of his knowledge of the world came from. He saw, in his mind's eye, an oversized cartoon bee being pursued by a grumpy clown with a flycatcher.

'What's this?' he asked, gesturing to the speaker.

'"Danse Macabre",' Iain answered. 'By Saint-Saëns. I think this is the Montreal Symphony Orchestra version.'

'It's a bit jaunty for this kind of work, isn't it?'

'It makes me smile, and not much does in this room. Is that all right with you?'

The 'all right' was a sharp shard of Glaswegian on Iain's tongue; Tom simply nodded his assent.

Iain led him to the table. The deceased MP was naked, his clothes having been removed and bagged by the evidence officer during the post-mortem, and handed over to forensics for closer examination. There was a tattoo on the left side of his ribcage: an elaborate collection of interlocking triangles drawn in stark black ink. It looked like it had been done recently. The lines of the tattoo had been infiltrated by a number of bruises which covered his torso and stretched as far as his forehead, as if he had fought ten rounds with Mike Tyson. Of course, the stab wounds confirmed his actual fate was much worse. The three dark holes, ringed with blood, stood out against the pallor of his mottled skin.

'Are those what killed him, then?' Tom asked.

'No,' Iain said. 'Surprisingly, the knife missed his vitals. The lacerations are deep, but nothing some stitches wouldn't have sorted. I'll walk you through what I've found. Shout if you have any questions, right?'

Iain moved around the body and stood by the head.

'There's a lot going on, and it's hard to tell in what order most of it happened, but I'll give you my best guess. First, I think our victim was bashed over the head from behind. Hard. The impact caused fractures in the skull and bleeding on the brain. Considering the area of injuries, I'd say the weapon was something long and hard like a baseball bat or a wrench.'

'Poor bastard,' Tom said.

'Aye, and that's just for starters. If you look at his face, some of the capillaries in the cheeks and the eyes have burst, indicating asphyxiation.' He gave Tom five seconds or so to take in what he needed to, before continuing. 'And now, have a look at the throat. There are clear bruises which would indicate pressure from a hand.'

Tom leaned closer to the body. On one side of the neck, there was a small dark circle which he supposed was the thumb print, and on the other side were four smaller marks. Fingers.

'Is *that* what killed him?' he asked, taking a few steps back.

'I'd say so. He was probably knocked out first with a bat to the head, and then choked when he was on the ground. There were small bits of grit in the head wound, like you'd find on a concrete floor. The stab wounds feel like insurance.'

'It sounds like the work of an amateur. Bash, throttle and stab. Cover all bases.'

'It does, but would an amateur have the presence of mind to move the body from wherever the killing was done, and pose him like an angel? It's an odd one.'

'It *is* odd, isn't it?' Tom said. 'Anything else?'

'There's no sign of any defensive injuries. No dirt under his nails, so he didn't scrabble around on the floor, and no marks on his hands to suggest he tried to stop any of this. If the first blow knocked him unconscious, he didn't even feel his end. I'd say whoever did it was right-handed, considering the angle of the knife wounds.'

'What about the knife?'

The music stopped and started again: now it was 'The Floral Dance', a song Tom recognised from the film *Brassed Off*. The high tempo pomp of the brass instruments was at odds with Iain's answer.

'Like I said, they're fairly deep wounds, so probably something like a kitchen knife. About five inches. Non-serrated.'

'And the killer: male, female?'

'No way of telling.' Iain shrugged. 'Someone of medium height, if we think about how the instrument was used to cause the head injury.'

'No more clues to narrow it down?'

Iain shook his head.

'So, they're right-handed, medium height, could be male or female, and used a standard kitchen knife?'

'That's about right,' Iain said.

'Fantastic,' Tom sighed.

He bid Iain farewell and left the room. As he got in the car, Tom let his head fall back against the headrest. *All jobs are challenging at first*, he thought to himself, as he shoved the key into the ignition, but this killer was going to be about as easy to identify as a single flake in a snow storm.

5

THE SUN WAS WATERY and hung low in the type of blue sky only a fine winter's day could conjure. Its rays illuminated the snow that covered the lawns surrounding Sarah and Richard Handsworth's home, giving them an otherworldly glow. It would have been beautiful were it not for the shadow of death that clung to the property.

It was an odd thing, Tom thought, as he pulled into the driveway. It was as if the bricks and mortar could sense the mourning happening within, and had expanded to lock the grief inside; to not let it spill out into the grounds, like it might somehow become airborne and contagious.

Tom parked behind an emerald-green Skoda estate, presumably the family liaison officer's car. He'd had his heating on the highest setting, and the sting of cold on his face as he stepped out of the car felt like a particularly vehement slap from Mother Nature for bringing grief to this family's door. Not for the first time, he considered growing a winter beard.

The house was something else. Half of it looked like an old church, hewn from ancient stone. The front door was enclosed in an alcove, its knocker the face of a lion, and on the roof, one of the tiles twitched with each gust of wind. The older parts of the house mingled with the new; huge windows stretched from the floor to the roof, showcasing pristine white walls and an elaborate, twisting staircase inside. An angular extension, made of glass and steel, gave the house a sense of movement. A small sign by the entrance to the garden told him the extension had been carried out by Woods Building Services. The whole house looked like a work of art, and Tom spent a few minutes taking it all in, thinking of the run-down rental house he was about to move into, and how he should have become a politician instead of a detective.

The door opened, and Lauren stood in the entranceway.

'How is she?' he asked when he reached her.

'She's doing all right,' Lauren replied, 'considering. She's down in the living room.'

Tom closed the door behind himself and slipped his boots off, leaving them beside the mat Sarah had stood on the night before, as they'd delivered the hammer blow of her husband's death. They walked down the airy hallway, and into a breath-taking living space.

Half of it was used as a sitting room, three velvet sofas arranged around a massive wall-mounted flatscreen. The floors were made of expensive oak, and covered here by a plush, yellow and orange patterned rug. The walls were a tasteful cream, aside from a red feature wall with a framed watercolour of a Little England scene: a cricket match set in a village square, with scores of out-of-focus spectators looking on.

An elaborately decorated Christmas tree took pride of place near the bi-folding doors that looked out over the enormous back garden, thousands of white lights twinkling on its branches. There was no ornament on the crown of the tree, and Tom wondered if an angel had been hastily removed.

The rest of the room was given over to a kitchen, an island the size of Tom's new front room acting as a divide. Several vases of brightly coloured flowers sat atop it. Alison, the family liaison officer, was busy making a pot of tea on a vast green Aga, whizzing around the space like she had been here many times before. Maybe part of a FLO's training was how to become an SAS soldier of the kitchen.

Sarah Handsworth was slumped in one of the sofas, a black cat snuggled beside her, its sharp claws pulling at a fleecy throw draped over its owner's knees. Tom and Lauren sank into one of the other sofas. He expressed his condolences, which were accepted with a barely perceptible nod. Tom studied her for a moment. Her eyes were puffy and red, perhaps not quite seeing what was in front of her. She looked dressed for a gala: a silk blouse under a black blazer, upon which a silver brooch in the shape of a birch leaf was fastened to the lapel. She wore a string of pearls around her neck, and Tom could make out diamond earrings glittering from under her coiffed auburn hair. He noticed the indented space on her fourth finger where a wedding ring should be.

'I know the timing isn't great, but I need to ask you some questions,' Tom said.

'Ask away,' she said, sighing with resignation. 'If you think it will help.'

'Tell me about Richard.'

'He's dead,' she said. Tom waited for her to continue, which she did with another sigh. 'Dicky was a Tory MP for Gateshead, and he was bloody good at it. We'd been married for over twenty-five years, which is no small feat these days.'

Richard was already being referred to in the past tense.

'Can you think of anyone who would want to hurt him?' Lauren asked.

'Didn't you hear me?' she asked. 'He was a Tory Party MP. We've been through Brexit, lockdowns, endless prime ministers and a million other things. Half the bloody country would love to have had a go, I'm sure.'

She held a finger up to the detectives, got up and strolled over to the kitchen. Her tatty old slippers were at odds with the outfit she was wearing, and every third step she had to stop and convince them to get back onto her feet. When she returned, she was slipper-less and carrying a small glass of port.

'Can I?' she asked.

'It'd be better…' Lauren started, but stopped as she threw the contents of the glass down her throat.

'Not to mention the locals around here,' Sarah continued, as if the drinks break had never happened. 'Knickers in a twist over the smallest of things, and it was always Dicky's fault, or so they said. Not enough car parking spaces, too many speedbumps, ambulance response times too slow… On and on it went. Honestly, a freak rainstorm could have hit the North East and the flooding it caused would have been my husband's fault. It was ludicrous. I don't know how he kept at it for so long. I'd have told them to stick it up their arses a long time ago.'

'Did *he* enjoy his job?'

'He loved it,' she said, and her eyes became wet. 'He never saw what they said as moaning, he considered it constructive criticism, and tried his best to do what he could for those he served. He was no angel, but he loved his job.'

'No angel?' Tom repeated, his eyebrows raised.

'Oh, no,' Sarah said, shaking her head. 'I didn't mean anything by that. I just meant in the eyes of his constituents… All MPs being tarred with the same brush, and all that, you know?'

She looked away, and Tom wondered if there was more to it than that. He'd double back to the comment later; give her time to think he'd forgotten it. It was an old police trick, and an effective one, in his experience.

'Had he been acting differently in the past few days?'

'No.'

'Was there anyone new in his life?' Lauren asked.

Sarah sat up a little straighter, a fearsome look in her eyes.

'What do you mean by that?' she asked, her rage becoming an almost physical thing in the room. Conspiratorially, the cat chose that particular moment to slink away, its claws tapping on the hardwood floors.

'Nothing,' Lauren said. 'Just that, I imagine, in his role, he met a variety of new people on a daily basis. Did he mention anyone new?'

'No. He did not.'

Tom caught Lauren's eye, and she scribbled something down in her notebook.

'Can you talk me through what he was doing last night?'

'He had a constituency meeting in the town centre. At the town hall, I think. That was at eight o'clock. He usually had a debrief with his team afterwards, and then they typically went for a drink. It was going to be their staff Christmas party last night, but Dicky said he didn't fancy it. That he'd be home around half past ten. When he didn't show, I assumed his fortitude had deserted him and he'd gone to the party. It wouldn't be the first time he'd given in to temptation. And then, once he's had a beer or two, he doesn't say no to three and four. I went to bed around eleven, and then you arrived in his place.'

'And you were here all night?' Tom asked.

'I hope you're not implying anything by that,' she said, raising a finger in his direction.

'I'm trying to establish facts.'

'I *was* here for most of the night; however, I did go into the village to get some milk and a bottle of wine.'

Tom would check this information was accurate on his way back to the station.

'Do you have an agenda for Richard's meeting?' Lauren asked.

'Why?' Sarah treated them to a look that suggested this line of questioning was pointless.

'Something that was up for discussion might have pushed someone's buttons. It could help us narrow down our search.'

'There is probably one in his office.' She motioned vaguely towards the ceiling. 'Upstairs, first door on the left.'

Tom got up and climbed the stairs. Lauren followed. They heard Alison leave the relative safety of the kitchen, and the low drone of stilted conversation began.

'She didn't like when you asked about someone new, did she?' Tom asked.

'No. And did you see she's already taken off her wedding ring? Seems like a pretty crass thing to do, doesn't it?'

'Maybe there was marital trouble before he died. Did you happen to notice if she was wearing it last night?'

Lauren shook her head and said, 'It never occurred to me to look.'

They reached Richard's office door and pushed it open. The room was large and well-appointed, painted in a neutral beige. The walls were lined with heavy wooden bookcases filled with mostly non-fiction titles, though a few recent crime novels had snuck their way in, too. An expensive-looking teak desk sat by another huge window, affording stunning views of the countryside.

Richard's computer had already been taken by forensics, but a pile of A4 paper sat on the desk. Some had fallen onto the carpet. Tom crossed the room and checked each page carefully, the tip of his tongue wedged between his teeth, as it often did when he concentrated.

Finally, he found what he was looking for. On it, the schedule for the meeting was printed. Some of the motions had been scribbled out, and some added by hand. Tom supposed this was a draft copy, and that a final one would have been typed up, perhaps by his secretary.

There were a number of items up for discussion: things like updates on planning permission applications and the possibility of a disabled parking space near the chemist on the high street. It was representative of small-town politics; nothing stood out as malevolent or underhand. Certainly nothing that could rile someone to a murderous rage. Tom showed the page to Lauren, who shrugged when she'd read it. She handed it back to Tom, and he put it in an evidence bag. It paid to be careful.

Outside the room, they peeled their gloves off and pocketed them.

'Do you think we should push her more?' Lauren asked.

Tom nodded and led the way to the twisting stairs. As he reached the bottom, his phone rang. He answered quickly, and Henry started talking to him the moment the call connected.

'Are you at the station?' he asked.

'No, I'm at Richard's house. Is everything okay?'

'You need to get back here, quick. We've found something.'

6

GATESHEAD POLICE STATION WAS not what you would call pretty. It was a rectangular slab of characterless brick and dull glass, built in the heady architecturally uninspired days of the eighties, when a proposed curve or arcade would've gotten you a reprimand for thinking above your pay grade.

Thankfully, the inside *had* been modernised. A lift carried Tom to the third floor where he and his team worked. The CID room was large and open-planned, if a little plain and utilitarian. The walls had been painted white some time ago and would need another coat at some point in the very near future. Fluorescent lighting cast a harsh glow on the cheap pine desks, though some officers who used the room had made an attempt at being homely, evidenced by the framed pictures of children and pets that adorned a few desks. On one near the back, someone had opted for a signed photo of Miguel Almirón, Newcastle United's current Paraguayan poster boy. A large whiteboard filled one of the walls. On it were pictures of the crime scene; of Richard's body, of the hole in which he was found and the injuries he had sustained. There were scrawled notes and names and annotated maps, and Tom felt like, already, the investigation was pushing on.

The room was quiet. Natalie, the DCI, was deep in hushed conversation with some of the forensic team. A man of about twenty-five, with a quiff and a sculpted beard, was staring at a computer screen, wireless headphones pushed into his ears and a look of deep concentration etched on his face.

The calm before the storm.

Tom caught Natalie's eye and she beckoned him over.

'Busy first day,' she said, and led him and Henry to one of the offices off the main room.

'This is yours,' she said. 'You can add or get rid of whatever you want once you've settled.'

Tom thanked her and surveyed the room. It was spartan, just the way he liked it. There was a desk, a padded blue office chair and a computer. One of those lamps with a green glass shade sat on the desk, lending the room a noir vibe. Grey blinds were pulled down over the internal windows that looked onto the main space. In his last job, Tom hadn't spent much time in his office, and he probably wouldn't here, either. He preferred to be in the main room with his team. It was where the buzz of the investigation happened; the graft and the bonding. It was also easier to pretend that paperwork didn't exist, if you weren't in the same room as it.

'What have we got?' Tom asked Henry.

From his pocket, he pulled out a sheet of paper encased in a clear evidence bag. It was a photocopy, but you could see that the top of the original page had been torn, like it had been pulled from a reporter's notebook, and thin grey lines ran across it. Henry handed it to Tom. The writing was childlike. Though whoever wrote it wasn't very confident with spelling, they clearly took great care with their presentation. The letters were well-formed, and they had made sure each word was separated with a finger space. The ink was black, but a red pen had been used to cross out the first item. Tom read the list aloud:

1. ~~No Angel~~
2. Red partee dress
3. Alien egg toy
4. Box of majic tricx
5. Suprise

A million thoughts ran through Tom's head, not one of them good. He looked at the other two: he imagined their horrified expressions matched his own.

* * *

Tom's team, comprising himself, Natalie, Lauren and Alan, sat around a circular table. Alan, who Tom had met the night before at the crime scene, had brought cups of takeaway coffee and a packet of freshly baked pastries from the local café. The bearded man who had been working on the computer got up, stretched, and made his way over. He clocked Tom and walked towards him, hand outstretched.

'Howay, pal,' he said in a broad Geordie accent. 'DS Gamble. Call me Phil. Pleased to meet you.'

Tom shook his hand and invited him into an empty seat.

The evidence bag, with the note inside, was in the middle of the table. Phil spun it so he could read it. He mouthed along as his eyes scanned the words.

'No Angel?' he said, followed by a low whistle. 'Jesus, are we dealing with some sort of joker here?'

'We'll get to that,' Tom said. 'I want us to have a think about who it could belong to first, before we get to what it means. Any suggestions?'

'We will be getting a handwriting expert in,' Natalie said, 'but on first impressions, it looks like a child has written this. It could obviously be an adult doing an impersonation, but it looks too real to me.'

A murmur of agreement.

'It was found in Richard Handsworth's jacket pocket, but we've checked with his widow, Sarah,' Tom said, pointing to a picture of her on the board. 'She has confirmed that he didn't have any children in his life. No kids of his own. No nieces, nephews. No godchildren, even. So why did he have this in his pocket?'

'Maybe he was masquerading as Santa at the Metrocentre in his spare time,' Phil said, to a titter of laughter. 'Politicians love a sneaky second job, don't they?'

Tom smiled, before moving the discussion on: 'What about the first item, then? No Angel. Bit creepy considering where the body was found. There's got to be a link, surely?'

'Maybe,' said Lauren. 'But we can't be sure. The note is obviously written by a child, and probably a girl, given item number two is a party dress…'

'What could "No Angel" mean on a little girl's Christmas list?' Tom asked.

'If I'm remembering right, there was an album by Dido of that name yonks ago.' She pulled out her phone, typed something on the screen, and passed it around.

On the screen was a picture of a CD cover. It had a silver background, with the name of the artist cut out in large block letters revealing a black-and-white photo of a woman looking out at them. The title of the album was written in smaller letters below. Tom remembered Dido from a song she'd performed with Eminem in the early noughties. He passed the phone back. The group sat in silence for a moment, each person trying to make sense of the note.

'What are we thinking, then?' Alan said, eventually.

'Does the first item date the list to back when Dido was big? That was twenty-odd years ago now, right?' Lauren said.

Phil fiddled with his phone, and then said: 'She had an album out quite recently, but *No Angel* was released in 1999.'

'Do you think it refers to a physical thing? No one buys CDs anymore, do they? It's all streaming now. Spotify and that,' Alan said.

'It could refer to vinyl, though. There are reissues all the time.'

Phil nodded, and seemed like he was about to add something else, when Lauren said: 'Sorry to go back to the first point, but could the letter belong to a kid in Richard's life that Sarah doesn't know about? Maybe he has a secret family, or something like that.'

'He's well known for being a bit of a touchy-feely prick,' Phil said. 'I've been trying to get a profile built up of him, and there's mutterings here and there on social media of him being a bit overfriendly at galas and those types of black-tie events. A guiding hand on the back turning into a pat on the arse, that kind of thing. Apparently, he was known as *The Right Honourable Handsy* in certain circles.'

'Maybe he wanted children and Sarah didn't, or she was unable to, so he's played away from home,' Lauren said.

'It's definitely a possibility,' Tom said, scribbling in his notebook. 'And a good motive. This is all great stuff, guys. Anything else?'

'It's horrific to even think about,' Alan started, 'but maybe he was grooming a kid. Why else would he have a list like that in his pocket? Maybe the kid's parents found out and took matters into their own hands.'

The temperature in the room seemed to drop a couple of degrees as the chilling thought settled. Tom had certainly seen his fair share of grooming cases, and it usually started with the promise of items like the ones on the list. It was wishful thinking that Sarah would have been able to see such behaviour in her husband: Tom knew criminals were very good at covering their tracks.

'Could be the killer is fucking with us,' Phil said, his voice stealing into Tom's thoughts. 'He or she could have written that list themselves in a child's scrawl, crossed off the first item and stuck it in his pocket before battering the poor fella to death.'

'Maybe. But the *No Angel* album being crossed off is bothering me,' Tom said. 'It feels like a deliberate message. The killer left someone near the Angel, and crossed that item off the list in a different-coloured pen. I don't know if that's significant. There are four more items on the list. Maybe it's a code for what he or she plans to do next.'

'Could be,' Phil agreed, 'or it could be a way of making us chase our tails while they watch and have a right laugh at our expense.'

Tom nodded, but he didn't buy it. He thought about the three possibilities they'd come up with. One where Richard had played away, one where he was grooming a child, and one where the killer was simply playing games. He didn't like any of the three. He began to formulate a plan.

'Phil, get down to forensics and tell Henry about the grooming angle. They already have his computer. Get the search started on that as a priority. I want it done by this evening. Sanction overtime, if needed. I'm sure that won't be a problem,' Tom said, glancing at Natalie, who shook her head.

Phil gave him a little wink and practically ran out of the room.

'Lauren, can you go back to Sarah's and ask a few more questions about Richard's life? Let's get right down to the nuts and bolts of their relationship. Mention the lack of wedding ring if you think it'll get her talking. Alison's already there and can help with the more...' he searched for the right word, '...delicate questions. Alan, get on the ANPR cameras. Henry thinks Richard's body was transported to the Angel after he was killed, rather than having been killed there. A list of any vehicles that passed through that area will be useful. It was snowing pretty hard, and I can't imagine there were many cars on those roads, so we might get lucky. Get onto the phone companies, too. Any unusual numbers catching the masts might narrow it down further.'

'I think I should probably do a press conference. An appeal for information relating to Richard's death,' Natalie said. 'The shit is about to hit the fan, so let's get moving. Any questions?'

Alan nodded towards the whiteboard. On it, above all the photos and notes and maps, someone had written, in thick black marker pen: Operation Fluffle. Investigations up and down the country were assigned a random code name by a computer in Scotland Yard, the only proviso being that the word can have nothing to do with the case, hence the strange term 'fluffle'. Other cases Tom had worked over the years had included Pin, Bagel, Bakertown and (bizarrely) Crevice.

'What does fluffle mean?' Alan asked.

'It's the collective name for a group of wild rabbits,' Lauren said, and the group rounded on her. She shrugged. 'I looked it up when I saw Gavin write it on the board earlier.'

'Why can't we ever have cool operation names like Zelda or Pharos?' Alan said.

'Because this way you've got some pub quiz trivia out of it,' Natalie said, with a tone suggesting the forum was officially closed. She stood first, and then everyone left the room. Tom hurried down the stairs, needing to get to the estate agent to collect his keys before they closed, then he could head up to Whitley Bay to grab his stuff from Anna's house. Maybe he would stay one more night – the thought of an already-made bed was heaven right now.

* * *

Anna's house was empty when he got there, the windows dark and the garden still. He parked in the vacant driveway and let himself in with the key she had given him. He called her name, though only silence greeted him.

He walked down the narrow hallway and into the kitchen. He fumbled for the light switch, which he had always found noto-riously difficult to locate. Eventually, light bloomed and from the fridge he grabbed the milk, ready for a nice cup of hot chocolate. While the Velvetiser worked its magic, he washed a mug in the sink and pulled his phone from his pocket. He was searching for Anna's number, when he noticed a note on the dining table. It was a single page, torn from a notebook. It had a thin purple border, with a smiling sunshine in the bottom left-hand corner.

He moved towards it and picked it up.

Dear Tom,

I'm working late tonight on a shoot. I didn't want to ring you during the day, in case you were interviewing or something. And who doesn't love a note?

There are some takeaway menus in the second drawer, and some cans of Coke in the fridge. Help yourself!

I hate that I can't see you tonight,

Anna

Tom found an Indian takeaway leaflet and ordered himself a chicken tikka masala with pilau rice. He was starving. He could've walked to the shop at the end of the road and chosen something a little healthier, but Anna had planted the idea of a takeaway and nothing else would do. While he waited, he threw himself onto the sofa and turned the television on, trying to forget about the case.

There wasn't much on, and his mind drifted to the state of his current relationship. He was enjoying being with Anna. Her job as a TV producer meant she worked all sorts of strange hours, and that suited him just fine. He loathed couples who needed to be in constant contact.

But, of course, no relationship in the early days goes without doubts. Being in a relationship at Christmas was nice, though. Snuggling up on the sofa watching *The Holiday* (a guilty pleasure) and strolling around a Christmas market were activities best done in a pair.

But what about the rest of the year? Was Anna simply staying with him while he was a lodger in her house? Now he'd got the keys to his own place, would she abandon him? He didn't think so, but doubts like these always seemed to play on his mind.

His takeaway arrived, disturbing his thoughts before they could spiral. He plated up (the takeaway had thrown in a free naan bread, and Tom felt his Christmas spirit soar) and then turned on a re-run of the *Gavin and Stacey* Christmas Special. His phone buzzed ten minutes into the show, a notification flashing up from BBC News. Richard's death was now public knowledge. The article told what little information they knew and was accompanied by a brief statement from Natalie.

It was standard fare. She urged the public to respect the family, and asked that any pertinent information about his death be passed on to the police. He finished reading and turned back to the TV. He couldn't concentrate, though. His mind kept drifting back to the note, and to the faceless little girl who might be tangled up in all of this. He felt sick to his stomach, but vowed that whoever killed Richard Handsworth would be brought to justice.

7 sleeps 'til Christmas

I can't wait! It's only one week until Santa comes! I've been trying so hard to be good, even though sometimes it's really hard. Mum told me to make a Christmas list, and I keep thinking about it. If ever think about doing something naughty, I just imagine the presents. I imagine them under the tree on Christmas morning, all wrapped up, even though I already know what's underneath the stripy paper and twirly ribbons. That helps me do the right thing.

Most of the time, anyway.

This year's Christmas is going to be perfect. Presents in the morning. Singing carols and watching a Christmas film, while the smell of cooking food makes us all feel hungry. Roast turkey,

Yorkshire puddings and all the cocktail sausages I can shove in my mouth all laid out on the table. I'll even eat some of the veg if that keeps everyone happy. The last thing I want to do is make everyone feel sad, like last year.

After dinner, we'll play with all the toys we unwrapped in the morning. The dancing robot and the art set I've asked for. I'll make everyone a Christmas card, or they can have some of the pages from my notebook, to start writing ideas for next year's lists. If I've been super good, I might even get that bike I wanted. The one with the basket that means I can go to the shops and be really helpful. It'll be like that video of France that my teacher showed us. A man cycling home with a baguette in his basket. That would make Mum happy.

I hope Santa doesn't mind that we don't have a lot of decorations. We don't have anything in the front garden, nothing to show we even celebrate Christmas. I suppose there's enough on the street already. The tree isn't great, either, but at least some of the lights still work on it. I wish we could have a real one, like the one in the hall at school, with its lovely smell and the perfect angel on top, but Mum says they're too expensive and are a nightmare to get rid of after the holidays.

I've been trying so hard to be like that angel.

It's always this part of the year that it's hardest to keep the act up. I like a normal school day – when it's just maths and English and science. Even though I'm crap at maths. At the minute, all the lessons are different, and there's some free time for art and singing. It's hard to concentrate, and that's when I can start to make silly choices. Like last year when I… when I…

Never mind, that was a long time ago.

I hope Dad remembers to buy everything we need this Christmas. I would hate for my year of trying to act like an angel to be all for nothing… especially when keeping up the act is sooo hard.

7

On television and in the movies, the detective doesn't eat or sleep. He survives on coffee and adrenaline and the hunt for clues, and only rests when the perp has been swept from the streets. Then, and only then, will he succumb to troubled sleep. Tom was a let-down in this department, as he didn't drink hot drinks, aside from hot chocolate (though he had taken one of the cups Alan had brought to the station yesterday, not wanting to seem ungrateful), insisted on a bellyful of food at regular intervals, and very much enjoyed a full eight hours of slumber, if the baddies of the world allowed.

In reality, life continues.

The morning after staying at Anna's, Tom drove to his new house in Kibblesworth, a picturesque village approximately twenty minutes' drive from Newcastle's city centre. It was there he had happened upon a problem: he didn't have anything he needed to start a new life. No spoons, no mugs, no towels.

And so, standing in his spartan new living room, he had phoned Natalie and explained his predicament.

She told him she could hold the fort as investigations continued, while he got himself sorted with the necessities.

He had barely made a dent in the ground floor of IKEA when he decided he would rather attend fifty crime scenes than tackle this place again. Trooping around the Swedish megastore was awful at the best of times, but throw in busloads of harried Christmas shoppers, indecisive couples on the edge of a full-blown argument, and incompetent seasonal staff, and the experience became akin to wheeling a trolley (with a faulty wheel) around the seventh circle of Hell. He emerged from the sliding double doors, slightly traumatised and squinting into the hazy sunshine like he had only recently arrived back on Earth.

In a further moment of madness, he decided to pay a visit to the Metrocentre. He didn't need to buy many presents but thought, if he could cross that job off his list, he would be done early, escaping the madness of the very last-minute shoppers. It made sense, seeing as he was practically already there.

The only problem was that the entirety of the North East of England and beyond had had the same idea. He pulled into one of the only remaining spaces, much to the chagrin of a woman in a Smart car who had been hovering nearby.

Inside, the colossal shopping mall was sensory overload. Fast-food restaurants lined one side of the walkway; the other dominated by a gaming arcade, from which pounding dance music and manic laughter poured.

Thankfully, Tom's Christmas list was short and (almost) simple.

Angela and Nigel were always easy to buy for, and this year had made the whole process even easier by asking for matching his 'n' hers towels, so he headed towards Next. There, in the homeware section, he picked a couple of navy-blue bath towels, as per their very particular specifications, and paid.

Seth, his younger brother, was a different proposition altogether. Though there were only three years between them, they didn't have much in common. Tom had always been serious and career-driven, whereas Seth had drifted from this job to that, never settling at anything for longer than five minutes. They got on all right when they were together, but neither made a massive effort to stay in touch when they were apart.

So, what to buy?

As he was in Next, he visited the men's section. He eyed some black socks, but didn't want to be *that* guy come Christmas morning. He moved to the novelty selection: blue socks with smiling hot dogs on them. He shook his head. Even kitschy socks were naff. In a gadget shop opposite, called Menkind, he browsed rows of pointless contraptions: a self-stirring mug, a robotic guard dog, a toilet bowl light and more besides.

Frowning, he left the shop before the assistant who had been trying to catch his eye could make his way over. He felt his mood darkening. Shopping had never been his thing, and he could feel himself hitting the threshold where his emotions might boil over. He walked as fast as the crowd allowed him back to his car and, as he got in, his phone rang. He didn't recognise the mobile number.

'Hello,' he answered.

'All right, pal?' a gravelly voice asked. 'I've been told to give you a call.'

'Who's speaking?'

'Frank Woods. I've just been up at the Angel to collect some building supplies and finish a few last bits, and I've been turned away. I was given your number by the bloke guarding the place. He said you'd explain.'

Tom had been trying to get in touch with Frank Woods since yesterday, but he hadn't been answering his phone.

'Ah, Mr Woods, nice to hear you are alive. I'm afraid there has been an incident, and the site is now a crime scene. Access is restricted until the forensic team are finished.'

'So, I can't get my stuff?' Frank huffed.

'Not until the forensic team are done with the site,' Tom repeated.

'Fuck's sake. I'm going to have to rearrange with the punter, then. That's a working day, not to mention a good amount of money, down the drain.' There was silence for a moment, and then he spoke again. 'A crime scene, up at Rusty Rita? Sounds serious. Is it a murder? Anyone I'd know?'

'Richard Handsworth, the MP for Gateshead. It's been all over the news.'

'Don't watch it, pal. Too much shit in my own life to be worrying about other people's, too. Shit your lot are currently adding to. When can I collect the stuff I need?'

Instead of repeating himself for a third time, Tom asked a question of his own: 'When were the pits dug at the Angel?'

'Couple of days ago now. I need to get up there to line them with concrete, otherwise I'm going to have to take the Bobcat again. Then the electrician I have on hold can get up and install the boxes and the lights. Do you know how much it costs to have an electrician on retainer? An arm and a leg.'

'I can only imagine. What date were the pits dug, exactly?'

'Why do you need to know?' Frank said. He sounded cagey, and Tom decided now was the moment to press home the advantage.

'Because, Mr Woods, the victim was found in one of the holes you dug. You giving me an exact date can help narrow down the time of death and, more importantly, it'll get me off your building site so you can crack on with your electrician. Of course, I'm more than happy to come up to your offices to go through the paperwork there if now isn't a convenient time. Industrial estate in Longbenton, right?'

Suddenly, the information became freely available. The holes were dug on the fifteenth of December, a day before the body was discovered. The council had decided now was the time to install some spotlights to illuminate the Angel.

Tom reckoned the killer had probably driven past the Angel, saw the diggers, and figured it was a pretty good place to make a statement by displaying the body, especially after the snow had turned it into a no-go zone for the workers.

Tom ended the call with a promise to let the builder know when the site would be free. He realised he'd had his reverse lights on for the entire duration of the conversation, and a very patient (or very committed) would-be shopper had been waiting for him to leave with her indicator on. Tom threw up an apologetic hand and got out of the car park as quickly as he could.

8

LAUREN'S MORNING WASN'T GOING as planned, either.

Sophie had woken her at just after half past five, and refused to go back to her own bed. There wasn't even a suggestion of light at the edges of her bedroom curtains, but (against all the parenting books' best advice) she let her daughter come into bed with her. Being a single parent was a lonely affair, and the double bed was more than big enough for the both of them.

Despite the early hour, sleep was off the menu. Sophie lay still for about thirty seconds, filling Lauren with false hope. Then, she began whittering on about breakfast, and *Bluey*, and what she wanted for her next birthday (which was 264 days away). Lauren kept telling her to be quiet, but it was no use. Before she knew it, she was in the kitchen, preparing Sophie's breakfast of Rice Krispie Shapes with a side of raisins. While Sophie ate, Lauren ran around the house, trying to tidy as much as possible.

Being a detective sergeant made the job of keeping a house tidy almost impossible. The hours were anti-social, and it was only the good grace of her own mother that kept her home from resembling a bombsite.

When Sophie had finished, they lay on the sofa together and watched a TV show about gymnastics. The little blonde girl, who resembled Sophie, was walking across beams and swinging from bars and generally screaming with sheer delight.

'Can I go to gymnastics?' Sophie asked.

'Maybe,' Lauren replied. 'I'll try and find somewhere close that does it.'

'Will it be after school today?'

'No. It'll take a while to find one.'

Sophie huffed for a few minutes, and then began talking excitedly about what type of leotard she would wear, before changing the channel. Lauren left her to it. There was washing to be done, uniform to be sorted, and a dishwasher to be filled. It seemed never-ending at times.

Finally, at half past eight, they set off out the door. Sophie's school was only a ten-minute walk away, and Lauren loved this part of the day. To some people, it was normal, and maybe even a hindrance to their working day. To Lauren, who had feared she may never become a mother, it was heaven.

On the way, they bumped into some of Sophie's classmates, and twice Sophie begged to stop so she could stroke some passing dogs. When they finally made it to the school gates, Sophie took off, running at full speed across the playground. Lauren watched her come to a stop next to Emma, her best friend. They stood chattering to each other, and when Lauren caught up, she heard Sophie say: 'We didn't see the smiling lady this morning.'

Weird, thought Lauren.

'Who is the smiling lady?' Lauren asked as casually as she could, while handing Sophie her book bag.

'Oh, just some lady I see on the walk to school,' Sophie shrugged.

'Does she help with reading in school or something like that?'

'No.'

'Do you know her?' Lauren asked.

'No. But I think she knows me, because sometimes she waves at me.'

Lauren presumed it was either Sophie imagining things, or there was a purely innocent reason for the lady smiling and waving. Maybe she was a lonely old woman who never had kids of her own, or perhaps she was unwell.

'If you ever see her again, tell me. Okay?' Lauren said.

'Okay, Mammy,' Sophie said, before toddling towards her classroom door, hand-in-hand with Emma.

Lauren's attention immediately turned to the case, and, for the moment, all thoughts of the smiling lady were driven from her mind.

9

LAUREN WAS SITTING AT one of the desks when Tom entered the third-floor office, leaning back in her chair, scanning the computer screen.

'How did it go with Sarah?' he asked.

Lauren shrugged. 'We pretty much went over everything you did. I even mentioned the possibility of an affair, and she laughed in my face. I didn't get much more out of her, annoyingly.'

'Maybe there is nothing more to get. Thanks for trying. Is she holding up all right?'

'She was okay. Flitted between stoicism and weepy mess. I'm just putting the case notes on HOLMES.'

'Let me know if you need anything,' he said, and went to his own office. Paperwork was already mounting on his desk, but there was a pink Post-it note stuck to the screen of his computer monitor that caught his attention first. He tore it off, and marched to the lift, punching the B button. He checked his reflection in the mirror. Bags were already gathering under his eyes, and the grey that had been threatening to invade the hair around his temples was gathering its forces for a prolonged attack. Maybe he'd ask for a box of Just For Men for Christmas.

When the doors opened, they revealed a brick corridor with multiple doors leading off it. He didn't know if Northumbria Police's decision to put the tech team in the basement was a logistical one, or one that was trying to keep the 'computer nerd' image alive – a holding cell for those with sallow skin, glasses with thick lenses and a vital need of some vitamin D.

Tom wandered down the hallway, searching for the door he needed. When he found it, he knocked and let himself in.

The room was small and dingy, lit only by a strip of narrow overhead light. The walls were decorated with posters of bands, mostly rock bands that Tom liked himself. A large desk took up most of the room; a variety of laptops and technology Tom couldn't even name spread across it. A small fridge hummed from the corner of the room; a six-pack of luminous energy drink cans visible through the glass door. Abrasive music blared from a speaker on the desk, so loud it put Tom in mind of those SAS shows where they try to make celebrity detainees spill their secrets by blasting heavy metal through tinny speakers.

'I love a bit of Slayer,' he called to the man behind the desk, whose back was to him.

The man jumped, dropping a wireless mouse to the floor in the process. He reached for the speaker and turned the volume down to almost zero.

'You scared the life out of me!' The man laughed. 'I use *Seasons in the Abyss* to help me concentrate, weird as it may seem.'

'I was always a *Reign in Blood* man myself,' Tom said, as the man got up from his chair to introduce himself.

Craig Jarvis had long, dark hair tied in a man-bun, and a thick black beard. A gold hoop hung from his left ear, and a stripy T-shirt was stretched over a rather pronounced beer belly. Tom wondered if he modelled his appearance on Jack Sparrow.

'Nice to meet you, mate. You said you had something for me?' Tom said, holding up the Post-it note.

'I do. I've run a series of tests on Richard's computer. I've trawled his e-mails, his internet search history and anything else you can think of.'

'And?'

'He's clean.' Craig shrugged. 'There's nothing to suggest he was in contact with anyone underage, certainly no children. His internet history is mainly political, with some social media stuff, too. Again, the social media usage is linked to his role as an MP.'

'So he *is* clean,' Tom said, his shoulders slumping. He had hoped something would be picked up on his computer to move the case along.

'Almost clean,' Craig said, holding a Columbo-esque finger aloft. 'Have a look at this.'

From a manila folder, he pulled a piece of A4 paper and handed it to Tom.

'What is this?' Tom asked.

'It's an e-mail I found in Richard's draft folder. The man certainly had a way with words…'

Tom read it aloud:

Delicious M,

I wish to extend to you a most cordial invitation to a meeting of the utmost sexiness. Please join me at 8 p.m. on 22 December in a location of unparalleled allure (you know the one I mean) where the champagne will flow as freely as the rivers of Venus. The dress code, I am delighted to say, is nothing short of tantalising, so don your most seductive attire and join me for a night of unbridled passion. Our agenda is simple: to revel in our desires and explore the ecstasy of our passions. So let us come together (hopefully) in the spirit of unapologetic sexual pleasure, and create a night to remember. I guarantee it will be the sexiest meeting you will ever attend. I look forward to seeing you there, my fellow connoisseur of the carnal.

Yours, Hands xxx

'Jesus,' Tom said when he had finished. He wanted to wash his mouth out with soap.

'I know,' Craig said, wincing. 'It was weird enough reading it on the screen, but hearing you say it out loud really took it to another level of repulsive.'

Tom laughed, before asking: 'Do we know who M is?'

'No. There are a number of names beginning with M who he is in regular contact with. I've written them here for you,' he said, giving Tom a second piece of paper. 'Annoyingly, he hadn't entered the e-mail address he had intended to send it to, just the body of the text, so we can't trace her, or him, that way. Sorry.'

'You've struck gold here. Thanks, mate,' Tom said, patting him on the arm. 'Mind if I keep this?'

He held up Richard's note.

'Please do. The thought of someone coming in here, finding that piece of paper and thinking I'd written those words doesn't bear thinking about,' Craig said. 'Now, can I attempt to purge his message from my memory forever?'

'You may.' Tom smiled, thanking him once more before leaving the room. He headed towards the lift, studying the words on the page, the wail of a guitar solo from behind Craig's door following him down the corridor.

The timestamp on the bottom of the drafted e-mail showed it had been saved on the sixteenth of December – the day his body had been found. So, he'd written the saucy missive just before lunchtime, gone to a constituency meeting at the town hall that evening, and been found dead just before midnight.

Quite the day.

His thoughts moved on to M. Craig's list provided him with five possible Ms – Madison Hutchinson, Millie Whitlock, Maria King, George Milner, and Lucy Boyle. Tom decided that he'd give the list to Phil and ask him to dig deeper into the people on it. As the e-mail had been saved in a draft folder, Tom assumed that this mystery lover never actually received the message, unless Handsworth had sent a similar text via a burner phone or something like that. It seemed unlikely – he had taken the time to type it up on his e-mail account. Why would he change tack?

But why hadn't he sent it?

Had he been rebuffed by M in the past, and was chancing his arm again, but bottled it at the last minute? But that couldn't be, if the 'you know the place I mean' part of the message was to be believed.

These were all questions only M could answer, which begged the question – who was she? Or he?

10

GATESHEAD POLICE STATION HAD five interview rooms. Four of them were par for the course; the blueprint for every television cop show drama: small, with a flimsy table – covered in coffee-cup stains and cigarette burns (depending on how old the table was) – cutting the room in half. Four chairs, two for the interviewing cops, one for the interviewee and one for their legal brief, should they feel the need for one. The decor – peeling paint and a distinct lack of natural light – was liable to give Laurence Llewelyn-Bowen a hernia.

The fifth room was different.

The walls were painted in pastel shades and, instead of a scarred table and plastic chairs, a low glass coffee table stood between two comfortable sofas. On a sideboard near the door, an assortment of mugs was piled, flanked by a selection of teas, coffees, and even hot chocolates. A stainless-steel kettle, recently purchased from the Argos down the street, was ready and waiting to be of service.

This was the room where interviews were done when the interviewee was not under arrest. When they came willingly and were not thought to be a threat. When it was thought that a quiet chat was better than going in all guns blazing.

This is where Sarah was sitting on a sofa, a mug of coffee on the table in front of her. She sat alone, absent-mindedly twisting the wedding band which had reappeared on her finger, a scowl on her face.

The two detectives sat on the sofa opposite, and smiled at Sarah. She did not return the favour. Instead, she fixed them with a glare that Tom was sure had put many a person in their place. He wondered if Richard had perfected the glare, too. He imagined it would come in quite handy in the politics game.

'Hi, Sarah,' Tom said. 'Thanks so much for coming in today.'

'I didn't have much of a choice,' she replied, tersely.

'I know it's already been explained, but you are not under arrest, and we appreciate you answering more questions that could take the case forward. We're going to record the interview…'

He couldn't tell if he had imagined it, but he thought Sarah's eyes had widened ever so slightly. Perhaps the cosiness of the room, and the softly-softly approach they'd taken with her so far, had lulled her into a false sense of security.

'Standard practice,' he continued, holding a placating hand up. 'You've chosen not to have a lawyer with you today. Are you still happy to continue, having made that decision?'

Sarah gave her best 'I've got nothing to hide' look (which bordered on petulant), and Tom started the recording.

'Interview with Sarah Handsworth beginning on the eighteenth of December at 1:37 p.m. Present are DI Tom Stonem and DS Lauren Rea. Sarah is here of her own free will and without a legal representative.'

He gave her a reassuring smile.

'Now, Sarah,' he began in earnest. 'I'd like to go through some details that you've already told us. To make sure they still stack up. On the night of Richard's death, you told us he was hosting a constituency meeting at Gateshead Town Hall. Agreed?'

'Yes.'

'And you were in the house most of the night, except for when you went to the village shop to buy some wine.'

'Yes,' she said again.

'We checked with Mr Satie, who owns the village shop, and he confirmed this. He has CCTV that proves you entered the shop at 8:37 p.m., and a receipt which proves you paid for your items at 8:43 p.m. I imagine you left not long after that. Did you go home straightaway?'

'I did.'

'And stayed at your home for the rest of the night?'

'Until you showed up and drove me to the mortuary, yes.'

'Thank you.'

He took a photocopy of the Christmas list found in Richard's pocket and passed the piece of paper to her. She took it, gave it a cursory glance, and set it on the coffee table beside her drink.

'Do you know what that is?' Tom asked.

'It looks like a little girl's Christmas list,' Sarah replied, her eyes darting to the piece of paper again for a split second.

'Agreed. It does look like the Christmas list of a little girl, going by the items listed on it. What I'd like you to try and help us understand is, why would Richard have that list in his jacket pocket?'

She appeared puzzled, and then emitted a sharp bark that could have been laughter.

'Are you seriously telling me you have dragged a grieving widow from her home to deal with this nonsense? Isn't it obvious? Someone probably gave it to him at the meeting, and, rather than throw it in the bin in front of them, he must have promised to pass it on to Father Christmas when the meeting ended. He was a kind man, and people knew that.'

'What about the No Angel reference in item one? Those were the exact words you used when we talked at your house yesterday. Don't you think it's suspicious?'

'I think it's coincidence, and nothing more. I also think you are wasting your own time. Dicky was a good man, and it seems to me like you are indulging a fantasy here, rather than getting out there onto the streets, and putting in the hard work that it takes to catch a killer. I know what you think he's done...' Tears formed in her eyes. 'You're trying to tar him as a paedophile. Trying to make it seem like he was trying to screw some young thing with the promise of music from before they were born and a fucking alien egg, whatever the hell that is. Do you have any actual evidence?'

'We have the list,' Lauren said.

'Sarah,' Tom said, as soothingly as he could, 'surely you must see how this could have looked to us. We had to explore the angle that your husband was attempting to groom an underage girl. Thankfully, we are fairly certain this was not the case.'

'Fairly certain? Oh, excellent! I've got to say, fantastic police work.' She applauded sarcastically. 'So, *do* you have anything else, or am I free to go and get on with the business of mourning my husband?'

Almost reluctantly, Tom passed a second piece of paper to her. The page with her husband's creepily unerotic epistle to M on it. Sarah took it, and Tom watched as her eyes drifted from left to right and back again.

'Do you know who M is?' Tom asked, when she'd finished.

'At a guess, I'd say it's probably George Milner,' Sarah replied, placing the page face down on the sofa beside her. He noticed that her face had lost some of its colour.

'George?' Tom repeated. He recognised the name from the list of Ms that Craig had given him.

'Milner, yes. He is an MP who my husband was good friends with. They used to send jokey messages like this to each other all the time.'

'We didn't find any related communication between the two—' Lauren started, but Sarah spoke over her.

'I know what you're trying to do here. You couldn't paint him as a paedophile, so now you are trying to make him out as a philanderer. Like I told you before, Dicky and I were married for a quarter of a century. We knew and trusted each other intimately. I can assure you, with God as my witness, he was not having an affair.'

'How can you be certain?' Tom asked.

'I just know, all right? Is that it? Can I go?'

Tom passed her the list of possible Ms that Craig had given him. 'Do you know any of the people on this list, other than George Milner? When DS Rea asked you last time if he had recently met anyone new, you didn't seem happy. Is one of these Ms someone new in his life? A friend? A lover? Someone who caused you to take your wedding ring off the day after your husband was killed?'

Sarah glanced at the list, and her face coloured. She looked both frail and utterly ferocious at the same time. Tom wondered if he had pushed her a little too far, suggesting her husband had a lover on the side. He hadn't even had chance to ask her about the reappearance of her wedding ring yet.

Before he could speak, Sarah stood up and glared at the two detectives. When she spoke, each word was so brittle, it sounded as if a misplaced syllable could break her.

'When we next talk, if you have the balls to come for me again, I will have a lawyer present, and he'll be the one asking you the questions about why you think it is necessary to hound a grieving woman. If you ever try to defame my poor husband again by suggesting he was some sort of womaniser, I'll have you in court for slander. Let me remind you, Detective Inspector Stonem, that my husband was killed. He is the victim in all of this. So do your fucking job and catch whoever was responsible.'

She walked out of the room, leaving Tom and Lauren on the sofa, mouths agape. As they packed up their notes and evidence, Tom's phone rang.

It was Natalie.

'I bet she's put a complaint in already,' Lauren whispered, glancing at his screen.

Tom snatched up his phone and answered.

'I need a word,' Natalie said, and hung up.

Fuck.

Tom hated being summoned. It must be some sort of evolutionary hangover, like the fight or flight reflex, or having an appendix. He remembered being told off by his headteacher for shouting out in assembly, and the time he snuck out of the window when he was seventeen to go to a club with his mates. The disappointment in Angela's eyes had been tough to take. It was no better as an adult, as it usually meant he was in trouble.

Not today, however. His summons had led to a very short discussion with Natalie which, in turn, led to a breakthrough. Of sorts.

She had a friend, a photographer who did the function circuits and sold his pictures of high society to the local papers. Natalie had contacted him after her press conference and asked him to have a look through his archive, on the off-chance something leaped out.

Something had, and so Tom had been dispatched by his boss to find out what.

CT Photography was in part of an old mill on the south side of Newcastle. The mill was huge and hewn from ancient red brick, now stained a dull brown from the years of industry that had gone on in and around it. Scaffolding covered part of the building, and a couple of workmen wearing hard hats and hi-vis jackets were milling around at the base, squinting up at some of their colleagues who were examining a cracked window frame with shards of glass that were only just managing to hang on. More workmen were gathered around a hot food trailer that took up a couple of spaces in the car park. The smell of bacon wafting from it almost convinced Tom to join them. Instead, he walked towards the studio and opened the door.

The woman behind the counter smiled at him as he approached.

'Hi, I'm here to see Charlie,' Tom said.

'I'll see if he's free,' she said. 'Hang on.'

She got up from her stool and walked through a door at the back of the room. She returned a minute later, her high heels clacking on the wooden floor, and told him Charlie was in his office and he could go on in.

Through the door was a much bigger space, split in two by a false wall, each side made to look like a bedroom. One half of the room was airy and bright, painted in classy ivory. It had a four-poster bed with too many pillows on it, a velvet chaise longue with a patterned silk throw spread over it, and a full-length mirror. The other half of the room was the complete opposite. A double bed with black satin sheets took pride of place. The beginnings of a black spiral staircase rose in the corner, though it led to nowhere. An assortment of whips stuck out of a big black vase where a bedside table might go. Tom didn't know what to think.

'Can I help you?' a voice said. Tom spun around and eyed up the man who must be Charlie. His grey hair was long and hung loose over his shoulder; his face was covered in a thick beard flecked with white. He was wearing a three-piece suit with a spotty pink-and-white tie. An unlit cigarette was clamped between his thin lips.

'Charlie?'

'That's me.'

'Tom. Stonem. Natalie sent me over.'

'I bet she did. She avoids coming here herself when she can help it.' He winked.

'What is this?' Tom said, nodding at the odd room behind him.

'Not what you think,' Charlie laughed. 'And certainly nothing you can arrest me for. It's a boudoir set-up. All the rage, these days. Very classy. Very sophisticated.'

Tom would have to take his word for it. Instead of asking any more questions about the space, he said: 'Natalie said you had something to show me.'

'Straight to business,' Charlie said. 'I like it. Follow me to my office.'

Charlie's office was off the main room. There was a desk, a computer, and a couple of chairs. Charlie sank into the spinning office chair. He pulled a pair of glasses from his jacket pocket and positioned them halfway down his nose. Tom stood, leaning against the door frame. He watched Charlie start up his iMac and click a few times on the wireless mouse.

'Natalie called me about your case, and I think these might help. They're from a party Richard attended last week. A Christmas party for the movers and shakers of the North East. I can tell you, it was about as fun as a kick in the balls. Too much money, not enough dancing. The DJ didn't even play "All I Want for Christmas Is You". Have a look through. See what you think,' Charlie said. Despite having one already on his person, he pulled a crumpled packet of cigarettes from one of the desk drawers, and headed for the door.

Tom did as he was told, clicking through the photographs of an aristocratic Christmas party. It didn't take him long to find what he needed.

6 sleeps 'til Christmas

Today, school was epic!

We all got to wear Christmas jumpers. Well – I didn't. Mum and Dad told me I didn't need one, even when I begged them. Usually, I know when to leave it, but I really wanted one. They made it pretty clear their answer would not change, so I just wore my school uniform and made a big show as I walked in, pretending I'd forgotten Christmas jumper day was today. I did that thing where you slap your forehead. It was probably a bit over the top, but it seemed to fool the other kids, even if I did see a couple of the adults exchange a sad look.

Most of the jumpers were pretty normal, with candy canes and Santa's face and things like that, but Harry had one with a reindeer's face that sort of poked out so it looked 3D. It had a bell wrapped around one of its antlers, and every time he moved, it would tinkle. The teacher was getting really annoyed, and just before lunch she'd had enough. She made him take it off.

He did, but when he came back from putting it in his bag, his T-shirt was playing a song. It had a speaker built into it some-where, and it was doing this really high-pitched version of 'Jingle Bells', and we all sang the Batman version. We'd just got to the bit about Robin laying an egg, when the teacher shouted. I don't think I've ever heard her yell like that. She made us miss a bit of afternoon play as punishment, and she made Harry take it off and put on this really grotty T-shirt she found in lost property. It looked like a PE T-shirt that someone must've left in school ten years ago. We all made fun of him and he was really annoyed. He even called Miss a rude name when she went to take someone to the office.

All of that wasn't even the best bit.

It was Christmas dinner day – the best day of the year. I think because the cook feels a bit tight for me, he loaded my plates with a few extra bits. I had cocktail sausages, turkey, mashed potato, some veg, and best of all: pigs in blankets. Whoever thought of those was a genius. I covered it all in gravy. Everyone else wolfed theirs down, because it was snowing and they wanted a snowball fight, but I took my time, enjoying each mouthful.

The only thing that ruined it was Holly's moaning.

'Mashed potato?' she whined to her friend Jessica. 'Everyone knows roast potatoes are traditional.'

I tried my best to block her out, to focus on each delicious mouthful. It would be a while before I ate a meal like this again!

When I finally finished, I waddled down the corridor. My tummy was sooo full, and I felt sleepy. That feeling was quickly knocked out of me by a well-aimed snowball as soon as I stepped outside. The freezing snow dripped down my collar and onto my chest, and I laughed, promising to get them back.

We made teams, and even when the bell rang, the teacher let us stay out for a while longer. When she blew her whistle, my team went on one last attack, and we managed to take their castle. Inside, we warmed up by the radiator and then Miss let us design Christmas cards, using the colourful card she keeps in her cupboard for special occasions.

As I walked home, I couldn't wait to tell Mum and Dad about my day. But, as soon as I opened the door, I knew something was wrong.

They were in the kitchen, and Dad was using his loud voice. It was scary, so instead of interrupting them, I tiptoed upstairs and into the bedroom.

My brother and sister were playing with a second-hand train set a neighbour had given us. Both of them looked like they'd been crying, so I told them Dad was probably just joking around with Mum, but that it was best if we stayed in the bedroom. For tea, we ate some dry crackers that I stored under my bed for times like these. I wasn't really hungry, but I had a couple just to try and keep everything as normal as possible.

And then, Dad shouted really loud and there was a big thump. Mum made a really weird noise, and the little ones started to cry. I held them close and told them everything would be all right. The noise from downstairs stopped, and eventually, so did the noise in the bedroom.

I pulled out some blank paper from my school bag that I had taken from class. I told them we were going to write our Christmas lists, but we had to keep them a secret, and if we were really, really good, Santa would bring us everything we wished for. They got busy, and I thought about my own wishes, but I didn't bother writing them down. My parents had sayings about wishes, and both made me sad.

Mum would always say: 'Be careful what you wish for.'

Dad's saying was: 'If you don't keep quiet, you'll wish you'd never been born.'

11

'Do you think they were shagging?' Lauren asked from the passenger seat, between mouthfuls of bacon butty.

She was holding the pictures of Richard Handsworth and Millie Whitlock that Tom had managed to find in Charlie's cache. The one on the top of the pile showed the MP standing close to Millie. She was probably in her mid-thirties, her long blonde hair cascading down narrow shoulders. Her green dress was covered in sequins and had a plunging neckline. Richard's eyes were a-wandering towards the flash of skin.

There were photos of them at the bar together; laughing by the edge of the dancefloor; and, in one of the final images he had found, Millie had her arm around his waist, their eyes locked in a tender moment

'I wouldn't like to speculate,' Tom said. 'Sarah is certain Richard wasn't having an affair, but the pictures suggest that he and Millie were pretty close.'

'And Millie was his PA?' she asked.

Tom nodded.

'Hardly original, was he?' she said.

She set the photos down and they munched on their greasy breakfast butties for a while, making small talk until they could knock on Millie's door.

Lauren asked: 'What made you want to join the police?'

Jesus, what a question, Tom thought. He decided to give her the abridged version.

'When I was little, I wasn't very academic. The teachers told me I wouldn't amount to very much. I always thought being a police officer was a status symbol.' He shrugged. 'Do you know what I mean? Like, if you wore the uniform, you were giving something back to society. My goal in life was to walk past my teachers while on patrol, and for them to see that they were wrong about me.'

'So, your whole career is built on spite?'

'And then some,' Tom laughed. 'What about you?'

'I just liked the idea of helping people. I wanted to be a vet for ages, but didn't like the thought of putting animals to sleep. We were robbed when I was about ten, and justice became more of thing for me after that.'

They sat for a while longer, watching Millie's house while wind buffeted the car. There was no movement inside.

'What are your Christmas plans?' Lauren asked. 'Are you going back to your family?'

'Probably not. We usually spend it together, but my brother is away at the moment, and I quite fancy staying put. I'm hoping the case will be done by then – the thought of a quiet Christmas on my own is perfect.'

'I'm sure Anna would be delighted to hear that.'

'Yeah, well, things aren't exactly rosy there, at the minute,' he said.

'What do you mean?' Lauren asked, before stammering, 'Umm, if it's private or whatever, I...'

'No, it's fine,' Tom said. 'I was supposed to go to her office Christmas party last night. She works for a television company. But I just couldn't bear it. The thought of getting all glammed up and going to a party where I only know one person didn't appeal to me. Especially during such a stressful case, you know? I didn't want to be papped going into a swanky bar looking happy in the midst of a murder investigation.'

'So you cried off?' she said.

'Yeah, I said I had a breakthrough at work and needed to put in some hours. Which was true,' he added, noticing Lauren's expression. 'I'd just found those pictures and needed to find out more about Millie. But she wasn't happy. She usually sends me a good-morning message, but I haven't heard from her yet. Anyway, enough about me and my relationship woes. What about you? How are you spending your Christmas?'

'Me and Sophie usually go to my mam and dad's. Just the four of us.'

'What about Sophie's dad?' Tom said.

'He's not around anymore. I was married for a little while, and I really wanted a kid. We adopted Sophie when she was a baby because I couldn't conceive naturally. Sorry,' she said, 'this is a bit heavy.'

'Not at all,' Tom said.

'Anyway. When she was one, Greg told me one morning that this wasn't the life he wanted, and he left. Just like that. So, Christmas is all about family for me. Honestly, without my mam looking after Sophie when I'm working, I don't think I could do this job. Lydia Rae is a legend.'

The car's clock hitting 9 a.m. acted as a starting pistol, stopping their conversation. They got out of the car, walked to Millie's house and up the path. Tom pressed the bell, and they waited. When nothing happened, he lifted the letterbox flap and let it go again, the clatter reverberating around the square of houses. Again, there was no movement from within.

'Maybe she's working at the charity shop today?' Lauren suggested.

'Good shout,' Tom said, and hurried back to the car.

* * *

The charity shop that Millie volunteered in was at the end of the street, snuggled between a haberdashery and a family-run coffee shop. It had a purple front and a Christmassy display in the window. Silver glitter acted as a blanket of snow, and tiny cardboard trees surrounded a selection of hardback books, an Arran jumper and a pair of pink football boots that would have Lauren's dad grumbling about how the game had changed and not for the better. She could hear him now: 'Alf Ramsey would never have been seen dead in a pair of those monstrosities'.

The door squeaked as they made their way inside. They were greeted by a welcome blast of heat, and a wide smile from the woman standing behind the glass counter. Her hair was grey and shoulder length, and a thick pair of lenses magnified her eyes to several times their actual size. The silver tag attached to her knitted cardigan named her as Ethel.

Lauren pulled out her warrant card and aimed for her most reassuring smile. Judging by the worried look on the poor woman's face, she wasn't sure she'd quite managed it.

'How can I help, pet?' Ethel asked.

'We were wondering if Millie is here. We'd like to have a word.'

'No, sorry. She's not due in today. It was our staff party last night, and I offered a while back to cover today. Not much of a drinker, me, and I thought she would probably be in need of a lie-in.'

'There can't be many of you,' Lauren said. 'I mean, working here.'

'You're right. We get everyone who works in the charity shops on the street and have a big party at the White Swan. Same every year – cheap and cheerful.'

'Did you stay until the end?'

'God no,' Ethel chuckled. 'The young ones did, I'm sure, but I ducked out at around half eleven or so. That's a very late night for me, these days.'

'Was Millie there when you left?' Lauren asked.

'Aye, pet. Why?'

'We'd like to talk to her regarding an ongoing enquiry,' Lauren said. 'Nothing to worry about, though. Did she appear upset about anything?'

'No,' Ethel said. 'We all thought she might've given it a miss. We knew she worked for Richard, but she didn't mention it, so neither did anyone else. We didn't know if she was holding it together, and no one wanted to open the flood gates, you know? Sometimes you need a distraction, don't you?'

'Did anything unusual happen last night?' Lauren asked.

'With Millie? Now that you mention it, yes.'

Lauren could feel her shoulders tense like they always did when potentially useful information was about to be disclosed.

Ethel continued: 'We were having a ball. The karaoke was on, people were on the pool tables, and the young ones were knocking shots into themselves like nobody's business. Horrible, sweet-smelling stuff. Anyway, she went outside for a cigarette—'

'Time?' Lauren interrupted.

'Oh, now you're asking. Must've been around quarter past eleven or so. I was saying my goodbyes at the time. When she came back from outside, she seemed totally different.'

The door opened, allowing an icy blast to penetrate. The old man who entered held up an apologetic hand and made his way over to the formal-wear section, where he began looking through the suit jackets.

'Different how?' Lauren prompted.

'I don't know.' Ethel shrugged. 'Like all the fun had been taken out of her. I asked what the matter was. She smiled and tried to reassure me everything was fine, but I knew it wasn't. I thought maybe it was boyfriend trouble, but she told me it wasn't anything like that and not to worry about her.'

'And then what happened?'

'She went and sat with her friends, and I left. Didn't think anything more of it, but now you've got me worried. Is she okay?'

'We believe so,' Lauren answered. 'Like I said, we're just following up a routine enquiry. You mentioned a boyfriend. Do you have a name?'

'He's a young lad called Johnny. He came into the shop one day while she was picking a few bits up for her nan. Seems like a nice fella.'

'Johnny,' Lauren repeated. 'I don't suppose you've got a second name?'

'Sorry, pet. I don't. Ginger hair and a nice smile is all I know about him, though she spoke about him very sweetly.'

'Thank you,' Lauren said. 'You've been very helpful.'

They thanked Ethel again and stepped into the rain. Tom nodded at the café across the street, and they hot-stepped it across the road.

* * *

It was busy, with hordes of people using the place to avoid the downpour. While Lauren queued for their food, Tom went upstairs and found a table; a two-seater by the window. The glass was fogged up with condensation, but he barely noticed. He was thinking about everything they had learned that morning.

What had happened to Millie when she had gone outside?

If she and Richard were having a fling, wouldn't she have been more cut up about her boss's death? It was all over the news, and he had barely been dead more than twenty-four hours. Surely, if your lover, or even your boss for that matter, had been murdered, you would give the Christmas party a miss.

Maybe they hadn't been romantically linked at all, and they were just very close friends. Even then, getting in the party spirit would be tricky, no? Maybe she had simply tolerated him as she liked the job. Maybe the pictures that he'd found at Charlie's studio of Millie and Richard intertwined looked sensationalised with the magnification of death.

Tom called Phil and asked him to try and get in touch with other people who worked with Richard and Millie. He wanted to know if a romantic relationship between the two was part of the water-cooler chat. Phil told him his request was in good hands and rang off.

Tom set his phone on the table and thought about Sarah. Maybe her cock-and-bull story about the sexy e-mail being a joke for a male friend was actually true.

Tom wasn't a fan of maybes, and there were currently too many of them flying around his head.

He tried to think of his next step.

Whatever happened to change Millie's mood outside the pub seemed pivotal, and Tom reckoned it should be followed up straightaway.

'Let's make this a takeaway order,' Tom said, when Lauren emerged at the top of the stairs with a tray of cakes and waters. 'We're off to the pub.'

12

THE WHITE SWAN LOOKED like the type of place a Hell's Angels biker would speed past, keen not to get caught up in anything too insalubrious.

It stood alone by the side of an A road, its once white façade now stained a murky yellow, like smokers' fingers. Rusted shutters were pulled over the windows, and the sign, creaking noisily in the wind, showed a lone swan gliding across a body of water, ripples spreading across the surface. The imagery of the sign did not match the grotesqueness of the building.

Still, Tom went by the old adage: never judge a book by its cover. Without any (or at least many) preconceived notions, he pulled the door open, let Lauren go first, and then joined her.

Ethel, not an hour ago, had described the place as cheap and cheerful. Tom couldn't help but think that her years of loyalty to the place were clouding her vision somewhat. As bad as it looked from outside, it was far worse inside than Tom had dared to imagine.

The only light came from the row of fridges behind the bar, meaning the rest of the room was mostly cast in a sickly darkness. Padded seats lined the outside perimeter of the pub, and it seemed that every available inch of table space was cluttered with dirty glasses. The bar itself was mahogany, with battered stools pulled close to it. The wooden top was scarred and scraped and sticky. Tom got the distinct impression that if a Hollywood set designer had produced this room for a dingy bar scene, critics would have slated it for being too over the top.

The man behind the bar looked fairly mythical, too, as if he had been carved from wood with no skill and abandoned once it was clear the outcome was unsalvageable. Long grey hair was matted and fell in clumps on his shoulders. His face was a patchwork of scars, and he was missing several teeth and part of his left earlobe. He was holding an empty pint glass in one hand and swirling a filthy rag around it with the other. The glass was becoming dirtier by the second. He glanced at it and, seemingly happy, slid it onto a shelf with others of similar quality. When he realised the newcomers wanted something other than a seat, he groaned loudly, got off the stool he'd been sitting on, and sidled over to them.

'How can I help you?' he asked.

Lauren introduced herself and Tom, and asked if the pub had hosted a party the previous evening.

'Yes, we had a party,' the barman, called Percy, mumbled. 'We closed for a bunch of charity-shop workers that come every year. Had to chuck Barry out for the night, didn't we, Bar?'

Percy turned and looked down the length of the bar. Sitting on a stool, mostly engulfed by the gloom, was a small bald man. He looked up from his pint and nodded slowly, like an ancient tortoise.

'That reminds me,' Percy said, and turned his back on Tom and Lauren. He reached into one of the fridges and pulled out a steak and ale pie. He tore off the wrapping and shoved it into a microwave that looked like it hadn't been cleaned since it had been bought decades earlier.

'Where was I?'

'The party,' Lauren prompted.

'Oh, aye. So we shut the place down, and let them go wild.'

'I don't suppose you have CCTV?' Tom asked, without hope.

'As a matter of fact, we do. We've got cameras covering the outside and the back. Had some cheeky buggers a while back think they could break in. I had the cameras installed a couple of weeks before, so we managed to sort it.'

Percy finished his sentence with a certain glee in his eyes.

Behind him, the microwave pinged and Percy turned to it. He ushered the steaming pie onto a plate with his grubby fingers, and set it on the bar in front of Barry. Barry nodded his head in appreciation, as a critic might do in a Michelin-star restaurant as they survey the presentation before tucking into a mouth-watering delight. Here, Barry picked up his knife and fork, and waited for the steam to abate from his heated-up pie.

'Anyone comes in and wants something, you do it for me, all right?' Percy said to Barry, who nodded once more. Satisfied, Percy beckoned Tom and Lauren down the narrow bar and into the back. A set of stairs led up, as far as Tom assumed, to the barkeeper's lodgings. Up the stairs looked dark, and he couldn't make out any features, except a pendant light hanging from the ceiling at an odd angle with no lampshade on it.

Here on ground level were two doors. One was slightly askew, not quite fully on its hinges, with another set of stairs beyond it that sloped down to the cellar. Percy opened the other door and led Tom and Lauren into a spacious room so out of keeping with the rest of the place, Tom felt like the door had actually led them to an alternate dimension.

The room was kitted out like a Premier League's VAR suite. There were banks of screens, sleek and thin as a couple of sheets of paper. The mahogany desk they stood on was free of dust and polished. A cup of tea sat on a coaster (a coaster!) and Percy shifted it out of sight, as if he was embarrassed of the small show of house-proudness. A modern desktop computer tower stood beside the screens. Percy sank into a comfortable office chair and jiggled the mouse. The computer screen came to life. He entered a password, logged onto the camera system, and gave Tom a quick run-through of how the system operated.

'If you need anything, shout,' he said, getting up from his chair and trudging away.

Tom navigated the menu and found the date for the footage he needed. He selected the camera he wanted (the main entrance to the pub) and fast-forwarded through the day, watching a few punters enter and many more passers-by zoom past the pub like blurry Usain Bolts. At 8 p.m., he slowed it down to real time, and let it play.

For a while, nothing of note happened, and then an influx of taxis began pulling up on the double yellows out front. Tom watched party-goers slam taxi doors and disappear into the pub. At 9:08 pm, Millie and her two friends arrived. Tom recognised her from Charlie's pictures. Her hair was pulled into a tight ponytail, and she was wearing a sequined red dress and a pair of black, knee-high boots. The trio thanked the taxi driver and went into the pub.

Tom clicked forward to just before the time they'd been told Millie came back inside shaken. At 11:17 p.m., Millie emerged from the front door, alone. She leaned against the wall and reached into her bag, fishing for something. She pulled a cardigan out, wrapped it around her shoulders, and then retrieved a packet of cigarettes and a lighter.

She lit up and took a few drags, before dropping the lighter back into her bag. She smiled at a passing man, and was about to put the cigarette to her lips again when a figure emerged from around the side of the building.

The figure must've spoken, because Millie's neck whipped around, and she took two steps back towards the safety of the pub door. The figure closed the gap, and Tom paused the video. It was clear to see who had materialised from the shadows.

Sarah Handsworth.

'She certainly doesn't look like the grieving widow now, does she?' Lauren said, surprise etched on her face.

'I know. Doesn't look good for her, does it?' Tom replied.

He pressed play again. On screen, Sarah and Millie simply talked for a while. Sarah wagged her finger a few times in Millie's face, but that was as juicy as it got. After three minutes, Sarah walked away, Millie dropped the cigarette she'd been holding and squashed it with the sole of her boot. Then she retreated into the pub.

At 11:32 p.m., Ethel left the pub and got into a waiting taxi. About twenty minutes after that, Millie appeared again. An Uber pulled up a minute later, and she got in.

Tom pulled out his phone and dialled Natalie's number. She answered quickly.

'Boss,' he said. 'Get someone to Sarah's house as soon as you can. Bring her in. I think things are about to go to shit.'

'How do you mean?' she asked.

'I think she killed her husband.' He explained what he had just seen on the CCTV.

'Is Millie safe?' she asked.

'We don't know. She didn't answer when we went round earlier.'

'Get there now,' Natalie said. 'Break down the door if you have to.'

13

Outside, the sun had set. The sodium hue of the streetlights mingled with a low fog: the day had become a scene from a nightmare. They jumped in the car, turned on the lights and siren, and set off at speed.

The fog followed them to Millie's house.

It felt ominous.

Nothing good could happen in this weather.

They parked up and got out. Lauren ran to the door and knocked, while Tom opened the boot. From it, he pulled an Enforcer – a metal battering ram capable of convincing even the most reluctant of doors to open. Tom lifted it onto his shoulder and walked towards the house.

'No answer,' Lauren said, as he joined her at the door. They knocked again and waited.

Same result.

Lauren nodded at Tom and moved out of the way. Tom took a practice swing, getting used to the heft of the metal. It had been a while since he'd had to bust down a door. He fixed his eyes on the area just under the door handle, took a deep breath, and swung. The collision of materials was loud. The door swung back on its hinges, a huge gash of splintered wood where the impact had happened.

They walked in, cautiously. Knees bent and bodies poised for action.

'Miss Whitlock?' Lauren called out, and was met with only silence.

They secured the ground floor and made their way to the stairs. Lauren flicked on the landing light and they climbed slowly. The faint tang of iron started to curdle the air as they reached the landing. Tom felt bile rise in his throat; he knew what that smell meant.

'We're too late,' he whispered to Lauren.

In the master bedroom, he was proved right.

14

HAVING SAT OUTSIDE MILLIE'S house in the car like a caged animal for what felt like hours, Tom was relieved to see Henry walking towards him.

'You can come back in and have a look at the scene properly now, if you want?' he said.

What awaited him in the bedroom was just as chilling the second time around.

Millie Whitlock was still on the bed. Her hair was a mess, fanned out across the duvet and covering some of her face. A ring with a small diamond on the third finger of her right hand caught the crime scene photographer's flash.

She was still wearing the same red dress she had chosen for the party the previous evening. It came down to just above her knees, with two delicate straps draped over her slim shoulders. It was dotted with tears where the knife blade had passed through the thin fabric. Most of the cuts had stopped spilling blood, but a couple were still oozing.

Lifeless fingers held a newspaper clipping. When it had been photographed in situ and then prised from her grasp, Tom saw it was a picture of Richard and Millie. He guessed it had been cut from one of those pages that shows society gatherings. Richard and Millie were part of a group, but their gazes were very much only for each other. Tom wondered how Charlie would feel about one of his photographs ending up in the hands of a dead woman.

The MP and his aide's relationship was obviously the link between their deaths. Could Sarah really be behind these heinous crimes? It was hard to believe. But a woman scorned and all that… Why else would there be a picture of Millie and the deceased politician?

They had to get Sarah in again. They had to question her properly, and put some bloody pressure on this time, regardless of her threats from the last interview.

Iain said, 'Do you want an estimated time of death?'

'My old DCI in Manchester always told me never to ask. That it was for police shows on TV and I would look stupid if I did it in real life.'

'Aye, well, usually I'd say he was right, but this one is fresh. She's still bleeding, so I'd say whoever did this did it no more than four hours ago.'

The news hit Tom like a fist to the face.

Four hours?

He checked his watch. That meant the killer had been here at 2 p.m. at the earliest. He and Lauren had been faffing about in charity shops and pubs while Millie was being stabbed to death. This was a death that, if they'd had a bit more gumption, they might well have prevented.

He could feel the anger swell inside himself. Anger at the killer for making a mug of him, and anger at himself for letting it happen.

'Anything else, you let me know, right?' he said to Iain, who nodded. Tom left the room and stalked downstairs, Lauren in his wake.

'Get to Sarah's and get her back in,' he said to her. 'No fucking around this time. She's playing us.'

Lauren's eyes widened. She hadn't seen this side of Tom before. Not wanting to agitate him further, she said: 'No worries' and made her way towards the door.

'Lauren,' he called after her, his tone softer this time. 'Sorry, I didn't mean to speak to you like that. That wasn't on. It's just...'

'I get it,' she said with a grimace. 'I feel the same as you do. We're on the same team.'

She nodded and left. Tom had a quick walk around the downstairs of the house. The living room was painted the type of grey that was considered fashionable, though he couldn't say he was a fan of the chintzy pink sofas. The detritus of pre-drinks was clear to see: empty bottles of Lambrini and Prosecco and stemmed glasses with bright lipstick marks littered the rectangular coffee table in the centre of the room. One had fallen off; its contents had soaked into the cream carpet. Had she not been brutally murdered, Millie might have woken up this morning and moaned about the stain, adding carpet cleaner to a mental shopping list. Or she might've brushed it off as the collateral damage of a decent night out, and bought a cheap rug to cover it.

He'd never know.

The room was busy with suited bodies going through drawers on the sideboards and dusting the door frames and handles with silvery powder.

In the kitchen, Tom found out how the killer had gained entry. The flimsy door lock had been destroyed, and the back door hung ajar, though Tom imagined the attacker would have closed it after themselves. A crime scene investigator was looking at the hinges with a magnifying glass, and was muttering something to another man nearby. The kitchen counters were uncluttered, though something caught Tom's eye. A box of paracetamol lay beside a pint glass of water. Tom could imagine Millie in here last night, popping a couple of tablets in the hope of staving off the worst of the hangover come the morning. What awaited her had been far worse.

Hanging on the wall above the circular kitchen table were two things: a clock and a framed picture. The clock was irrelevant, it simply ticked on, oblivious to the horrors visited upon the house in the previous few hours, but the picture was not. It showed Millie, smiling and alive, arm in arm with a tall, muscular man with fiery red hair. They were by the coast. The sun was setting, splashing the blue sky with the first touches of pink. A lighthouse and a number of wind turbines seemed to rise from the sea, and Tom recognised the scene as the beach at Whitley Bay. He'd strolled along it with Anna not so long ago, marvelling at the vastness of the ocean and the unparalleled power of the rushing waves as they broke on the shoreline. A sadness gripped Tom, and he swore to himself there and then that no one else would die at the hands of this fucking killer.

As well as Sarah, he was also keen to talk to the boyfriend. He pulled out his phone to take a photo of the picture, and when he went to check it was in focus, his eyes fell on a different photo stored in his phone instead.

The Christmas list.

The second item caught his eye – a red dress – and he thought of Millie's party dress.

What did it mean? Was it coincidence that Millie was wearing a red dress when she died? Would the killer have chosen another target if Millie had emerged with a white dress on instead? Frustration rose in his chest. He didn't know what to think, but he knew he needed fresh air.

Tom edged past the technicians looking at the back door and emerged into a well-maintained back garden. A small lawn was home to an ornate bird table, and a flimsy-looking table and chair set sat on a patio area. A low fence separated her garden from her neighbours, but it was the back of the garden that interested Tom. He walked to the back fence and peered over.

Millie's garden backed onto a playing field. Two football posts, without the nets attached, faced each other over a vast expanse of grass. It was overgrown, and the metal posts had gone rusty at the joins. There were streetlights, though a few were flickering and more had given up the ghost altogether. It would be easy for anyone to hop the fence and make their way through the garden towards Millie's back door without being spotted.

He looked back at the house. A security light was fitted above the door, though this looked like all she had in the way of deterrence. He pulled out his phone and called Alan, who was back at HQ. He answered quickly, and Tom asked his DC to check the playing field's CCTV cameras. It was probably a futile, not to mention time-consuming, exercise, but one that could not be skipped. Alan promised he would get straight on it, and as they hung up, Tom could already hear Alan's fingers racing over the keys of his computer.

Tom left the garden by a creaky side gate, and knocked on Millie's neighbour's front door. The whole area would be canvassed by uniforms in the coming hours, but Tom had a few questions for the man who lived next door.

'Bad business, I'm guessing?' the man, who introduced himself as Jack, said, when he opened the door.

'You're not wrong,' Tom answered. 'I'm hoping you can help me.'

'What's happening?'

'I'm sorry to say that Millie is dead.' Tom wouldn't normally give this away at this point, but he thought the man might go the extra mile if he thought he was in Tom's confidence. 'We're treating the death as suspicious.'

'Oh, Jesus,' Jack said, the colour draining from his face. 'Oh, God. Am *I* in trouble?'

'I know it's a lot to take in,' Tom said. 'For your safety, we'll be sending police cars as a deterrent for the next few nights. Just for extra peace of mind, but we're hopeful that the threat has passed.'

'That's awfully good of you. The poor wee lass.' He took a few moments to compose himself, and then said: 'Is there anything I can do for you, to return the favour?'

'Actually, there is,' Tom said. 'We're told Millie had a boyfriend. I'm wondering if he ever came here?'

'If it's a ginger lad, then he has.'

'Do you know a name or anything like that?'

'No,' Jack said, shaking his head. 'Sorry.'

'Do you know what kind of car he drove?'

'He drove a van. A transit, I think.'

'I don't suppose you know the colour or the reg plate?' Tom asked.

'Not off the top of my head, but I can check.'

'How?'

Jack pointed at the doorbell. 'It's got a camera on it.'

'Doesn't it wipe itself at a certain point?'

'Aye,' he nodded. 'But the boyfriend was here this afternoon.'

He shuffled away and came back with his mobile phone. He thumbed through menus and selected an app, before turning it so that Tom could see.

'There's you and the wee lassie,' he said, referring to Lauren.

He watched Jack swipe through time. The only change was the passing of clouds and the occasional darkened figure moving in the distance. At 14:34, a van pulled into Millie's driveway, and the man Tom knew to be Johnny got out. He was wearing a thick sweatshirt and a pair of cargo shorts. He knocked on the door and waited. When nothing happened, he knocked again and took out his phone. He pressed a few buttons and held it to his ear. He squinted in the front window, and then disappeared around the side of the house.

Tom expected him to reappear quickly, or to dash around the house with his phone to his ear, reporting the break-in. But none of this happened.

In fact, nothing did.

'When does he come back?' Tom asked.

The man whizzed the footage on and stopped when Johnny reappeared.

'Twenty-three minutes later,' he said, and seeing Tom's quizzical look, asked: 'Do you think he did it?'

5 sleeps 'til Christmas

Things were weird in our house. Mum came and woke us up, like normal, but there was something very different.

There was a big bruise under her eye. It was already really dark blue, with bits of orange around it. I knew it had come from the big noise I heard last night that made the little ones cry.

Dad had hit Mum.

Again.

I'd give all my Christmas wishes to make him go away. I think Mum would be really happy if that happened, too. When he's gone to the pub or out with his mates, she's really different. One time, she let me stay up for a while to watch telly. We had fun and joked around, but she kept looking at the clock, and then told me to get to bed before he got home.

Anyway, after the latest punch, I had to get everyone ready and get to school. Mum needed to go back to bed, she said. It was pouring down, and because we were running late, I forgot my coat.

Great – I probably wouldn't be allowed out at playtime now.

On the way, we talked about Christmas, and the little ones kept going on about the lists they made last night. But they wouldn't say what was on them. It was bad luck, they whispered. Only Santa could know. Except, I know they told each other. Twins have a habit of doing things like that – like the rules don't apply to them.

It was only when we turned onto the school's road that my brother asked about Mum's face. I told him she probably smacked herself with the door, the way she always did. We joked that Mum was clumsy.

I distracted him. We talked about what our best Christmas meal would be, and, if we could have any present in the whole, wide world, what would it be?

My sister said a trampoline. My brother wanted a games console and a television the size of a cinema screen.

I'd want a new family, but I didn't say that. Instead, I agreed with my brother. His idea *was* pretty cool.

I left them at their classrooms, kissing my sister's cheek and attempting to rub some grime off my brother's face. His teacher rolled her eyes in a jokey way, as if to say, 'What is he like!' I smiled at her, but I didn't feel very happy. In fact, I felt miserable. I was soaked, and kept thinking about Mum. I wanted to run home and give her the biggest hug.

But I couldn't. If I missed any more school, I'd be in trouble. I made it through the doors as the bell rang, and ran down the corridor to my classroom.

The teacher took the register, and then asked Gemma if she would collect in the homework.

My stomach dropped.

I'd forgotten to do it. Again.

15

THE SUN WAS JUST about rising, its weak beams barely making a dent on the sombre room. Natalie, Alan, Phil, Lauren, and Tom were sitting around a table. Each nursed a cup of coffee (aside from Tom), the warm ceramic used to heat cold hands. Pads of paper lay before them, with today's date (20 December) and Sarah Handsworth's name written on the most recent page, surrounded by scribbled notes.

'What have we actually got, then?' Natalie asked.

'Sarah lied about where she was on the night of Richard's murder. She said she hadn't left the village where she lives, but we have an ANPR hit of her car on the other side of Gateshead, near Millie's house,' Tom answered.

'Anything else?'

'Not really. Alan has checked cell site analysis, and apart from it pinging a mast near the pub where Richard's Christmas party was taking place, it was at her home before and after.'

'Could she have gone home after passing the pub, dropped her phone off, and then gone out again to kill her husband?' Natalie asked.

'It's possible, but, with all due respect, guv, she is a grieving widow, not a criminal mastermind,' Phil said. 'Surely an old lady like that wouldn't know about things like cell site analysis.'

'Old?' Natalie repeated. 'She's the same age as me.'

'Oh... ah... what I meant was...' Phil stammered.

'I know what you meant, you cheeky bugger,' Natalie said, though there was a smile on her face. 'So, where are we?'

'We've got nigh on fuck all, except for the CCTV footage of her speaking to Millie,' Lauren said. 'But maybe the accusation of lying will open her up a bit.'

'Let's see,' Tom said, rising to his feet. 'Anything on the boyfriend yet?'

'Nada,' Alan said. 'Without a last name, it's difficult.'

'Nothing on her Instagram page?' Natalie said. 'I'm led to believe that all the young ones these days spill their deepest, darkest secrets on social media.'

'They're set to private, so only her friends can see. We could send it to the tech team, but there's a backlog and I reckon it would take a few days. Maybe even into the new year.'

'Fuck that,' Tom said. 'I want the case sewn up in the next few days. Can you get some officers out to more of Millie's friends and family? Someone is bound to know who this Johnny is. It's vital we speak to him, to account for those twenty-three minutes that he's round the back of her house.'

'I'll get on it, Tom.' Alan nodded, and sped off towards his work station. Tom called a thank you after him, before turning to Lauren. 'Let's do this.'

They walked in silence towards the interview rooms. Long gone was the hospitality they had afforded her last time. This time, they'd chosen room one for Sarah. Rather than sofas and pastel colours and all-you-can-drink coffee, this one was decked out with a small table, a quartet of uncomfortable chairs, and an array of audio-visual recording equipment.

There was no window, and in the unnatural, ugly glow cast from the strip light above her, Sarah looked ill. The skin under her eyes was purple and saggy, and her lips, devoid of lipstick, looked thin and cracked. She wore an ill-fitting ensemble and held a plastic cup of water in her hand. She was absent-mindedly squeezing it, and when it cracked, she flinched as if a gunshot had torn through the room.

A lawyer sat beside her, in every way her polar opposite. He was huge but his pinstriped suit was a size too small, as was his cream shirt which accentuated the size of his paunch. His face was clean-shaven and uneven, and he reminded Tom of a modern-day Henry the Eighth.

'Hi, Sarah. How are you?' Tom asked, as he and Lauren took their seats.

Sarah stared a hole through both of them, and said, 'I've been better.' A sound escaped her lips that was something between a laugh and a death rattle.

Tom started the recording device and stated the necessaries, before fixing his gaze on Sarah.

'Sarah, why did you lie about your whereabouts on the night of the sixteenth of December?' he started.

She cast a glance at her lawyer, who nodded.

'I know I'm innocent. I know I did not kill my husband, but I thought if I mentioned that I'd driven to the girl's house to see if they were together...' She spat that last word.

'What girl?' Tom asked.

'The tart he'd been sleeping with. I left my house, went to the village shop, and before I knew it, I was at her house. It was supposed to be their Christmas party, and I just wanted to see if the lights were on in her house, to know if she was in there alone or with him at the pub. Of course, once I was there, I lost my nerve. I didn't knock or anything like that. I knew it would look bad on me if I told you that I was there.'

'It looks worse that we had to find that out for ourselves,' Tom said.

'I know that. And I feel awful. I knew about their affair. He didn't tell me, but I've been to functions and she's been there too. He couldn't tear his eyes away from her. He didn't tell me, but he didn't have to. It was obvious.'

'So why did you go and see her on' – Tom made a show of checking his notes, flipping through the stapled document deliberately slowly – 'the eighteenth of December?'

'I… I don't know. Richard was dead, and with him died their affair. I guess I wanted to see if she was as upset about it as I was. Obviously she wasn't. She was out on the tiles as if the man she was fucking hadn't just been stabbed to death.'

'What did you say to her?'

'I told her I didn't know how she could live with herself. She told me the affair was long over, that it was a two- or three-time thing she did because he was the boss and she thought she should if she wanted to get anywhere in her career. She apologised over and over again, and I believed her. But I could never forgive her.'

She broke down into wracking sobs. The lawyer pulled a packet of tissues from a jacket pocket and handed them to her. She wiped her eyes, took a sip of water, and breathed deeply, trying to regain her composure.

'Look,' the lawyer said. His voice sounded like Kermit the Frog, completely at odds with the heft of his body, and took Tom by complete surprise. 'Yes, Sarah miscalculated the situation. She should have told you, but she has expressed remorse and explained why she did what she did. A woman wanting to find out if her husband is having an affair is not a crime. She did not attack the woman in question, as you can see on the video footage. She was calm and left when she had the answers she so desperately needed.'

He took a sip of water and looked like he was relishing the opportunity to play the knight-in-shining-armour role. He continued:

'Now, I've reviewed the evidence you have, and I use the word evidence very loosely, because what you have doesn't amount to anything worthwhile at all. There's no forensic evidence to link my client to any crime scene. After seeing Millie, she went straight home. A neighbour can testify to this, as he has a video of her car passing his drive that he captured from CCTV cameras set into his gate. She was nowhere near the Angel where her husband's body was discovered at any point that day. To sum it up, you have nothing at all. Sarah is innocent.'

Tom let the dust settle on this well-prepared monologue, and then dropped a bomb of his own: 'Millie Whitlock has been murdered.'

'What?' Sarah gasped. Her hand flew to her cheeks. 'When?'

'Yesterday.'

'Obviously, that is horrific news,' the lawyer said. 'But, Sarah has absolutely nothing to do with it. She was in all day, with the liaison officer *you* provided to guide her through this difficult time.'

'Except Alison didn't arrive until four o'clock yesterday,' Lauren said.

'And you think my client could kill someone, and an hour later be home, having discarded any forensic evidence, showered, changed and transformed into a welcoming host?'

'At two,' Sarah said, shakily, 'if you check my phone, I was on the landline, talking to my brother in South Africa. He's arranging to come over, and we were discussing pick-up arrangements from the airport.'

'I'd suggest checking those records quickly,' the lawyer warned. 'If my client is kept a single second longer than required, there will be hell to pay. Honestly, whatever happened to innocent until proven guilty?'

He stood. 'Sarah, we're done with this fiasco. I'll make sure you are out of here as soon as I possibly can.' He turned to Tom and Lauren. 'Now that all of your avenues have been exhausted, I assume you'll see to that.'

'Am I in danger?' Sarah asked, her voice small.

'No, we don't believe so.' Tom said, and ended the interview.

A uniformed officer entered the room and led Sarah out to go back to her holding cell.

'Off record,' the lawyer said to Tom and Lauren, 'you need to lay off her. Her husband has been murdered, and you've hauled her in here not once but twice. I beg of you, do what you need to do as quickly as you can, let her go and leave her to fucking grieve.'

He left the room and marched up the corridor, Lauren accompanying him to make sure he didn't go where he wasn't supposed to. Tom sat a while, feeling anger and revulsion mingle in his stomach. The lawyer's words stung. He needed to do something, but nothing he was doing was getting him anywhere.

His phone pinged. It was an e-mail from Craig, the tech guy in the basement, saying he had trawled through Millie's computer and phone, and she had apparently ended things with Richard weeks ago, just after she and Johnny got together. It seemed they had arranged to meet up at a hotel in Newcastle's city centre three times before the date of the draft e-mail, but that was it. The rest of their communication had been professional, though Richard had been using an e-mail address unregistered on his own devices that the police had seized.

Had Millie's boyfriend found out about their fling? It seemed weak, considering there was barely (if any) overlap, but maybe it was a pride thing. No one liked to think about their partner being intimate with someone else, and maybe Johnny was the overly sensitive type. Maybe the thought of the two ex-lovers working together was enough to tip him over the edge.

16

ALAN WAS HOLDING THE phone receiver between his ear and shoulder, and scribbling something on a notepad on the desk. When he saw Tom, he widened his eyes, nodded and smiled. He finished his call with a couple of thank yous, and told Tom the good news: they had a name and address.

The bad news was that the address was near Manchester, in the town of Stockport. It turned out Johnny Golding worked at a builders' merchants, though what had brought him to Gateshead in the first place was anyone's guess.

'So he must be staying somewhere around here with someone known to him?' Tom said.

'Nope,' Alan said, shaking his head. 'I just called the tech guys with the reg plate of Johnny's van, and he's pinged a tonne of cameras all the way down the A1 and then the M62.'

'What time?'

Alan checked his notes. 'He hit the first motorway camera at about 15:23.'

'So not long after he left Millie's.'

'Looks like he's fled a murder scene,' Alan said.

'Possibly,' Tom nodded. 'Though, if he was fleeing, surely he'd use the back roads to try and stay away from cameras.'

'People do silly things when they think they might have got themselves in trouble,' Alan said, before suggesting they get on the blower to their colleagues in Greater Manchester. Tom shook his head. The fire in his belly that the lawyer had stoked was raging on. He wanted to be the one to talk to Johnny.

Tom thanked Alan for the breakthrough and left the room. He strode over to Natalie's office and knocked. He ignored the offer of a seat, remaining standing, the energy coursing through him making him bounce on the balls of his feet.

He told his boss about their breakthrough and reasoned that the trail had run cold in the North East. Johnny *had* to account for the time he had spent around the back of Millie's house. The investigation could hinge on what he had to say. Tom had done interviews over video call before and hadn't liked it. According to research, non-verbal communication accounted for 55 per cent of how humans expressed themselves, and losing that much to the lens of a laptop's camera wasn't acceptable. Tom wanted to look into Johnny's eyes, to hear the words pour from his mouth. *He* wanted to be the judge of whether he was telling the truth or not.

Tom thought she could sense his agitation, because she immediately agreed that him travelling south was the best course of action.

'Great,' Tom said. 'I'll head on.'

'What, now?' she asked.

He nodded.

'How much sleep have you had in the past three days?'

'Not nearly enough, but I have a copper's best friend to help me.' From his pocket he pulled a crumpled packet of Pro Plus. She looked at it dubiously, but did not argue.

'Will you go straight to see him?' she asked.

'I looked at his website just now. It says his shop closes early today, so I'll get there first thing tomorrow morning. I think I'll stop in with my parents for the night.'

Natalie told him to be careful, to get in touch should he need anything, and then turned her attention back to her computer.

Tom went home and packed an overnight bag. While he was finding bits and pieces from his bedside drawers, he made the mistake of sitting down on the bed. The previous night had been a scramble to bring Sarah in and get an interview strategy worked out. After that, Tom had come home, but the image of Millie lying dead on the bed had not left him. Sleep had not come easy, if at all, and the pull of the duvet now was too much. A few hours wouldn't hurt, he reckoned.

* * *

It was almost 8 p.m. when Tom pulled into his parents' driveway. He sat for a moment, taking in Angela and Nigel's house. Their festive decorations would put Times Square to shame. In the front garden, flashing reindeer guided a neon-red Santa upon his sleigh. Every single window in the place had florescent snowflakes dancing and flashing. The brickwork was covered in twisting coils of lighted rope, spelling out a brightly lit 'Merry Christmas'. The rest of the cul-de-sac was the same, like something from a bombastic Elton John video. Tom was wondering how the national grid was coping, when the door opened, and Nigel appeared in the doorway with a huge smile plastered on his face.

'Tommy boy,' he said, walking towards Tom and enveloping him in a massive hug. 'How are you, son? To what do we owe this pleasure?'

'Do I need an excuse to drop in on my family?' Tom laughed.

'Not at all!' Nigel boomed, clapping him on the back.

'Actually, as nice as it is to see you, I'm here for work. There's a bloke I need to speak to in Stockport in the morning.'

Nigel nodded sagely and led Tom into the warmth of the house. Inside, Tom was expecting more neon, but it was actually very tastefully decorated. In the living room there was a tall tree, a lit garland across the fireplace and a sideboard filled with cards.

'Cuppa?' Nigel asked.

'One of your famous hot chocolates would be perfect.'

They walked to the kitchen, and Tom sat at the breakfast bar while his dad started up the fancy barista-grade machine he'd got for Christmas last year. It began to cough and splutter as Nigel pulled packets and mugs from various cupboards.

'Where's Angela?' Tom asked.

'Choir. They're singing in some church in Hazel Grove, but I didn't fancy it. She's been practising her harmonies around the house for months, and if I hear 'Ave Maria' one more bloody time, you might be needed to take me to the cells. It's been torture.' He checked his watch. 'She should be home soon, though, and if she asks, I never said a thing. Got it?'

Nigel slid a mug towards him with a wink, and a sudden sadness hit Tom. He missed living here. Nigel was a legend – all his friends agreed. He was the cool dad. He played bass guitar in a pub band. He had bought Tom a car when he passed his driving test, and made him compilation CDs of good driving music – Bowie, Hendrix, Queen. He was dependable and nice and had saved Tom's life in more ways than he would ever know.

Had he made a mistake moving to Newcastle?

No, he thought. He hadn't. It was a good move. A good promotion. He liked his team, and once he'd given his house a bit of a once-over, he'd like it, too. It wasn't like it was the other side of the world, was it?

The front door opened and Angela wandered into the kitchen, setting her keys in a bowl on the side.

'Tom,' she squealed, enveloping him in a tight squeeze. 'Why are you both sitting in the coldest room in the house? Get into the living room.'

They followed her down the hallway like a pair of badly behaved ducklings, and took up residence in the front room. It was much cosier, and Tom could feel his eyelids begin to droop as soon as he sank into the soft upholstery of his favourite armchair.

'How was choir?' he asked.

Angela cast a side-eye at Nigel. 'Has he been moaning?'

'No,' said Tom, a little too quickly. 'He was just saying he was sad he couldn't go.'

'You're an awful liar, Tom Stonem.' She laughed, before throwing a cushion at her husband. 'It was great, actually. They've asked us back next year.'

'You'll be booked for the Bridgewater Hall at this rate, love,' Nigel said. Another cushion narrowly missed his face.

'Have you heard from Seth much?' Angela asked, once Tom's laughter had abated.

'Not much, no,' Tom said. 'Have you?'

'It's hard to pin him down,' she replied. She pulled out her phone and navigated the menu, before handing it to Tom.

'Since when have you had Instagram?' he asked her.

'What are you saying it like that for?' She laughed. 'Are the over-60s not allowed to look at photos?'

'Depends what photos you're looking at.' He smiled back.

'You know me. I'm a nosy cow. I want to see what Mary is having for breakfast every day, and what shirt that lovely weatherman has chosen…'

'Which lovely weatherman?' Nigel piped up.

'And, of course, how Seth is getting on,' Angela carried on, as if she'd never heard her husband.

Tom flicked through photographs on his brother's account. There were Malaysian temples and vast, turquoise waterfalls. Bright sunlight glinted off the famous waters of Venice's canals. There was Machu Picchu, and Petra, and the Colosseum, and dozens of other famous places Tom would love to visit. And in front of each and every one of them was Seth, mostly alone, though occasionally with another person or as part of a group.

He was tanned, in good shape, and most importantly: he looked happy. Each picture had a lengthy caption under it, which Tom ignored.

'He seems to be having a lovely time,' Tom said.

'An enlightening one, by the looks of it. Every time he goes somewhere, he describes the experience in such detail. I'm wondering if he has found God.'

Tom wasn't sure if God was to be found in ancient killing fields or towering monuments built at the cost of many human lives, but he didn't say anything. It did make him wonder if there had been a switch of babies at birth, though. Seth and he were so unalike, always had been really, but the filtered photographs and lengthy spiritual diatribes were a million miles away from Tom's own life. He'd never been a fan of social media (though he was grateful that many were: countless cases he had worked on recently had been blown wide open by people oversharing and being loose with their privacy settings) and he'd always been a career man; he was unsure if Seth had ever had a job that had lasted longer than six months. He must have done, unless Nigel and Angela were funding this round-the-world excursion. Maybe Tom was being harsh. He should send his little brother a message and catch up.

One thing was for certain though: the last post Seth had put up was a picture of himself standing on the snaking Great Wall of China. It was stamped with yesterday's date, which meant Tom wouldn't need to worry about buying a Christmas present for baby bro for at least a couple more weeks.

Tom smiled at the thought of picking something up in the January sales, for a fraction of the price he would pay now. And, with that frugal thought, he excused himself and made his way upstairs to bed, the heaviness of the day tugging at his eyelids.

Before he lay down, he phoned Anna. The conversation was stilted. It was clear that she was still pissed off at him for missing the party, and further annoyed by his sojourn in the North West.

'When will I see you?' she asked.

'Tomorrow night,' he said. 'As soon as I get back.'

Her tone brightened slightly. 'Do you promise?'

'Pinky promise,' he said.

He hung up and hoped he could keep his word.

His dreams that night involved castration. It didn't take an oneirocritic to work out what that meant.

4 sleeps 'til Christmas

Miss was straight with me. Because I missed a lot of school, I was behind where I should be for someone my age. She kept talking about responsibility, and how I needed to be in charge of my own learning. I told her I would try harder, and begged her not to tell Mum and Dad. I didn't want Mum to have anything more on her plate. I didn't think Dad would care that much, but sometimes he was weird about things like this.

She agreed to keep it between us, as long as I stayed in at lunch to do the work I'd forgotten. When the bell rang at twelve, I walked with her to the staffroom. She grabbed a chair for me and told me to sit outside while she ate.

I got on with it for a while, and then I got bored. I'd worked hard all morning. I needed a break. I was sitting back in my chair when Mr Gibson walked past.

He told me to stop daydreaming, and to get on with it —I wasn't here for a jolly. He disappeared into the staffroom.

A minute later, Mrs Berney – my brother's teacher – came out of the room, but stopped midway out of the door. Someone had shouted her name, and now she stood listening to them.

It was hard to hear what they were saying, because elsewhere in the room Mr Gibson was talking loudly about me. He was talking to another teacher about my clothes, and how smelly I was. I'd always wanted to know what went on in the staffroom, but now I wished I hadn't. I started to cry. I covered my eyes with my jumper, and tried to stop, but couldn't.

Mr Gibson's voice was drifting out of the room, louder now. He was telling anyone who would listen that I was a lost cause, because I was from the wrong side of the tracks. My teacher was standing up for me, but I didn't want to listen anymore. I'd probably get in trouble, but I got up from my seat and ran towards the toilets. The corridors were mostly empty, luckily. But, as I rounded the corner towards the toilets, Holly walked out of our classroom. She was with a friend, and when they saw me, they stopped and stared at my red eyes, and the tears streaming down my cheeks.

Holly started to laugh, and her little puppet friend did the same. I pushed past them, and ran into the toilet. I locked myself in one of the cubicles, and pounded on the walls with my fists until my knuckles were swollen and bloody.

As I calmed down, I thought about Christmas. If I had written a list, I'd add on that I wished Mr Gibson would be involved in a car accident over the holidays, or that masked men 'from the wrong side of the tracks' broke into his house and robbed him at gunpoint. Maybe then he'd know how it felt to live a life like mine.

17

A CAR ROLLED PAST, coming too close to the kerb and spraying icy water all over Lauren. Her trousers got soaked, and her Converse were so waterlogged they felt like she was walking on the bottom of the ocean.

Just great, she thought.

She looked down at Sophie, who was carrying a green umbrella with big frog eyes. She seemed to have been missed by the water completely. Small mercies – Lauren did not have time to take her daughter home to get changed. Nor, for that matter, did she have any spare uniform to change her into. She really needed to get on top of things.

They walked on, among the sea of bodies, towards the school gates. Suddenly, Sophie tugged on Lauren's sleeve and said, 'There she is.'

'There who is?' Lauren said.

'The smiling lady.'

Lauren looked to where Sophie was pointing, but could see only a mass of umbrellas and people hurrying along the street, eager to get out of the downpour.

'Where is she?' Lauren asked.

'Where I'm pointing,' Sophie said. 'I think she might've gone round the corner of the bank.'

Lauren fixed her attention on the corner of Moor Lane. The Santander sign glowed red, and there was a man in a dark suit and a long overcoat using the ATM. He was jabbing the buttons angrily, as if that would make the machine go faster. Aside from him, and a few passers-by, Lauren couldn't see any smiling lady.

'Are you sure it was the same person you've seen the other times?'

'Yes. She was waving at me.'

'What does she look like?'

Sophie shrugged. 'Her hair is brown, and she was wearing a big silver necklace, like a mayor.'

'Look...' Lauren started, but got cut off by her daughter's excited squeal when she saw Emma and her mum crossing the road towards them.

'Would you mind walking Sophie the rest of the way?' Lauren asked Emma's mum. 'I've got a work thing that's urgent.'

'No problem,' she said.

Lauren kissed Sophie and handed her her water bottle, before threading through traffic on the main road and looking down Moor Lane. The man who had been at the ATM was gone. Some parents who had already delivered their children to school were heading back down the road, walking in groups and taking up most of the pavement. Lauren joined them and was halfway down when she saw a head peek out from a doorway near the bottom of the street. It was a woman with brown, curly hair.

Lauren took off, pushing past the dawdling mothers. One of them shouted something after Lauren, but the noise hardly registered. The woman with the brown hair left her hiding place and walked briskly around the corner at the bottom of the street. Lauren spotted the oversized silver necklace bouncing against her chest. She sped up and was about to cross the road when an Amazon delivery van emerged from a side street and blocked her way.

Cursing, she jinked around the van and ran as fast as she could down the centre of the road. At last, she reached the corner and careered around it, to find the street mostly empty. There were a few straggling children, their parents barking at them to get a move on. A couple of people leaving their houses and rushing to parked cars, dressed for a day in a city-centre office. But there was no sign of the woman Lauren had been chasing.

She checked the alleys, doorways and front yards of Lower Moor Lane. But the smiling woman was nowhere to be found.

Maybe Lauren was overacting. After all, Sophie was five and hardly the most trustworthy witness. The woman with the brown hair might be a parent of a child at the school; she might have been waving at one of her friends. Maybe she had simply been on her way home and lived in one of the red-brick houses on the street.

Lauren wasn't convinced, though. Something didn't seem right. But she didn't have time to go knocking door to door to find the smiling woman. Tom was galivanting around Manchester, and she needed to get to the office as quickly as she could.

18

MEANWHILE, IN MANCHESTER, TOM was running late.

He had woken to the smell of food frying and, by the time he'd showered and made it downstairs, a feast fit for a king awaited him. The table was covered in plates and bowls, offering sausages, bacon, croissants and those little mini muffins favoured by upmarket hotel chains. Angela had even deemed the occasion worthy of 'the good plates'.

Though he'd told her in the past that this amount of effort was unnecessary, he knew better than to complain or remonstrate with her today. It had gone unsaid, but him moving to Newcastle was a big deal. With Seth trailblazing around the four corners of the globe, Tom had been the constant. The reliable one.

And now, he wasn't. He had moved one hundred and fifty miles away.

So, despite having a rather time-sensitive task on his day-planner, he sat down and piled his plate high. Angela flitted around the kitchen like a whirling dervish, filling his glass with more orange juice the moment he drained it and topping up his plate until he was worried the button on his trousers was going to pop under the strain of his groaning gut.

His plan to get to Johnny's place of business bang on 9 a.m. was scuppered, but he hoped half an hour wouldn't make a difference.

At 9:35 a.m., Tom pulled into the car park of DW Building Merchants on an industrial estate on the outskirts of Stockport.

He hung up on Alan, who had phoned him with more information on Johnny. Information that shone a harsh light on Millie's boyfriend.

The building was a large rectangle made of corrugated iron with a sloping roof. Above the door was a wooden sign emblazoned with the company's name, in need of a lick of paint. To the back of the building was a massive yard filled with lengths of wood and heavy bags of stones, cordoned off from the public by a tall metal fence, accessible through a locked gate.

There were vans in the car park, emblazoned with a stylized red DW, but aside from them, it seemed like a quiet morning at the office. Builders had probably done half a day's work already, Tom thought, as he pushed open the door of the shop.

Inside was a DIY nut's dream. Everything was on one floor: rows and rows of shelves, housing seemingly every tool ever invented. Some of the higher ticket items were security-locked with flashing tags. At the back of the shop was a collection of ladders, hung up by their rungs, and at the front, behind a wooden partition housing a till and a green charity collection pot, was Johnny.

His ginger hair looked shaggy and unwashed, and his blue eyes were obscured by drooping lids. He wore a grey T-shirt and a pair of workman chinos, the side pockets bulging. The scent of a citrusy shower gel was prominent, yet still failed to cover the obvious stench of a night on the tiles.

He smiled at Tom and asked for a moment's patience as he finished changing a receipt roll in the till. He disappeared through a door and reappeared a couple of minutes later holding a cylindrical wad of paper. He busied himself at the till, mumbling apologies to Tom every ten seconds or so.

'Sorry,' he said once more, and straightened up. 'How can I help you?'

'I'm Detective Inspector Tom Stonem, and I'd like to ask you some questions.'

Johnny looked nervous but tried to mask it. He lifted a mug with a bawdy joke inscribed on it and took a swig. Tom had seen the move a million times before – Johnny was buying himself some time. He set the mug down again, with a little more force than intended. Tea slopped over the side and soaked into a ledger on the counter, though Johnny didn't seem to notice.

'What's this about?' he asked, as coolly as he could.

'Maybe you'd like to take a seat,' Tom said, and motioned to the padded office chair behind the counter. Johnny followed his advice, worry etched onto his weather-beaten face. 'Millie Whitlock was found dead two days ago, on the nineteenth of December.'

'Dead?' he repeated.

'Yes, I'm sorry to be the one to break it to you. There will be a media announcement soon, but I wanted to tell you face to face first. Millie was murdered, and we are trying to catch her killer,' Tom said.

'Fuck.' Johnny looked at Tom like he was waiting for a punch-line, or for Tom to realise he had walked into the wrong builders' merchants and informed the wrong guy of his girlfriend's murder.

'I know this news must come as a shock,' Tom said. 'But I'd like to ask you some questions about your relationship with Millie.'

'What? You can't think that I had anything to do with it!'

Tom didn't know whether that was a question or a statement, and didn't answer it anyway. He was thinking about the time Johnny had spent round the back of Millie's house, and how, at this point, he very much did think Johnny had something to do with it.

'Mr Golding, please could you tell me about your relationship with Millie? How did you know each other?'

'We met on a night out. I was up in Newcastle on business, and me and a mate went out. I bumped into Millie in a club, and we got talking. She was nice, and we agreed to meet up again.'

'What were you in Newcastle on business for? Do the builders of Newcastle rely on materials from Stockport?'

'We have contacts where we can source materials that are hard to get.' Johnny shrugged. 'Once you supply to builders once, you tend to do repeat business. It's an unreliable business at the best of times, but if you can show yourself to be dependable, people come back time and time again. The amount of money we were earning made a two-hour trip up north worth it. Throw Millie into the bargain, and I was thinking of moving up for good.'

'You saw a future with her?'

'Definitely.' His eyes misted over, and Tom allowed him a moment.

'How many times did you see her?'

'Maybe six or so, over the space of a month and a half.'

'Run me through what you did on the nineteenth.'

Johnny took a moment to put the pieces together. When he'd done his mental jigsaw, he spoke: 'I had a few calls to make in the morning in the north of the city. When I'd done that, I went round to Millie's. We'd agreed to meet for brunch, but she never turned up. I assumed she'd had a heavy night at her work party, so went round to see if she was about. She didn't answer, and I had to get back home for a mate's birthday party. I tried calling her a few more times during the day but could never catch her, so assumed maybe she'd lost her phone or something. When I didn't hear from her at all yesterday, I was getting worried that something was wrong, or that she'd dumped me and not told me.'

'We have CCTV footage of you disappearing around the back of her house for twenty minutes or so. What were you doing?'

'I went round the back to see if she was in the garden or in the park behind her house. Sometimes we'd jump the fence and go for a walk in the park, so that's what I did, to see if I could spot her.'

'Did you try the back door to see if it was unlocked?' Tom asked.

'Yeah.'

'And was it?'

'No,' Johnny said. 'She was a bit OCD about locking her doors. She liked to watch true crime documentaries, even though they scared the life out of her, so when she went to bed, she'd check every door and window was locked like five times.'

'We know that whoever murdered Millie gained entry through the back door, so if you are telling me it was intact when you got there, it helps us narrow down the time of death,' Tom explained.

'I swear.' Johnny nodded. 'Everything looked normal. Door locked. No windows open.'

'Thank you. Just one more question, if that's okay?'

Johnny nodded.

'Did you know Millie and her boss once had an affair?'

'Mills and Richard Handsworth?' Johnny asked. 'The politician she worked for? Ha, no way. Someone has given you wrong information somewhere down the line.'

'I can assure you—'

'Whatever you think you know,' he interrupted, 'you don't. Millie would never have gone out with a man like Richard fucking Handsworth in a hundred years.'

Johnny sounded like a man trying to convince no one but himself. Calmly, Tom explained the evidence that they had. The drafted e-mail. The gala pictures. Sarah's confession.

'I'll never believe you,' Johnny said. 'She always went on about what an arse he was. I can guarantee you they never got together in that way.'

It was time to play the trump card that Alan had given Tom over the phone.

'Here's the thing, Johnny. I know about your past. Six months in juvie for assault. Assault involving an ex-girlfriend.'

'That's different,' Johnny stuttered. 'That was a long time ago. You can't think…'

'I can think. It's something I'm very good at. And what I think happened is, you found out about Richard and Millie, and you went round to her house to teach her a lesson.'

Johnny's face paled, and he started to gasp. 'I need water…'

He pushed himself up from the chair and went into the back room. Tom ran around the counter and followed him into the back, just in time to see an external door smash back into its frame.

'Fuck.' Tom ran at the door, throwing his full weight at it. He burst through it into the huge lot at the back, crammed with machinery and wooden panels. Johnny was running towards a gate at the back, faster than Tom imagined a hungover man could move. Tom took off, the contents of his breakfast roiling in his stomach. He was at a disadvantage: Johnny probably knew this area like the back of his hand, and, if Tom lost him, he would surely go to ground.

Still running, Tom watched Johnny burst through the gate and turn left. Thanks to the amount of stuff piled against the fence, he lost sight of his prey. He pulled his phone from his pocket, phoned GMP and requested immediate back-up, his words coming in staccato bursts, punctuated by heavy breaths. Luckily, the dispatcher was an old friend and understood him, assuring him help was on its way.

Spilling through the gate, Tom turned left but knew the chase was over. Johnny could have disappeared into any one of the multitude of warehouses or alleyways that snaked their way through the estate. He slowed down to a walk, and patrolled back and forth until two police cars arrived.

Tom filled the officers in on why he was there, and how apprehending Johnny was a matter of urgency. They told him they would leave no stone unturned and traded numbers. Tom made his way back into Johnny's shop with one of the officers, keen to have something to show to his boss when his failure to detain the little scrote came to light.

He must be hiding something: why else would he have run away?

The back room of the shop was messy. There was a small TV screen fastened to one of the walls, and a table upon which a variety of magazines lay haphazardly. A paper bin was full of polystyrene cups and protein bar wrappers.

A filing cabinet in the corner of the room caught Tom's attention. Each drawer was given to a financial year, so Tom opened the most recent and pulled out the contents, laying them on the faux-wood floor. There were a number of ledgers, and what looked like thousands of receipts and invoices. It was going to take serious manpower to get through them.

Tom asked the officer with him to get on the blower to his DCI and ask for more bodies. The officer pushed himself up and got his phone from his pocket. While he was chatting, Tom got the distinct impression the DCI on the other end was none too happy about being told what to do by a DI from Northumberland. He reached out for the phone, thinking if he explained the case his officers would be pouring themselves into, it might smooth out some of the creases. However, his own phone rang.

It was Natalie.

Had she heard about his failure on the wind? Bracing himself, he pressed the green button.

'Tom,' she said. 'I need you back here. There's been another one.'

19

Tom spent the drive back to Newcastle trying to get a handle on the case. He'd asked Natalie not to tell him anything about the latest body, because he didn't want someone else's observations to cloud his own first impression of the crime scene.

Instead of looking forward, he returned to the past.

Richard Handsworth had been found at the Angel of the North on the sixteenth of December; just five days ago. He had the Christmas list in his pocket and had died from massive trauma to the head and strangulation, with a side order of stabbing. Two days later, Millie had been accosted outside her Christmas party by Richard's wife, who wanted to know more about her and the MP's affair – an affair Sarah had denied any knowledge of before the CCTV footage made a liar of her. The next day, at some point in the afternoon, someone broke in to Millie's house and stabbed her to death. They left a picture of Richard and her looking rather cosy.

The suspect pool had grown and shrunk. Sarah had an ironclad alibi for Millie's death and a pretty good one for Richard's. Johnny was currently looking like the most compelling suspect, having abandoned his own business to get away from Tom. Tom had a pretty good idea that Johnny knew more about the affair than he was letting on. He also could have been lying about the back door of Millie's house not being smashed in when he visited; he *had* been around the back of the house for a long time. Tom had asked for CCTV from the park in order to corroborate Johnny's story about going for a leisurely walk in search of his girlfriend.

Unfortunately, there'd been no sightings of Johnny on the industrial estate at all. Tom had a sneaky suspicion that a mate was currently sheltering him, unwilling to give him up to the fuzz.

When he got bored of going round and round in torturous mental circles, he turned the radio on. It was a phone-in about the case, and he listened with detached interest. Most of the callers thought Sarah was behind the killing.

Without the evidence that Tom was privy to, he too would probably have thought that. Of course, she was the only suspect who had been named in the papers, so Joe Public had no one else to point the finger at.

Jane from Dundee thought the police had been very short-sighted in letting Sarah go. According to her, they should have kept Sarah in the cell until she confessed. Quite a medieval tactic, Tom thought, and one that would certainly not go down well with any lawyer. The next caller, a chap called Gareth with a West Country twang, was adamant that a concoction he had devised would have Sarah spilling her guts in no time. When asked what ingredients had gone into his truth brew, he became wary, and started talking about live-action role play instead, where he had just obtained the role of spiritual healer.

The public were idiots, Tom decided (not for the first time), and turned the radio off.

* * *

Tom was sick and tired of industrial estates. This one, Benton Square, was in the north of Newcastle, and looked like every other one across the country.

A rabbit warren of roads wound through enormous corrugated-iron buildings. No-nonsense signs adorned the front of the structures. Those that tried to go a bit fancier with their branding ended up looking like they'd been designed by an overly ambitious but wholly underqualified sixth-form art and design student.

He passed the offices of Frank Woods – he of digging-holes-at-the-Angel-of-the-North fame. Was it odd that the builder had a connection to that murder scene, and this one? After all, a troop of police cars and other liveried vehicles were only a few doors down from his place of business, their strobing blue lights pulsating in the dying embers of sunlight. As Tom pulled up behind a pool car and got out, he made a mental note to get in touch with Frank.

A heavy sheet of rain was falling, and the already icy ground was slick beneath his boots. So as not to fall, he held on to each vertical pole of the fence that ran along the length of the path. The last thing he needed after losing a suspect was to turn up at the next crime scene with a shattered coccyx, so he took his time.

He made it, without incident, to the small tent that served as the in/out access to the crime scene. He showed his warrant card to the waiting uniformed officer. Inside the tent, he signed in and suited up, and made his way in. Behind the tent, the car park that served Benton Fabrics was cordoned off with the standard blue and white tape. A couple of suited bodies were floating about, deep in quiet conversation. One of them pointed Tom in the direction of the action, and Tom nodded his thanks.

He walked to the back of the car park and passed another officer who was standing guard at the edge of a path that led around the back of the building. The path was lit by a series of motion-sensor bulbs fixed high on the side of the building, and the forensic team had laid down a series of stepping plates. A good thing, too, because the path was made from crazy paving. Tom could only imagine how treacherous the journey would've been on the icy, uneven walkway.

He walked through a gate leading to a wide patio that was home to an oil tank made of a white plastic. It was raised on a concrete cradle, ovaloid in shape, and much taller than Tom. The safety stickers were still attached, though torn at the edges and discoloured from years of exposure to the elements. A platform of wooden boards and scaffolding poles was set up beside it, upon which the crime scene photographer stood, lighting up the late afternoon with a succession of flashes.

Natalie's eyes met Tom's and she made her way over.

'Tom, are you all right?' she asked.

'I'm fucked off that I let Johnny get away,' he replied.

'Let it go,' she said with a smile. 'We know where he works, we know where he lives, and the tech guys are going through his computers as we speak. If he didn't want to tell you who he's been dealing with up here, that tells us he has something to hide. We'll find out, and that's thanks to you.'

Natalie was showing good leadership. While she might have been pissed off with her newly appointed detective inspector, publicly she gave him what he needed: encouragement, rather than a dressing-down. Though Tom was grateful, he still felt like a failure. Her words felt to him like the dreaded vote of confidence footballing boards give to their ailing managers just before the chop.

'I need to get off,' she said. 'But Iain will talk you through the scene. Keep a cool head, yeah?'

She patted him twice on the shoulder and left. What did she mean – keep a cool head? Was she patronising him?

'Shall I get you up to speed?' Iain asked, before Tom could psychoanalyse her comment any further.

Tom nodded and was invited to climb onto the platform the crime scene photographer had vacated. Tom did as he was asked. The metal was cold against his hands, and suddenly a wave of exhaustion hit him. He longed to be back in the warmth of his car or, even better, his bed.

Still, he knew there was a job to be done, and silently rebuked himself for his moment of weakness. Something awful awaited him, and that something awful was someone's son or daughter, wife or brother. When he got to the top, he peered into the opening of the oil tank and could hardly believe his eyes at what awaited him.

Inside was the body of a man. He was lying on his side, half-immersed in the oil in the foetal position, knees pulled up to his chest and his arms by his sides. The oil tank was mostly empty, with only a small amount of liquid resting at the bottom.

Tom saw that he was completely naked.

'Has anyone been in?' he asked.

'Aye. Henry has. Moaned the whole time about getting oil on his good shoes. You'd think he'd know not to wear his Sunday best to a fucking crime scene by now, eh? Daft bugger.' Iain laughed.

'What's the thing around his neck?'

'A lanyard.'

'ID card?' Tom asked, hopeful.

'Nope. The wee bit where the card would slot into is there, but the card is missing.'

Of course it was.

'And we have no idea who it is?'

'Nada.' Iain shrugged. 'But now that you've seen him in situ, we can get him moved. Try and get an identification as quickly as we can.'

'Do you think this is related to the Richard Handsworth case?'

'We assumed that might be so. You'd think if the killer is trying to make some political point, he'd be targeting people of similar stature or from the same party as Handsworth, but Henry didn't recognise this guy, and he's pretty clued up on current affairs. It would be nice if it was connected, as it would give us more to play with, but it seems it might be just another killer hoping the Dicky Hands case might be taking up most of our time.'

Tom thanked Iain and climbed down off the platform carefully. He went around to the car park. As he made his way towards the fabric shop's door, Lauren emerged from it. She looked tired, and it was the first time he'd seen her without lipstick on.

'Fucked up, eh?' she said by way of greeting.

'Just a bit. What have you got?' he asked.

'Well, the man who found the body was the oil delivery man. Guy named Lewis Henderson. He said the lady who owns the fabric shop' – Lauren checked her notepad – 'Ivy Finnan, had asked for the delivery to be today, as she was expecting a Christmas rush and wanted the place to be nice and warm. Said she'd just finished brewing a fresh batch of mulled wine, but I didn't get a drop. Lewis turned up when he should've, took the top off the tank, looked inside to make sure everything was spick and span and nearly fell off the ladder when he saw what was in there. He's properly shaken up. Threw up all over the car park.'

'Poor guy,' said Tom. 'What about Ivy?'

'Devastated, as you'd imagine. The story Lewis told us checks out. I've checked her call logs, and she phoned the oil company when Lewis said she had. She had the appointment in a Google calendar. Obviously, the tech guys will look at her computers and what have you, but, to me, they're both innocent in this.'

Tom agreed. If Ivy had been behind the murder of whoever the guy was in the tank, she wouldn't have left him in there to be discovered. He was thrusting his hand into his pocket to grab his own notebook, when it brushed against something else.

He pulled out the plastic wallet, inside which the photocopy of the Christmas list rested. He looked at the first two items: No Angel and the red dress. Both of those could be crossed off now. The third item made his blood run cold.

Alien egg toy.

An image of the toy flashed in Tom's mind. He'd never had one, but his mate had. He could see the moulded plastic container in the shape of an egg. He could feel the squelchy goo between his fingers and the stretchy body of the alien. The body in the oil tank replaced the image of the alien in the egg, and Tom fought the urge to yell in frustration.

'It's the Christmas List Killer,' he said, shoving the photocopy into Lauren's hands.

20

AFTER A FRUITLESS FEW hours at the station, where all he and Lauren could do was review what scant evidence they had and speculate on what they might learn from their John Doe, exhaustion hit Tom like a ten-tonne hammer blow.

He asked Natalie to let him know the moment they had anything new, and then drove home to the house he'd had little time to do anything with. When he pulled up outside, he struggled to remember a single moment of the journey. He made sure his car was locked and trudged up the path towards his door.

As the case was taking up most of his waking moments, most of his belongings were still in boxes scattered between the rooms. He *had* made a point of ensuring the bedroom was accessible and mess-free. He'd read something once about a direct correlation between clutter and sleep deprivation, and had always made an effort to keep his bedroom clear.

On the day he moved in, he had made it to the off-licence, and so had a four-pack of beers chilling in the fridge. He had only ever been drunk a handful of times, and hated how it felt. He didn't enjoy being out of control. However, he did enjoy a beer before bed. It calmed him and helped him switch off from the stress of the day.

He took a bottle out, opened it, and sat down on the sofa. He drank it quickly. Usually, he would use his beer-before-bedtime to go over what had happened in the day, to try and separate his job from his life. However, tonight, it felt like his brain was a runner trying to speed through treacle. It wasn't happening, so he finished his beer, climbed the stairs, brushed his teeth, and lay down on his bed fully clothed.

And then he remembered where he was supposed to be.

He grabbed his phone and called Anna.

'You pinky promised,' she said.

'I know,' Tom said. 'I'm so sorry. I…'

'Tom. I don't want any more excuses. It's obvious you aren't as into me as I thought you were. If you were using me for a place to crash, that's pretty low, but I'd rather you be straight with me.'

'It's not that. At all,' Tom said. 'I do like you. There was another body found. Nothing's been reported to the media yet, but it's kept me busy all day. I'm sorry. I know we said we'd go out tonight, but it just completely left my head.'

'That's nice to know.' She sighed loudly. 'Look, I don't know if I can do this. I want someone I can trust. Who wants to spend time together. This feels like… I don't know… a bad omen. If this is the start of our relationship, what's it going to be like down the line?'

Tom didn't know what to say, so stayed quiet.

'I thought you were one of the good guys,' she said.

Before Tom could reply, she hung up. He tried to call back, but it went straight to voicemail. She'd obviously turned her phone off.

Tom threw his phone onto the pillow, and mentally chastised himself. He had a nice girlfriend, who he genuinely liked and who didn't expect too much of him, and yet he still couldn't live up to his end of the bargain. He vowed to make it right in the morning. He'd send her flowers and make dinner reservations for the evening. Killer or no killer, he'd be there.

Despite his exhaustion, sleep wouldn't come. Before plugging his phone in to the charger, he texted her an apology. Then he checked Instagram. He wasn't a prolific user, and rarely posted, but he was interested to see where Seth had visited today.

Turned out he was in Hanoi, Vietnam's capital. He was sitting on a kerb, next to a street vendor's cart. In his hand, he had a bowl of something that looked delicious. The accompanying caption was full of hippy crap, thanking the Gods for safe passage, good food, and even better friends.

Tom's last thought before he fell into a deep sleep was that maybe he would get his brother a Bible for Christmas.

3 sleeps 'til Christmas

The police came to school today.

The headteacher came round the classes and told us all to come to a special assembly immediately. He gave Miss a look, and he had this stern expression on his face. We were right in the middle of converting fractions to decimals, mid-question, but Miss cut maths short and told us to line up as quickly and quietly as we could. Jamie was whispering to Ross as we went into the assembly hall, and the headteacher went bonkers, shouting at him to show some respect. I've never seen him so cross. His face was bright red.

Then we found out why he was so stressed. A copper walked in.

He was a big man. His shoulders were wide and square, his face like a concrete block with furry sideburns.

He pushed the double doors open like he was a cowboy walking into a saloon, and strode slowly down the side of the hall. When he got to the front, he stood there like Billy Big Bollocks, looking out at every face. I swear his gaze lingered on mine for a fraction too long. He pointed at the radio that was tucked into his chest pocket and told us he wasn't supposed to turn it off.

Ever.

He could get in serious trouble if he did.

But I watched him reach for it and turn the little knob on the top of it. The red light flickered and died, and he fixed us with his glare again. He told us the message he was here to deliver was more important than anything that was happening on the streets outside.

One of the little kids down at the front, a Year One (I think) started to cry, and Miss Thompson, one of the teaching assistants, went and took her out.

When the copper spoke again, his voice was a bit softer, and he started to talk about 'a recent spate of bad behaviour'. I had to ask Miss what spate meant when we went back to class. She said it means a load of the same type of stuff, or something like that. When he told us what people were doing, it didn't sound too bad. A bit of graffiti on some buildings, some fights down where all the pubs are. To be fair I was sad when he talked about the nasty things someone's been doing to some families' pets. But I've seen worse in my own house. I thought about telling him about some of the stuff my dad got up to, but decided there was no point.

I noticed Gemma was crying now, and Miss was trying to calm her down. The worst thing she's ever done is make a spelling mistake, and I doubt the police are going to lock her up for forgetting i before e except after c. But she still kept blubbing like a ninny until the policeman had left.

When I was little, I thought coppers were so cool. I even thought I might like to marry one someday. Someone kind who would keep me safe and on the right track. But I know that was stupid now. It's obvious that cops didn't really care about people like us.

21

Tom was pulled from his slumber at just after half past five in the morning by loud ringing. He groggily reached for his trusty iPhone in the darkness, his sleep-filled eyes squinting against the harsh light emitted by the screen.

'We have a name,' Natalie said.

'I'll be right there,' Tom replied, his voice croaky.

He got dressed quickly and rushed out the door. The roads were quiet, and he reached the station in no time at all. The car park was surprisingly full, and he had to park near the back. The cold of the morning was biting and unpleasant, and Tom hurried towards the relative warmth of the station.

Inside, Natalie had called a meeting. The briefing room for Operation Fluffle was already full, but Lauren had kept him a seat near the front. A few bleary-eyed officers were crowded around the coffee table, duly emptying sachet after sachet of sugar into their brews. The hushed, expectant chatter that preceded any important briefing seemed to echo around the room.

'She said anything yet?' Tom asked, as he sat down.

'Nothing,' Lauren replied shortly. 'She's waiting for everyone to get here.'

Under the table, Lauren's foot was tapping impatiently. It seemed he'd caught her in a bad mood. 'Makes sense,' he said innocuously. He glanced over at the drinks table. 'It's times like this I wish I drank coffee. Even just for something to warm my hands up on.'

'I don't know how you survive without it,' Lauren said. 'I think I've had too much caffeine already today though. If I'm not careful it makes me jumpy.'

Grumpy, more like, he thought to himself, as Natalie took to the floor. She stood in front of a large whiteboard with wheels. It was covered in pictures and notes and maps. The DCI cleared her throat and allowed a moment for the would-be baristas to scurry back to their seats. Silence descended on the room.

'Thanks for getting here early,' she said. 'The press are going to be all over us with this, so I wanted to get the ball rolling as soon as I could.'

She pointed to a photo of a man on the board, stuck next to Richard's and Millie's. Before she spoke again, there was a mass grabbing of notepads and pens from pockets.

'This is our third victim. His name is Zachary Willis. Thirty-nine years old. His mother identified the body in the early hours of this morning. Apparently, he had been missing for a couple of days, and she'd been phoning the police each morning to find out if any bodies had been discovered. Her daughter drove past the crime scene last night on her way back from work, told her mam there was a big police presence near Zach's house, and the mam came down to the station.'

'Do we know anything about him?' Tom asked.

'We know he was a teacher at the local comprehensive. He lived in Longbenton, so not far away from where his body was found. The forensic report will be along today, but the headlines are that he had been stabbed multiple times in the abdomen. There's a big chunk of his thigh missing, too, but we're not sure why. He died from massive blood loss.'

She gave the room time to absorb all the information she'd dished out, before continuing.

'At the moment, we are working on the assumption that the perpetrator is the same person who killed Richard Handsworth and Millie Whitlock. We don't know if there is a concrete link, but hopefully we will establish that before the day is out. Tom has a theory about the Christmas list found on Richard's body, but as the link from that to this one is tenuous, we're keeping an open mind. It may be related; it may not.'

This was a sign of good police work, but Tom still felt a jolt of annoyance. To him, the link was far from tenuous. Richard Handsworth had been posed like an angel near the Angel. The *No Angel* CD was item one on the list. Millie's Christmas party dress was red, and a red party dress was number two on the list.

As for Zach, Tom couldn't think of any other way to replicate an alien in an egg other than a dead man in an oil tank. Tom wasn't sure how Natalie wasn't seeing the link, but didn't want to speak out of turn.

He was sure there was a connection and intended to prove it.

Natalie went through the day's actions, and divvied out who would be doing what. Tom was still feeling raw about letting Johnny escape, so volunteered for more than the lion's share, much to the palpable relief of those around him, who no doubt saw sitting in the office and making enquiring phone calls rather than trooping round Newcastle in sub-zero temperatures as the lesser of two evils.

Tom and Lauren's day was planned. As the three locations were fairly close together, they would go to Zach's home and see what they could uncover there, before heading to the school where he taught, and finally the fabric shop to find out if him being dumped in their oil tank was some sort of message.

Before any of that, Natalie planned to host a press conference, in the hope of relaying the news to the breakfast crowd. Perhaps someone on their way to work saw something they'd dismissed as nothing the night before but may reconsider in light of a death.

'Tom,' Natalie said. 'I'd like you in on it, too. Let's show them we're not fucking around.'

* * *

Despite the late notice and early start time, the conference room was crowded. All the seats were taken, and the space at the back of the room, usually allocated to bigger cameras on tripods, was filled with bodies, too. Some reporters had arrived too late and been relegated to a hastily set up viewing suite (a rather grandiose name for a nearby cupboard with a computer screen set up on a makeshift table).

Tom was a bit nervous. The case was high profile, and so far he had managed to keep his mug off the telly. Now, he'd be front and (almost) centre. He and Natalie were outside the room, listening to Joanne Batt – the Media and Communications Manager – prep the waiting journalists with the standard greeting and rules. Everyone in attendance knew them all already, but protocol must be adhered to.

Finally, he heard his own name and the door swung inwards. He ignored the retina-burning camera flashes, instead keeping a steely gaze on his seat. The table at the front reminded him of a footballer-signing. On it was a jug of water and two glasses; a couple of microphones emblazoned with television channel insignias; around ten Dictaphones, and a selection of mobile phones, already set to record. Tom took a seat, and Natalie followed suit.

'Good morning, everyone,' she started. 'Sorry to get you out of your beds so early. There have been a number of developments in the past twenty-four hours. A body has been found on an industrial estate in Longbenton. We are keeping the name to ourselves for now, but we are treating the death as suspicious. If any member of the public was in that area in the past few days, and noticed anything suspicious, we'd like them to get in touch.'

A tall man raised his hand, a pen gripped in it. He stood before speaking. 'Archie Walker, *The Guardian*. Is this death linked to the murders of Richard Handsworth and Millie Whitlock?'

'We aren't ruling anything out at the moment,' Natalie said, before addressing the room at large. 'I'd appreciate it if you kept questions until the end.'

Archie Walker sat down, like a scolded boy. Natalie continued.

'We are keen to talk to Johnny Golding, as a witness. Johnny was last seen in Stockport, but has links to the North East. Again, any information concerning his whereabouts would be gratefully received.'

'Is he a suspect?' Archie again.

Tom could feel heat rise in his cheeks. Not only did he consider Archie rude, he was also concerned the truth about him being the one to lose Johnny would come to light. As he opened his mouth, Joanne thankfully got there before him.

'A reminder that questions should be saved to the end,' she said, before a rather pointed 'thank you.'

The rest of the press conference ran as it should. Natalie handled any awkward questions with the skill of someone who has attended too many media-training courses. It was like listening to a footballer give the bland, non-offensive answers to questions that inevitably came after a loss:

We'll try harder next week; we let the fans down; #WeGoAgain

Thankfully, he and Natalie were on the same team. After the last question, they got up to leave. As they walked down the aisle, Archie had positioned himself at the end of the row of seats.

'They don't have a fucking clue what they're doing,' he said, perfectly timed and loud enough for Tom to hear. Tom stopped in his tracks and eyeballed the reporter. Archie had a couple of inches on Tom, but he was thin and looked like he spent more time discussing the intricacies of vintage wines with friends at a country club than lifting heavy weights. Tom took a step towards him, but Natalie hissed in his ear to get moving. He held Archie's gaze for a second longer, and followed Natalie's order.

'Prick,' Tom said, when they'd left the room.

'Agreed. He is a prick,' Natalie replied, 'but it's no good coming across all threatening. Never become the headline.'

Tom nodded.

'Now,' said Natalie, 'don't you have a busy day ahead of you?'

'Ma'am,' he said, and strode down the corridor, keen for some fresh air and a catch-up with Lauren.

22

ZACH WILLIS LIVED IN a flat not far away from where he died.

Three identical blocks rose out of the ground, arranged in a triangular formation that overlooked a grey swathe of car park. The structures rose to seven floors and looked as if they had been manufactured from the cheapest materials available at the time of building. The bricks were grey, the window frames were grey and, coupled with the gunmetal sky, it was the drabbest scene Tom had ever seen in his life.

The car park, at least, had some colour. Whatever money those who lived here had saved, they had blown on their cars. It looked like a scene from *The Fast and the Furious*: vehicles with flip paint, oversized spoilers, and ridiculously large alloy wheels took up most of the car park. If there had been a boy racer doing donuts in a souped-up Saxo, Tom would have been unsurprised.

The two detectives pulled up between a purple Ford Focus and a metallic blue Vauxhall Corsa, and got out. Each car was polished to within an inch of its life, and Tom could imagine the owners' annoyance at any adverse weather, an occupational hazard when living in one of the rainiest places in the UK.

Tom double-checked the address they'd been given, and he and Lauren made their way to the correct tower block. A re-inforced glass door with a web of cracks in it led to a depressing foyer. One of the walls was taken up by a bank of lockers that served as letterboxes. Tom had lived in a similar place when he first moved to university, and had resented having to go down four flights of stairs just to grab his post, which had been mostly made up of takeaway flyers and the free local paper. He made a note to check Zach's mail on the way down.

Zach lived on the third floor. They eschewed the lift in favour of the stairs. There were always a few cautionary tales thrown out during training about lifts. A couple of months ago, Tom had been made to watch a YouTube video that had gone viral, showing a police force in New Zealand. They were stuck in a lift and spent the time making up Stomp-style rhythms using only the walls, floor, and body parts. The thought that he might be coerced by the PR team into making a similar video had haunted Tom's nightmares for weeks.

The third floor was much the same as the entranceway. The carpet was worn so thin you could see the concrete floor below, and the walls looked like they hadn't been painted since the building had been completed. Zach, at least, had tried to inject some colour into the place. His door, 307, was flanked by a couple of potted plants, not yet dead, but heading that way. A Christmas wreath with little white flowers hung underneath the brass numbers.

'It's a bit of a shithole, isn't it?' Lauren said, glancing at the broken light switches and flickering bulbs dotted down the hallway.

'Not everyone can live in luxury,' Tom said.

'But he was a teacher. You'd think he could afford somewhere a bit better than this.'

'I suppose. No one can afford anything at the minute, though, can they?'

Tom inserted the key they had got from the landlord and eased the door open. He let Lauren lead the way, and then closed the door behind them. They found themselves standing in a narrow hallway with a couple of framed pictures hanging on the cream walls. The pictures looked like the cheap prints that were already behind the glass when you bought the frames; a place-holder for whatever you wanted to put there instead. The first door on the right opened into a small room with a toilet and a sink. The walls were an aquamarine blue and the floor was covered in a laminate designed to look like black tiles.

The second door on the right opened into a laundry room. The washing machine's door was open, and lots of shirts (mainly light blue) were dangling off a plastic drying rack. The lemony smell of detergent hung in the air.

The door at the end of the hallway led to the living space. The main room was open-plan. It was rather small. Maybe a savvy designer had considered that an open plan gave the illusion of more space than there actually was. On the right was a kitchen with limited surface area. An empty fruit bowl sat next to a microwave, which looked like it saw considerably more action than the hob and oven. The walls in the kitchen were painted a garish yellow, as if someone had taken a risk in a moment of madness and been too proud to admit their error in judgement.

The living area was modest. Two cracked leather sofas had been squeezed in, leaving little room for much else. A small IKEA television unit had been shoved into the corner with a massive television set on top of it. A tangle of wires connected a PlayStation 4 and a Nintendo Wii to it. Games cases were stacked haphazardly on the floor nearby, with some finger-smudged discs on top.

'Two consoles,' Lauren said. 'Bet he didn't get out much.'

'Aye, and when he did, he gets killed. There's a lesson to be learned here,' Tom replied. 'Maybe endless seasons of FIFA are the way forward.'

For a few minutes, they poked their noses into the corners of Zach's life. The kitchen cupboards turned up what you would expect: a range of pots and pans, bin bags and the like. There were no hidden bags of cocaine to be found in the DVD cases that sat on the windowsill or between the small number of paperbacks stuffed down the side of the sofa, so they trooped upstairs.

There were only two rooms up here. The flat was a one-bed, which turned out to be a mezzanine. The bed was made up like in a hotel, with one corner of the stripy red and white duvet turned down. There was one wardrobe, inside which his work apparel hung. The shirts (more blue) had already been ironed, and each pair of trousers hung with its matching jacket. One clothes hanger was home to ten or so ties, which were a mixture of block colours and stripes.

The bathroom was where they turned up their first clue into the life of Zach Willis. This is where he chose to be messy, something the rest of the place was not.

Dried lumps of toothpaste covered the sink. White towels (why not blue?), some with obvious skid marks, littered the floor and caused the room to smell like wet dog. A blanket of green mould was creeping across the parts of the walls that were untiled. Lauren toed the towels out of the way, and into a little pile in the corner near an overflowing bin. In a medicine cabinet above the sink, there was the usual mix of unopened toothpaste tubes and over-the-counter medication. There was also something unusual: a small brown bottle with the label partially torn off. Tom picked it up and turned it over.

The label told him the little pink tablets inside were amisulpride. A quick Google search gave Tom all he needed to know. He shook the bottle at Lauren.

'What is it?' she asked.

'It's a tablet to help treat schizophrenia and acute psychotic episodes.'

'You think it's his?'

'I'd guess so.' Tom shrugged. 'It looks like he lives alone, and, even if he was in a casual relationship, do you think whoever they belonged to would leave them here in this shit tip?'

'Maybe not. But would a school hire someone who they knew suffered from an illness that can alter their mood if they forget to take their medication?'

'Good point,' Tom conceded. 'There's only one way to find out.'

From his pocket, Tom produced an evidence bag. He dropped the bottle of tablets into it and filled out the details on the front. They took one last quick look around the house, before heading for the car.

23

THE TRAFFIC WAS LIGHT, and the journey from Zach's flat to the school he taught at took less than five minutes to drive.

Benton High School was served by two elaborate wrought-iron gates. On either side, a hedge of towering evergreen bushes wound its way around the perimeter of the grounds. The drive looked like it had been tarmacked recently and was without bump or pothole. Old oak trees lined the approach, and, through the tangle of bare branches, Tom could see the school's playing fields. On one side, several rugby pitches were marked in white paint; the grass was filled with divots and huge swathes of mud. On the other, the space was given over to football nets and a circular cricket green.

It was all very impressive, until they reached the car park and got their first sight of the school. The school buildings themselves were tired and grey. Silver letters, declaring the school's name, were drilled into the concrete wall beside the entrance to the reception area. Someone had got rid of the O and the N, so that it read BENT HIGH SCHOOL. Tom could only imagine the hysteria that would've caused on the day it was discovered.

Lauren rang an electronic buzzer fixed to the wall beside the door. A fisheye lens was encased behind a thick sheet of plastic, and Tom was unsurprised when they were buzzed through without being asked through the intercom who they were.

The receptionist looked like she had been pulled straight from a CBBC show. She was plump, wearing solely primary colours. Her T-shirt was yellow, and the baggy cardigan she had pulled over the top was red. A huge smile was plastered across her face and, when she spoke, she sounded like she was greeting a couple of nervous children on their first day of nursery.

Tom liked her immediately, and imagined every kid who passed through these doors did, too.

'Officers,' she said, with enthusiasm. 'How can I help you?'

'We were wondering if it would be possible to speak to the headteacher?' Tom said.

'I can check. I think she might be in a meeting, but just give me a second…' She picked up her phone and scanned a laminated page with a list of internal numbers on it with her finger. When she found what she needed, she punched three numbers and held the phone between her shoulder and ear while the other hand moved to the computer's mouse.

'Marjorie, are you free at the moment?… mmhmm… all right, it's just we have a couple of police officers here who would like to speak to you… Yes, I should imagine it's urgent… Okay, then. Thanks.'

She set the phone down again and looked back at Tom.

'She'll be right with you. If you'd like to take a seat…' She swept an arm at the area behind them where a number of seats were scattered. The waiting area was decorated with posters advertising upcoming events, including a Winter Ball.

Not long after, the internal doors opened with a buzz, and a tall woman introduced herself as Mrs Marjorie Perkins.

She was wearing a thick Christmas jumper with smart black trousers, beneath which deep-red Doc Marten boots poked out. Her hair was dark brown, though her greying roots were betraying her. She had keen eyes that darted about, taking in every detail, and Tom reckoned it would take an awful lot of effort to pull the wool over her eyes.

She led them down a corridor with colourful displays. They passed a French board showing young adults posing near an array of Parisian monuments, and an English board on which older children, perhaps sixth-formers, were huddled outside the Swan Theatre in Stratford-upon-Avon. Some held quills aloft; others were dressed in full bard garb. Everyone was smiling.

Marjorie's office was small and neat. There was a television screen mounted to the wall, on which the school's open-evening video seemed to be playing on loop. Tom wondered if she secretly used it for a sneaky episode of *Homes Under the Hammer* when she had a bit of downtime. Not that it looked like she had much of that, judging by the amount of paperwork waiting on her desk. It was filed neatly in a plastic tray next to an ancient computer monitor.

'How can I help you?' she asked, when she had taken her seat and made sure Tom and Lauren were comfortable in their own.

'We'd like to speak to you about Zach Willis,' Lauren said.

'Mr Willis, yes. What about him?'

'We're sorry to have to tell you, but Mr Willis was found dead yesterday.'

'Dead?' Marjorie's hand shot to her mouth. 'How?'

'We're keeping that to ourselves, for the time being.'

'Oh, Jesus.' Her arm was shaking, and she was staring at the detectives like she had only just noticed they were in the room. Lauren gave her a moment to let the news sink in.

'We know it's a lot to take in, but any information you can give us will help the investigation enormously.'

Marjorie nodded and pulled a couple of tissues from a box she pulled from a desk drawer . She blew her nose and dabbed at the corners of her eyes. Once she had gathered herself, she said:

'Zach is a lovely man. And very reliable. He has worked at Benton High for around seven years, I think. Never had a sick day, to my knowledge, so I was very surprised when he didn't turn up for work the past few days without letting us know why. We have had to get a supply in, but it never occurred to me that he might be...' She trailed off, her voice faltering. 'Sorry, it's just inconceivable that he's dead.'

'It's a lot to take in,' Lauren said again, and once she'd given the head a few moments to compose herself, added: 'Is there anything else you can tell us about him?'

'Umm... I only really knew him in a professional capacity. No one lets their guard down around the boss, you know?' She allowed herself a sad chuckle. 'His department head, Mr Fisher, is about to go on lunch. They were best mates, so it might be worth talking to him.'

Tom nodded, and Marjorie got out of her seat and left the room. Five minutes later, Mr Fisher knocked on the door, curiosity etched into his face. He was probably around the same age as Zach, with a buzzcut and a thick beard. His white shirt was a tad too small, though it did emphasize the wide shoulders and muscular arms. His body tapered into thin legs and polished pointy shoes.

Not a fan of leg day at the gym, Tom thought.

'Matthew Fisher,' he said, showing them the ID card that swayed from his lanyard, as if to prove he was telling the truth.

'DI Stonem and DS Rea,' Lauren said. She went through the same rigmarole with Matthew as she had with Marjorie, announcing the death of Zach, and allowing time for teary computation.

'Anything you can tell us may help,' she said.

Matthew didn't say anything for a while. He was staring into space, his Adam's apple bobbing up and down. Occasionally, he shook his head and muttered something under his breath. Tom and Lauren knew not to interrupt this moment of self-regulation. They were sure he would speak when he was ready. And he did, though his voice was thick with emotion. 'Ah, Zach was a total dude. He'd give you the shirt off his back if you needed it. That's more than can be said for most Mackems!'

'What's a Mackem?' Tom said.

'Someone from Sunderland,' Lauren clarified, before turning back to Matthew. 'Did you know Zach long?'

'Aye, for five years or so. He was here for a couple of years before me, but never wanted to progress. He loved the classroom, but he hated the paperwork and the meetings and all the bullshit that comes with management, you know? He was a fantastic teacher. Better than I will ever be.'

'I don't suppose you could help us with a timeline? When did you last see Zach?'

'Aye. It was two days ago. Me and him went to the Crown to watch Newcastle play and have a few pints. An unofficial Christmas party for the ones who don't like to dance. In the end, it was just me and him.'

'The Crown?'

'It's a pub. Close by, actually. About a five-minute drive from here. Pretty near Zach's place. Walking distance, but not quite stumbling distance.'

'Did anything unusual happen?'

'Well, now you ask, aye. Zach wasn't much of a drinker. He usually stuck to one pint. Didn't like a hangover. I mean, who does? But he really hated them. He was right up for it that night, though. He was proper rat-arsed by the end of the night. Proper gone. I had to help him outside come closing time. My Uber came first, and he insisted I go. I left him on the bench outside the pub. His taxi was only a couple of minutes away. Oh, God…' Matthew put his head in his hands. 'Did something happen to him then?'

'We're not sure yet,' Lauren said. 'But none of this is your fault. No one could have known what was going to happen.'

Matthew nodded and took a breath.

'Was Zach different in any way these past couple of weeks? Anything out of the ordinary, aside from the heavy night?' Tom asked.

'Ah, well, he had just started seeing a bird. Don't know much about her, mind; it was early days and he was trying not to get too excited. They'd been on a couple of dates, but that was about it. I don't think there was anything else. He seemed happy enough. This time of year in teaching is mental, it's so busy and it can get you down, but he seemed like the same old Zach.'

'Do you have a name for his new girlfriend?' Tom asked.

'No,' Matthew said, shaking his head. 'Sorry. I don't think he ever said. I can ask around, though, see if anyone else knew.'

'That'd be hugely appreciated. Thank you.'

'One last question, if that's okay?' Lauren said.

Matthew nodded.

'Did Zach take regular medication?'

'Not that I know of,' Matthew said, shaking his head slowly.

'Did he ever mention schizophrenia?'

'No, nowt like that. Why?'

She explained the medicine in his cabinet, but Matthew had never heard of it or seen him take regular medication. They thanked Matthew for his time and left the office. Tom assumed word would have spread about Zach's death, and also assumed the news had not yet reached the bubbly receptionist. She waved them off as enthusiastically as ever.

'What next?' Lauren asked, once they were back in the car.

'Pub?' Tom said, and Lauren nodded.

24

THE CROWN WAS A two-storey affair. The bottom half of the building was red brick and bay windows; the top half constructed in the black and white style favoured by the Tudors. The strange mixture worked rather well. The building was surrounded by a green, filled with picnic benches that Tom was sure would be full when the sun was out. A sign swung in the wind, showing a very realistic illustration of St Edward's Crown, with its famous purple velvet cap and multitude of glittering diamonds.

The car park was mostly empty, and Tom chose a space near the door.

Inside was the picture of cosy. A fire crackled in a hearth, made safe by a metal fireguard, though its heat could be felt from some way away. A mahogany bar ran the length of one wall, while the rest of the space was taken up by tables and chairs. A couple of fruit machines flashed in the corner, partly obscured by a plastic Christmas tree, though their jingles could not be heard over the music playing in the pub. Thankfully, it was not Christmas music; whoever was in charge of choosing had put on Radio X's albums of the year rundown. Tom recognised the jaunty, indie guitars belonging to Two Door Cinema Club.

They chose a seat near the fire, and took their coats off. As it was lunchtime, they thought it rude not to at least look at the menu. They sat in silence, aside from the rumbling of their stomachs, and each decided that, since they were here, they may as well choose something from the extensive list.

A woman in her early twenties with blonde hair scraped into a severe ponytail and a black apron tied tightly around her waist approached them a couple of minutes later, introduced herself as Amelia, and took their order. Tom, after much soul searching, chose the fish and chips, while Lauren plumped for a vegetable lasagne.

'Drinks?' Amelia asked.

The thought of a pint by the fire made Tom's tastebuds quiver in anticipation but, being on the job, he couldn't give them what they wanted. Instead, he plumped for an orange juice, and Lauren had the same.

'The manager wouldn't happen to be around, would he?' Tom asked.

'Why?' the waitress asked, nervous. 'Do you want to complain about something?'

'No, nothing like that. We're hoping we can have a look at your CCTV footage.'

'Oh,' she said, clearly thankful that the police's visit did not concern her personally. 'Tony is upstairs. I can get him for you, if you like. We've not had any fights or anything like that, though.'

She walked away, slid behind the bar, and typed up their orders on a touch-screen till. When she was done, she disappeared through a door and up a flight of stairs. They could hear her heavy footfall on each step. Clearly, she wanted to be rid of the situation, and was only too happy to pass it on to Tony.

Tony looked like a football hooligan. His head was shaved to the scalp, though some stubble remained where sideburns would grow. He had two waxy scars on his left cheek that ran parallel to each other. Thick black chest hair bloomed from the neck of his T-shirt, and his arms were covered in a patchwork of tattoos: some faded; some new. He had a toothpick in his mouth, and when he strutted over to their table, Tom thought they were going to have a problem.

However, when he opened his mouth, Tom changed his mind.

'Hello,' he said in a high-pitched voice. 'How can I help you today?'

'We're investigating a murder, and we have reason to believe that the deceased may have visited here on the night he died. If possible, we'd like to look at your CCTV footage.'

'Of course,' he said, 'of course. Can I get you a drink first, or some food?'

'We've ordered already,' Tom said.

'In that case, I'll get Amelia to bring your food into the back. That way, it won't get cold while you're looking for what you need.'

He led them through the bar and into the back. There was a flight of stairs, and beside it a narrow corridor with a door at the end. This is where he took them. The door opened into a small room that no doubt served as his office. There was a cheap wooden table and a low bar stool, and a filing cabinet. There was a dartboard on the wall, and Tom thought it nigh on impossible not to hit the number you were aiming for every time, considering the size of the room.

On another, sturdier-looking table sat two monitors. One showed the area at the front of the pub, the other showed the interior. The camera was positioned near an exit, and took in most of the bar and the entrance to the toilets.

'We invested in the best cameras we could get, so hopefully you'll get what you need,' Tony said. He explained how to operate the system, and said, 'I'll leave you to it but, if you need me, I'll be in the bar.'

Tom found the date they needed. He clicked on it, and the footage on the monitor immediately jumped from the live feed to the recording they needed.

The footage was not the grainy scourge of television detectives – pixelated beyond belief to stop them in their tracks – nor was it crystal-clear HD: it was somewhere in the middle. A streetlight provided some light, and the greenish hue of night vision provided the rest. They watched on double speed as punters came and went, some having been to a pre-drinks session, judging by their Bambi-on-ice missteps.

At 7:56 p.m., Matthew and Zach rounded the corner and entered through the main door. Tom had checked the fixture list in the car, and Newcastle had played Everton that night with an 8 p.m. kick off.

Tom switched to the interior camera, and watched as Zach secured a table while Matthew waited at the bar. Zach took his phone from his pocket and appeared to be looking through Twitter or Facebook. He didn't type anything; he simply used a thumb to scroll. When Matthew returned with two pints, Zach pocketed his phone and they turned their attention to the widescreen television in front of them. Tom knew of the intense rivalry between Newcastle and Sunderland fans, so was unsurprised when Zach jumped from his seat and celebrated when Everton went 1-0 up. It earned him some disapproving looks from other punters in the pub, but he didn't seem to notice. Occasionally, one of them would head to the bar and return with fresh drinks. Matthew was right, though: Zach was getting through them at a rate of knots.

After a while, Matthew returned with a pint for Zach and a smaller glass for himself. Tom supposed it was a soft drink, as Matthew had made it clear that he had not been drunk when they left. At no point in the evening did anyone approach either of the men, save for Amelia, who was on glass collection duty.

At 11:46 p.m., they gathered their belongings and headed for the door. Zach almost tripped down the two steps that led from their raised seating platform to terra firma. Matthew grabbed him, nodded a goodbye to Tony (who was wiping glasses behind the bar), and led Zach outside.

Switching cameras again, Tom watched as Matthew deposited Zach on a bench beside the door. He tapped on his own phone for a minute, and then put it away again.

'That's probably him ordering his Uber,' Lauren said.

Matthew then took Zach's phone from his pocket. He held it up to his friend's face, unlocking it, and then navigated the menu. He shook his head, tapped the screen some more, and then held the phone to his ear.

'What do you think he's doing there?' asked Tom.

'It looks like he was going to order an Uber for Zach from his own phone. He might not have had the app, or maybe there weren't any free, so he probably phoned a local taxi company instead.'

'Why wouldn't they go in the same taxi?'

'It looks like Zach could spew at any minute. Maybe Matthew didn't want to take the chance of having to pay a soiling charge if his mate threw up in the back seat.'

'Or maybe they lived in opposite directions.' Tom made a note to check up on this, though, from his actions, Matthew certainly didn't look like he planned on killing his mate.

Ten minutes later, a car turned up, Uber's distinctive logo emblazoned on the side. The two friends spoke. Matthew looked like he was saying he would wait, but Zach was waving a drunken hand towards the taxi, telling him to go, presumably. Which Matthew did.

Alone, Zach leaned his head back against the wall and chuckled to himself. A car pulled into the car park and beeped its horn, shocking Zach into movement. He stumbled across a flower bed and hunkered down unsteadily, his face inches from the car's passenger window. He seemed to be chatting to the driver, though his body swayed like a thin reed in the wind.

Perhaps the driver sensed he'd be mopping vomit if he took the fare on, because, a moment later, the car suddenly took off, turning in the car park and indicating onto the main road. Zach aimed a pointless kick in the car's direction, and stumbled onto the grass, where he fell flat on his face. He rolled around like a beached whale, but was unable to get onto his feet.

From the side of the building, cloaked in shadow, a figure emerged. It stole over to Zach's prone body, helped him up and led him off camera towards the car park.

Five minutes later, a car sped out of the car park and onto the main road, nearly colliding with another vehicle. The driver who was already on the main road had to slam their brakes on, and the car fishtailed across the centre line. Luckily, nothing was coming the other way.

They rewound the film and paused it when the figure was approaching Zach. The first time they watched the footage, Tom had been too keen to take in the bigger picture. Now he stopped to study the figure, he knew who it was.

25

FRANK WOODS WAS LEANING against the wall of the tiny interview room.

Tom and Lauren had purposely chosen the most drab, inhospitable room they had on offer, but Frank looked like he would be comfortable sitting in a muddy trench, so it was probably not working on the psychological level they were hoping for.

He had a black woolly hat pulled low, covering his bald head. Despite the temperature almost dropping into the negatives, he was wearing a polo shirt with his builder's business logo sewn onto a breast pocket. Tom had been watching him for about ten minutes via a video feed, and might have thought he was asleep, except that his heavy eyelids drooped over his shark-like eyes every ten seconds or so. They never once moved from the Styrofoam cup in front of him.

'Ready?' Lauren asked.

Tom nodded, and they made their way to the interview room.

Tom had expected an eruption of anger; a machine-gun burst of swear words, or a chair lobbed in their direction (had it not been screwed to the ground). Instead, Frank's eyes remained on the empty cup of water.

'All right, Frank?' Tom asked.

The builder raised his head and glared into Tom's eyes. The intensity of his gaze almost caused Tom to tear his eyes away, but the psychological side of policework had been drummed into him. He held Frank's stare, until the moment passed and Frank lowered his head again.

Tom turned the recording device on, stated the date and time, and those present.

'Are you sure you don't want a lawyer here with you? We can get a court-appointed lawyer for you, if you don't have your own,' Tom said.

'I ain't got nothing to hide, so why the fuck would I need a lawyer?' Frank snarled.

'Suspect has declined the offer of a lawyer,' Tom said, for the recording's benefit. 'Now, Frank, can you tell us about your relationship with Richard Handsworth?'

'The MP?'

'The very same.'

'I never had a relationship,' Frank said. 'I never met him in my life.'

'That's not strictly true, is it?' Tom said. From a manila folder, Lauren slipped a picture of the Handsworths' garden. It showed a huge swathe of grass, well-tended flower beds and a recently built conservatory. In one of the windows was a sticker, showing the same logo as the one on Frank's T-shirt.

'Did your company build this conservatory?' Tom asked, sliding the picture towards Frank. The builder spun it around and gazed at it for a moment.

'It's an orangery,' Frank replied. 'And yes, we did. Like I said, I never met Richard, but I did meet his wife. Only once. Me and Trev—'

'Trev?'

'My second-in-command. Trevor Richmond. We went there to price it up together. His wife liked the price and the plans, and we did it. Trev was in charge of the project, and I never set foot on their land again. Her husband was not there when I was.'

'Would Mrs Handsworth confirm that?'

'I doubt she'd be able to pick me out of an identity parade.' He shrugged. 'Like I said, we were there for half an hour, max, and then only Trev and a few of the lads returned to do the work.'

Tom changed tack.

'Do you know Johnny Golding?'

'I buy materials from him. Last time I checked, that wasn't a crime, so why don't you tell me why I'm here?'

'Johnny Golding's girlfriend was murdered not long after Richard Handsworth. It's interesting that you deal with a chap from Manchester who happens to be tangled up in both murders. Can you see how it might look bad for you?'

'Not really,' Frank said. 'I buy bits from him because he can get what I need. I also import glass from Belgium and most of my machines come from China. Are you going to tell me fucking Tintin or Chairman Mao is going to crop up in all of this, somewhere down the line?'

Tom ignored the sarcasm. 'When did you last see Johnny?'

'Probably a couple of weeks ago. We've been buying from the company he works for for years. He told me he was seeing some bird up here, and that I might be seeing more of him; that he was planning to move up here if it kept going the way it was going with her. Johnny's all right, but I wouldn't go out of my way for a pint with him.'

It was time to play the trump card.

'Can you tell us where you were on the evening of the twentieth of December?'

Frank scratched his head. 'Home, for most of it.'

'And the part you weren't?'

'I went to the pub to pick up my daughter. Must've been near midnight.'

Lauren pulled a laptop from her bag and set it on the table. She opened the lid and brought up a video file, before spinning the computer so Frank could see, and pressing play.

The footage started, showing the figure creeping from the shadows, making its way towards the motionless body of Zach Willis. She paused it as the figure lifted Zach to his feet.

'Is that you?' she asked.

'Yes,' Frank replied. 'That is me.'

'What are you doing?'

'Like I said, I went to the pub to pick up my daughter. I tried calling her from the car, but she wasn't answering her phone, so I was on my way into the pub to grab her. I saw some poor sod lying down on the grass, and thought I'd help.'

'Did you know who it was?'

'Only when I got him up. It was Mr Willis. He is my son's English teacher. I felt bad for the bloke – he kept mumbling about how his friend had fucked off on him – and thought I'd give him a lift home.'

'And did you?'

'Well, no, actually. I started walking him towards the car, but when we were in the car park, his mate must've felt bad and come back for him. He took him off my hands and bundled him into his car. When I checked my phone, my daughter had texted me to say she was on her way, so I got into my own car and waited. I did worry about Mr Willis, though. His mate was driving like a fucking nutter, wheel-spinning out of the car park and nearly smashing into someone on the main road.'

'What car were you in?' Tom asked.

'Volkswagen Golf.'

They let the footage play on, and a couple of minutes after the first car hared away into the night, a young woman with blonde hair left the pub and disappeared around the corner. A minute later, a dark Volkswagen Golf drove carefully out of the shot.

Tom's theory that Frank had been behind the murder of Zach Willis had been completely blown to smithereens. The builder was telling the truth.

'Can you describe the friend who took Zach off you in the car park?' Lauren asked.

Frank pursed his lips and frowned.

'I'm not sure,' he said, finally. 'He…'

'It was a man? You're sure of that?'

'Not 100 per cent. They were wearing a baseball cap and had a mask covering their face. I wanted to tell them Covid has gone and there was no need for the silly mask anymore, but I was more concerned about the bloody teacher chucking up over me.'

'What was the person wearing?'

'Do I look like Stella fucking McCartney?'

'Think,' Tom said, with a little more vigour than he meant.

'Jesus,' Frank said. 'All right, they were dressed head to toe in black. I can't give you any more than that, because I don't know. All I remember thinking was they looked like a ninja.'

'Did Mr Willis seem to know whoever it was?'

'Mr Willis didn't know his own bloody name, let alone who anyone else was. He went quite willingly, so I thought nothing more of it.'

'You must've spoken to whoever took him,' Lauren said. 'Surely you would've known whether it was a man or a woman from that.'

'All they said was the word "Zach", but I didn't really take their voice into consideration. I think it was deep, but I can't be certain.'

Tom and Lauren shared a look of irritation, which Frank picked up on.

'Oi, you two! Just because I don't have the memory of an elephant, doesn't mean you two can look at each other like that.

I'm right in front of you, for Christ's sake. I was there to pick up my daughter. At no point did I think I'd be in the fucking nick trying to identify a killer, so go a bit easier, eh?'

'Sorry,' Tom said. 'It's just, you're our first eyewitness to whoever took him. It's the closest we've been.'

Frank nodded, and then sat awaiting the next question, which Lauren delivered: 'Did you see the car they got into?'

'It was a Ford Focus. A black one.'

'Reg?'

'Jesus Christ. Again, I didn't realise I'd become an honorary policeman.'

'Officer,' Lauren corrected. 'We don't use the term "policeman" anymore.'

'Ah, the snowflake brigade! No, *officers*, I didn't get the car's registration. Now, am I free to go?'

With nothing else to learn, they stopped the recording, walked Frank up the stairs and watched him as he sauntered out of reception. He was already on his phone by the time he left the building.

'Fuck's sake,' Lauren said. 'I thought for sure we had him.'

'Me too,' admitted Tom. He thought of the murder board, and how the glowering face of Frank Woods could now, in all likelihood, be taken down. He had a genuine link with two of the victims, but it seemed the only crime Frank was guilty of was being in the wrong place at the wrong time. That, and also being a bit of an arsehole. It was frustrating, but narrowing down the suspect pool was no bad thing, either. It was some sort of progress, and it meant they could focus their attention elsewhere.

'He handed Zach over to his killer,' Lauren said.

'Frank is a bruiser, but I believe he thought whoever took Zach off his hands was genuinely a mate.'

'So, what now?'

'Well, we have a make and model of the car the killer was using. We can assume it wasn't his own, so we can have a look at any black Ford Focuses that have been stolen in the past month or so. We can get Alan to have another look at the Angel of the North footage, see if any black Focuses turn up there.'

It had been a long day and it was getting late. They walked to their desks with the intention of grabbing their belongings and going home. In the maelstrom of CCTV footage, they'd had to abandon their meal at the Crown, and Tom suddenly realised how hungry he was.

The adrenaline that had carried him through the day was wearing off, and his mind was so focussed on food that he missed the package sitting on his desk.

'What's that?' Lauren asked.

With his stomach rumbling, Tom reached for the envelope and had a cursory glance at the front.

It was addressed to him personally. It also had the station name and address, and in the corner, there were three first-class stamps. A postmark covered them, but Tom didn't bother to check where it had come from.

'If they've doled out for first class,' Tom laughed, 'I'm expecting the keys to a Ferrari in here. Whoever sent it is obviously wodged.'

He tore the top of the envelope and let the contents slide out onto the desk. It was a Christmas present, wrapped in red paper with a multitude of laughing Santas covering it. It smelt odd; a strange mix of something rotten being covered over by something fresh.

'Do you think you should put your gloves on, in case it's something fishy?' Lauren asked, catching a whiff of whatever was inside the wrapping paper.

Tom reached into the pocket of his coat and pulled out a pair of blue gloves. He pushed his hands into them and began to unwrap the present. Carefully, he pulled one strip of Sellotape away, and then another. The paper fell away.

'Fuck,' shouted Lauren, backing away.

Tom took a few steps back, too, horrified at what he was seeing. On the desk sat a flayed, decaying lump of flesh.

26

In less than twenty minutes, the quiet office had become a bustling crime scene. The forensic pathologist was among the first to arrive, and quickly set about trying to determine where the flesh had come from.

Tom was unsurprised when the verdict came back. It *was* fairly obvious. Iain didn't want to attach his name to anything with 100 per cent certainty before he ran a battery of tests in the lab, but he would hazard a guess that it belonged to Zach Willis and was probably the missing chunk of thigh that the killer had cut off the deceased's leg. Iain deduced that it had been hacked off antemortem, judging from the fact it was still covered in a thin layer of oil found universally on living human flesh.

Now, at least they knew why the killer had sent it: they were playing a game with the police, and with Tom, specifically, it seemed.

Once Iain was happy he had everything he needed, he let forensics take over. He and Henry had a bit of banter at the door, and Tom once again marvelled at the need for light in the darkest black. The job would chew you up and spit you out if you didn't compartmentalise. Before the CSI team went about their business, Tom took a picture of the thigh muscle and walked out of the office. He had already given a statement, along with Lauren, so was free to leave.

He went outside for some fresh air and pulled his phone from his pocket. He called Anna. When she answered, she was crying.

'Anna,' he said.

'You said in your text you were going to make it up to me tonight.'

'I know, and...'

'Don't bother, Tom,' she sobbed. 'I don't want to hear it. Don't call me again.'

She hung up, and Tom stared at the screen. He'd known this moment was coming, and a little part of him was glad it was now. It was in his DNA to fuck relationships up, so it may as well happen right at the start to save Anna some heartache further down the line. He wasn't good enough for her, and he knew it.

He stayed outside for a while longer, fighting the urge to call her back, and then went in search of Lauren. He found her in the canteen, looking a bit green around the gills and holding a mug of steaming coffee in her hands.

'You all right?' Tom asked. She nodded, but he wasn't convinced.

'I'm fine,' she said, 'just not been sleeping well lately. I've got some stuff on my mind.'

'Want to talk about it?'

She smiled and took a sip of her drink. 'Honestly, it's fine. What sort of sick fucker are we up against, though?' she asked, as he slid into the seat opposite her.

'I don't know.' Tom shrugged. 'What I do know is, whoever is behind all of this is getting a bit too sure of themselves. This is how murderers get themselves caught. They get too big for their boots. They slip up, and then we've got them where we want them.'

It was true. There seemed to be a pathological need for killers to show they were always one step ahead of the police. Dennis Rader, dubbed the BTK Killer, had been caught when a floppy disk he'd sent to a television station was traced to the church computer he had used to encode the message. His boasting had led to his downfall.

John Allen Muhammad and Lee Boyd Malvo, nicknamed the Beltway Snipers, had left tarot cards at the scenes of their crimes. When police failed to make satisfying headway, the killers had called a hotline asking for information, and bragged about past crimes, including a robbery committed by Malvo. Police were able to use fingerprints from that scene and the two gunmen were caught relatively quickly.

Of course, there were other cases where killers, such as the Zodiac Killer, had taunted the police and had never been caught. Tom chose not to linger on those.

'It doesn't feel like we've got them where we want them,' Lauren said. 'It feels like he or she is running rings around us, while we chase our tails. Truthfully, we're no further forward than we were after the first body.'

'We are,' Tom said. He flicked through the menu of his phone and brought up the picture of the thigh.

'Why are you showing me this again?' Lauren said, pushing the mug of coffee away from her, disgust etched on her face.

'Because he has left us a little clue.'

He zoomed in on the screen and set it in the middle of the table so they could both see.

Carved into the flesh were a series of numbers. Two lines of them. The digits were made up of straight slices, and Tom could imagine the horrible fucker they were chasing bent over the piece of flesh, cackling maniacally as he set about it with a small knife or scalpel. Maybe the way the digits had been carved would tell them something about the perpetrator. Maybe it wouldn't.

'Coordinates,' Lauren said.

'Exactly.'

Tom navigated his way onto a website where coordinates could be inputted, and typed in the numbers from the thigh.

The website thought about it for a few seconds, and then the map zoomed in on a point to the west of Gateshead. It was a country road, near an area called High Spen. The website reckoned it would take approximately twenty-three minutes to get there.

'You think he's guiding us towards another body?' Lauren asked.

Tom puffed out his cheeks. He had been looking forward to a slap-up meal and his bed, but he knew this couldn't wait. He also knew that if someone else offered to take the lead, he'd say no: the killer had addressed the letter to him. They'd made it personal. If there was another body to be found, he would be the one to find it.

'There's only one way to find out.'

27

THE SAT NAV LED them to a narrow country lane. Fields stretched for as far as the eye could see, the plots separated by ancient stone walls and hedges. The distant sound of cows mooing was carried on the wind, and Tom felt a pang of pity for them, having to be outside at the mercy of the elements. The rain was falling as heavily as he'd ever seen it.

While Lauren drove, Tom consulted the Christmas list. They'd had the Dido CD, the dress and the alien egg toy. Tom imagined the glee on the killer's face as they'd taken their red pen and scored out each item. It made him feel sick.

Eager to get ahead of the game, he tried to figure out what the next item meant. A box of magic tricks. The possibilities were endless. Magicians made items disappear. Did that mean the killer was going to kidnap someone? Were they going to get in touch with the police and demand a ransom? Or, just rub Tom's nose in it that they were still a few steps ahead on the chessboard?

Magicians also blew things up, but Tom didn't want to think about that.

The country lane narrowed, and Lauren had to slow to a crawl to make sure they didn't drift into one of the ditches either side of the track. Thankfully, they were in a small car – Tom smiled at the potential language being used by the teams inside the fleet of forensic lorries that were having a nightmare trying to navigate the lane behind them.

Lauren indicated into a driveway when instructed, and came to rest in front of a farmhouse built from old stone with rickety-looking wooden-framed windows and a thatched roof. It looked like a drawing a five-year-old might do; like a strong gust of wind or even a nearby sneeze could topple it.

Tom and Lauren wiggled into their paper suits. Not an easy feat in a standard pool car, but they were keen to spend as much time inside as they could. Heavy gusts of wind buffeted their car, and the windscreen wipers were having a hard time keeping up with the torrents of rain that fell from the heavens.

When they could resist no longer, they opened their doors and ran across the yard, which was pockmarked with a series of uneven holes. Tom could imagine sinking into the deeper-looking ones, *Vicar-of-Dibley*-style, if he wasn't careful. The canopy above the weather-beaten door did little to shelter them from the elements, and as there was no bell, Tom hammered on the door with a balled fist.

There was no answer, nor was there any sign of life. Inside, all was dark, and in the yard there was no car or tractor or anything else associated with life on a farm.

They ran back to the car and got in. They'd been outside for a grand total of sixty seconds, and both of them were soaked to the bone. Tom pulled his phone from his pocket and called Alan. The detective constable was in one of the vehicles currently blocking the lane. Tom asked him to go to the neighbour's house. Tom always took care not to abuse his higher rank, but what was the point of all those exams if he couldn't delegate during a biblical downpour? He had spied a similar farmhouse about two hundred yards up the road and there had been a light in one of the lower rooms. Alan confirmed he had seen it, too, and he would call back as soon as he had answers.

They waited in silence for a few minutes (aside from the chattering of their teeth and the whoosh of hot air spilling from the vents on the dashboard) until Alan called back. He sounded out of breath, his words coming in couplets.

'The woman who lives there says Grant, the man who owns the farm you're at, is in Australia visiting his daughter,' he said. 'He's been gone since the start of December. She's been down to check on the house every couple of days, to tend to the plants and things like that.'

'So, whoever brought us here might've known they wouldn't be disturbed when they were hiding whatever they were hiding,' Tom replied. 'Thanks for checking it out. I'll foot your next dry-cleaning bill.'

'I'll hold you to that,' Alan said. 'I'm as wet as a—'

Tom didn't wait to hear the comparison. He hung up and got out of the car. Whatever was waiting to be discovered had to be found: if there was forensic evidence attached, they needed to get to it before the weather made it unusable, if it hadn't already.

Before leaving the station, the team had assembled and studied an aerial view of the land. They'd formed a plan: they divided the area into manageable sections, and, in pairs, they would each search their own bit of ground. It was a large plot of land, and someone had suggested it was an almost impossible task: finding whatever had been left for them, in the dark and inclement weather, was akin to searching for a needle in a haystack.

Tom would usually have agreed, but not this time. The killer wanted what he had hidden to be unearthed; they wouldn't have sent the chunk of thigh meat otherwise. It was theatrical, and he had a feeling the killer would make it easy for them.

Tom and Lauren headed for a copse of trees to the south of the property. As they passed the side of the house, Tom shone a torch through the windows and peered in. One of the rooms was a large, spartan sitting room. There was a small television perched on what looked like a handmade stand. There was a sofa that sagged in the middle, a low coffee table, and not much else. The other room was a small kitchen. Again, it was as if Marie Kondo had swept her wand around the place: there was nothing there that didn't need to be. A large Aga took up most of one wall, and a Belfast sink the other. There was no microwave; no clock on the wall; no human touches at all, save for one childish painting attached to the fridge by a magnet.

A large patio at the back of the house looked as though it was used as a dumping ground. Two rusty trailers with wheels missing had been abandoned in one corner, and piles of rotting planks of wood and bits of machinery were clearly ready for the scrapheap. A length of blue tarpaulin that had been covering an old car had come loose and was blowing in the wind like a spectre.

To get to the trees, they had to walk across an area of grass. It was slick beneath their feet, and, coupled with the undulating terrain and deep divots, they had to work hard to cross the terrain without breaking their ankles. Once or twice, one of them slipped, and reached out for the other.

The trees offered a modicum of relief from the weather. The thick branches snaked up to form a sort of canopy, though some rain did still get through.

'Reminds me of *The Blair Witch Project*,' Tom shouted above the howling wind, as he looked around.

'Why the fuck would you say that now?' Lauren shouted back.

'Fair point,' Tom said, before miming zipping his lips together.

They walked the boundary together, separated by a couple of metres. They took a step and checked around them, their torches moving methodically like searchlights combing the area for an escaped prisoner, before moving on. When they found nothing, they manoeuvred towards the centre of the circle of trees and did it again. It was gruelling work, slowed by the rain, the wind, and the inescapable darkness. Tom could barely remember what sleep felt like anymore. Still, like the good soldiers they were, they pressed on without moaning. Much.

Near the centre of the trees, they found what they were looking for. The earth had been disturbed recently and left in a small, raised mound. An inverted cross, made from two branches, had been stuck into the ground. A thin piece of red fabric attached to the vertical branch fluttered in the wind.

'We've found it,' Tom said into his radio. He gave their location and waited.

In the space of a few minutes, the area was swamped by crime scene investigators. A forensic tent was erected (with some difficulty, thanks to the unrelenting wind) over the disrupted earth, and the demonic marker was deconstructed and safely stowed in an evidence bag.

Tom and Lauren were told to wait on the boundary of the trees until forensics were happy that the area had been thoroughly swept.

'What do you reckon is under the soil?' Lauren asked, her teeth starting to chatter again.

'Not sure,' Tom said. 'I was expecting a body, but the area disturbed isn't big enough.'

'Another body part?'

'Maybe,' Tom said. 'It won't be from Zach, as the thigh was the only missing bit.'

'Another victim, then?'

'Jesus, I hope not.'

A white-suited figure drifted out from among the trees and told them they were about to dig it up. Henry had decreed they could be present if they wished.

They did wish, and set off after their messenger.

The mood around the makeshift grave (if that's what it was) was tense.

When the crime scene manager was happy that everything had been photographed in situ, and the video was rolling, they began their excavation. With little trowels, they dug through the wet earth, taking care not to disturb whatever lay down there. It was like a ghoulish episode of *Time Team*.

After ten minutes of careful digging, they found something. There was a shout, and the photographer quickly moved into position. He took pictures of the hole, and what lay in it. When he was done, one of the besuited techs lifted a package out of the ground and set it beside the hollow they had created.

It was small and wrapped in the same paper as the thigh muscle. Here, the smiling Santas looked even more incongruous: still beaming despite having been buried under the cold, unwelcoming ground.

The tent was doing its job, keeping out the elements, and it was decided to open the package there and then. Each step was logged and photographed.

First, the wrapping paper was taken off to reveal a sealed sandwich bag. Whoever had left it there had obviously been worried about their message being lost to the inclement weather of the North East. The relief that a hacked-off body part was not inside was palpable.

The sandwich bag was opened and, from it, a red, square envelope emerged. Tom half expected his name to be scrawled on the front, but it was blank.

Finally, the envelope was prised open with a thin, metal instrument. Whoever had sealed it may have left saliva behind on the flap, and the tech was doing all he could to preserve whatever evidence there may be.

From the envelope, the tech slipped a Christmas card. On the front was a typically delightful Christmas scene: a red-breasted robin perched atop a snowy branch. A bough of holly floated in the top right-hand corner, with a gold embossed 'Merry Christmas' stamped across it.

There was a collective intake of breath as the card was opened.

Inside, it was blank save for a carefully scrawled missive:

> Lucky me, tick tick tick.
> I've got most things on my list.
> Two more sleeps and then we're quits,
> but will you guess my final trick?

2 sleeps 'til Christmas

It was the last day at school today. It was fun – we didn't have to do any work at all. Miss had got a load of colouring pages, and we were allowed to have as many as we wanted. I coloured in Father Christmas, a village scene with a big church and lots of elves wandering around delivering gifts, and a Christmas tree with loads of presents underneath.

We made snowflakes by drawing round a paper plate, cutting out the circle, folding it and then snipping bits out of it. Then, you unfold it and – hey presto – you have a unique pattern.

Then Miss got us into a circle. We pushed the tables back and we sat in the middle of the classroom. She explained she was going to pass around a cuddly toy, and you could only talk when you were holding it. That meant everyone had a fair go. She told us that when we were holding the toy, we had to tell the rest of the class about our plans for the holidays.

I started to panic. My family never did anything fun. We had a plastic tree and, if Mum and Dad weren't too drunk or hungover, we'd have a Christmas dinner. But not a great one, because they weren't very good at cooking, and we couldn't afford meat from the butcher, so we always had cheap, almost out-of-date stuff. The meat would be dry and the potatoes would be burned. I decided I'd try and put a positive spin on things – to make it sound like my Christmas was going to be as good as any of my classmates'.

Michaela said she was going to visit her grandparents in South Shields. She was looking forward to it because she didn't get to see them that often, and it was always special when she did. Her grandpa had a darts board in the shed, and she liked to play with him.

Nathan was going to Paris! His parents had told him already they were going to Disneyland, and maybe even the Eiffel Tower if they had time. Miss asked him to take lots of pictures, as we were going to start learning some French after the holidays. He said 'Oui' and everyone laughed. David stood up and pretended to do a wee in the corner of the room, but Miss shouted at him and told him he was ruining it for everyone.

I had my go and passed the toy to Holly. Holly lived nearby, but on the other side of the street. Everyone in town knew the main road acted as a sort of divide: scum on one side, nice families on the other. David had said it once and no one had disagreed. Holly lived on the nice side, obviously. She said it was going to be the best Christmas ever. She was getting a puppy. A little sandy-coloured Labrador she'd decided to call Penny. She said that when she went to see it for the first time, the dog had licked her and whined when she'd had to go. They'd cuddled the whole time. She said they were already best friends and she was never going to love anything as much ever again.

I could just imagine a little puppy trotting around her massive house, its nails tippy-tapping on the expensive wooden floors.

Most kids had finished after a few sentences, but not Holly. She was still going. Talking about mince pies, and carolling, and wrapping dozens of presents for all her family. How she'd saved her pocket money and bought her own presents for her siblings this year. David pretended to stick his fingers down his throat and throw up. Even Miss had a weird look on her face, but I couldn't figure out what she was feeling.

Holly finally passed the toy on, and the little fuzzy tiger completed its circuit. Miss said she was going to have a quiet holiday with her husband, and looked a bit sad.

After that, we went and got our coats. Holly and me were alone by the lockers. I don't know what I was thinking. Maybe it was the thought of her warm house with the pile of presents and the pine scent from the tree, but I'm not sure.

I asked her if I could come over on Christmas Day.

Dumbest thing I've ever done.

She looked at me for a couple of seconds, and then laughed. Laughed right in my face.

And, while she was laughing, more of the class came out. They asked Holly what she was laughing about. I shook my head, pleading with my eyes for Holly not to tell.

But she did.

The rest of the class started laughing, too. What I'd asked Holly spread like wildfire until it felt like everyone in the class was laughing. I felt tears trying to escape my eyes. But I didn't let them. Instead, as Holly tried to squeeze past, I stood on her undone shoelace. She stumbled, and as she started to fall, I pulled my locker door open. It smacked her in the face and she fell backwards. Blood bubbled from a deep cut in her lip. Tears rolled down her face.

'Fuck you,' I spat.

Of course, that was when the teacher came out of the room. She looked like a fish stuck on land, with her mouth opening and closing, as she took in the scene. Without saying a word, she marched me straight to the headmaster's office.

There, I sat in a seat in front of his desk and did what I had to do. I apologised. I grovelled. I even treated him to some crocodile tears, which seemed to do the job. He told me that he'd have to phone my parents and explain what had happened.

Good luck, I thought. If he got through, which was unlikely, I assumed Dad would tell him what I did was the right thing to do in that situation, and hang up.

I left his room, collected my stuff from my classroom, and got out of the building as quickly as I could. I saw Holly and her mum talking to my teacher further down the corridor, and found myself wishing I had someone who cared about me that much. When I split me knee open falling off the monkey bars last year, Miss had to be the one to take me to hospital, as they couldn't get in touch with my parents.

Do you know how embarrassing it is for your teacher to hold your hand while the nurse threads stitches through your wound while you cry in pain?

Holly doesn't, and she'll never have to.

I wish I could wave a magic wand, and swap places with Holly, even just for a day. Just to know what it feels like to be wanted and loved. How it is to live in a mansion and not have to worry about food, or clothes, or heating, or money.

I trudged home in the dark and opened the door to my house. It was freezing cold, and, in the living room, my breath came out like steam. The little ones were on the sofa, cuddled under a blanket, holding each other in an attempt to warm up.

'Where's Mum and Dad?' I asked.

'They left a little while ago,' my brother said. 'Daddy said you have to look after us until they get back.'

28

Tom was livid.

He was in the toilet at the station and wanted to smash the place to bits. He imagined broken sinks and cracked mirrors; shards of glass littering the floor, covered in blood from his own knuckles.

The killer was fucking with them. With *him*. They were so far behind the perpetrator that they weren't even playing the same game. The police were dancing to a murderer's tune, waiting for another titbit of information in the vain hope they would slip up, allowing Tom and his fellow officers to catch up. It was infuriating, and it was starting to feel personal.

Instead of wrecking the toilet, Tom splashed cold water onto his face. His eyes felt like they were full of grit, and when he checked the time on his watch, he was unsurprised to see that it was approaching 9 a.m. He tried to do the mental calculations of how long he had been awake, but his fuzzy brain wouldn't play ball. Well over twenty-four hours, anyway.

On his way to the briefing room, he stopped at a vending machine and bought a can of Red Bull, hoping that whatever magical ingredients gave others wings would at least keep his eyes from slamming shut. Angela would be appalled if she could see him, downing energy drinks before breakfast and looking every inch the dishevelled detective she would so regularly rail against when they were depicted that way on television. She liked them clean-shaven and with a good work-life balance.

Well, if only you could see me now, Angela, he thought. His trousers were caked in dried mud, his hair looked as though it had been washed in a chip pan, and the purple spreading under his eyes made him look like he was coming down with a serious illness.

Throwing these thoughts aside, he marched into the briefing room, keen to exude confidence. Gathered in the room were a huge number of police officers. The case was continuing to attract big press interest and, as Natalie kept reminding everyone, they needed an arrest yesterday. So far, the Christmas list, and the killer's fucking around with them for fun, had been kept out of the papers by a scrupulous press officer.

'Hi, everyone,' Tom said, as he walked across the room towards the front. He pulled the murder board closer to the group, so that everyone could see the finer details. Most of the officers had pens in hand, poised to make any salient notes.

'Lots to go at,' he said, pointing to the board. 'What I thought I'd do is a roundup for those of you who are joining the case from this point, if that's all right. I think it's useful for everyone, actually.

'So far, Richard Handsworth, a local MP, and one of his aides, Millie Whitlock, have been murdered. It is believed they were having an affair. Their deaths occurred close together and we assumed the murders were part of some political or sexual ploy. That still may be the case. We questioned his wife, who had a solid alibi. We are still looking for Johnny Golding, Millie's boyfriend, whose whereabouts are currently unknown, though we believe he is somewhere in the Greater Manchester area. The GMP are on it. We're still working on contacting everyone who was in attendance at a community meeting hosted by Mr Handsworth and attended by Millie. Could be something was said or seen then. A team of very diligent officers are working through that list of attendees.'

Tom paused to take a drink of water, before continuing:

'Then, Zach Willis' – he pointed to the picture of the teacher – 'was murdered in the north of the city. So far, there is no obvious affiliation with either Richard Handsworth or Millie Whitlock. He was a secondary school English teacher and was uninterested in politics, according to his mate.' Tom motioned to the map on the murder board, with the three red pins sticking out of it. 'As you can see, the location of Zach's murder is out of whack with the others, too.'

'What makes you think it's linked, then?' someone with a thick Yorkshire accent asked from the back of the room.

'Because the way he was killed suggests it's the same killer. Whoever is behind these murders, they seem to be following a Christmas list. We think it belongs to a little girl, judging from the items on the list. I've included a photocopy it in your packs…'

Tom paused as the fluttering of paper started.

'Richard Handsworth's body was found at the Angel of the North. If you look at the list, the first item is *No Angel*, which we believe may be a reference to the Dido album from 1999. When Millie was killed, she was wearing a red dress – that links with item two, and Zach was found in an oil tank, which links to the alien egg toy.'

'Which leaves a box of magic tricks and a surprise,' the same Yorkshireman said. 'Doesn't give us much to go on, does it?'

'Agreed,' Tom said. He nodded at a woman who was waiting at the side of the room. She walked to the front. 'This is Amanda Cooper. She's a psychologist, and she's been looking at the case notes and trying to put together a profile of our killer. I'll leave you in her hands.'

Tom walked to the side of the room, and let the psychologist do her thing.

'Hi, everyone. Having studied what's gone on so far, I think it's safe to assume that the killer is in a regressive state. They seem to be reliving a period in their life that was traumatic for them, trying to take some control from a situation where they had none the first time around. The Christmas list is interesting, as is the timing of the murderers. It's obvious this time of year means something to them, though these murders were not spur of the moment. Their plan is no doubt months or even years in the making. The owner of the list certainly seems like a female child, and the killer could either be that child grown up, a parent to that child, or a sibling. Either way, someone is trying to make up for something that did not go well once upon a time.' She looked up at the board. 'The toys on the list are fairly standard, aside from the alien egg toy. They used to be in every toy shop in the late eighties, early nineties, but aren't as common anymore. Perhaps that's something to think about.'

Though she dealt mainly in hypotheticals, there was a confidence about her that what she was saying was gospel. Tom felt vindicated. He had been the first to float the idea that the killer might be using the Christmas list as some sort of murder bible. His theory had not been taken as seriously as he would've liked from the start, so it was a shot in the arm to hear an expert confirm his hunch. She left the front with a hearty 'good luck', and Tom returned to his place in the spotlight.

'The priority now is to find out who the list belongs to. We believe that will lead us directly to the killer. DCI Freeman will assign tasks moving forward. Thank you for your time.'

Natalie took the floor. As Tom was about to take his seat, Alan stuck his head through the door and signalled for him to leave the room.

Tom snuck across to the door.

'What is it?' Tom asked, keen not to miss Natalie's assignments. He liked to have an overview of the case and to know who was doing what.

'We've just had a missing person's report filed.'

'And?'

'It's a woman who lives in the same apartment block as Zach. Caitlyn Hamilton. Her mother, Linda, called it in an hour ago, and it's just made its way onto the system. Apparently, her mum hasn't heard from her in three days, which is unusual because the pair of them talked on the phone most days.'

'Have officers been to her flat?'

Alan typed on his computer, studied the screen, and said: 'Yeah. We've been twice, and there was no answer both times.'

'Shit. Have you got the mother's address?'

29

LINDA HAMILTON LIVED IN an end terrace in Jesmond, not far from the city centre. It was your standard affair – red brick with a very small front garden devoid of green.

She was waiting for them by the door. She was a tall woman in her mid-fifties with vibrant red hair styled into two plaits that draped over her shoulders. She wore a long-sleeved blouse and jeans, and had a long, woollen cardigan pulled tight around her torso.

They followed her down a short hallway, painted a deep green and lit by a decorative faux chandelier, into a small living room.

'I'll get us some drinks,' she said, and left without taking an order.

Lauren used the time to look around the room. The walls were a baby blue, the carpet cream, but marked here and there from years of wear. Two sofas and an imitation oak coffee table took up the middle of the room, arranged to make the most of a huge television. There were biblical references on the walls – framed pictures of famous quotes and heavenly images. On the mantelpiece was a series of photographs, most of them showing the same four people: Linda, a man who Lauren assumed was her husband, and two sisters, one of whom must've been Caitlyn. She had brown curly hair and wore glasses. She reminded Lauren of someone, but who…

And then Lauren froze. Her hands grew clammy.

Was this the same person who had been waving and smiling at her daughter?

Surely not.

That would be too much of a coincidence.

'What's up?' Tom said, but Lauren simply shook her head.

She didn't want to get sidetracked or worry Tom when there was no real evidence that Caitlyn was the smiling woman. Or that there even was a smiling woman. Caitlyn was missing, wasn't she? She was hardly likely to be hanging around a school, wasting her time waving at a five-year-old.

Lauren joined Tom on the sofa, and a few minutes later, they heard footsteps and Linda reappeared. She was carrying a tray with three glasses of water on it.

'I'm so sorry,' she said. 'The house is a mess. Usually, a missing person's report doesn't mean the police come straightaway.'

'You've filed one before?' Tom asked, surprised.

'Loads, yeah. You see, Caitlyn has disappeared several times. She suffers from a psychotic disorder. We speak on the phone every day. It might seem a bit over the top, but it helps me sleep at night. I've not been able to get in touch with her for a couple of days now, and it's worrying me.'

'Do you mind if we ask a couple of questions?' Tom said.

'Go ahead,' Linda replied.

'Can you confirm your daughter's address?'

'14 Brookfield Tower. It's a block of flats in Longbenton. As you can see, we aren't swimming in money, but we've offered to help her get a nicer place. She insisted she wanted to earn her own money, live her own life, and who were we to stand in her way?'

'You say "we". Are you married?'

'Yes. My husband, Neil, works away a lot. He drives for Walkers Transport. It's a haulage company. It means we spend a lot of time apart. Her big sister, Alison, works in Dubai.'

'Have you checked Caitlyn's home to see if she is there?' Tom asked.

'Of course,' Linda said, looking at him as though he were an idiot. 'I wouldn't have rung the police if I hadn't checked first. I know how stretched you are. She's not there.'

'Have you checked with friends to see if they have heard from her or if they have let her stay?' Lauren said, hoping not to stoke her ire further.

'Yes, the ones I know, anyway. She was due to go and see friends in Edinburgh last weekend, though I don't have their numbers. I haven't heard from her since then, but she could be there.'

'How would she have travelled? By car?' The idea that they could track her journey by ANPR was almost too good to be true; which of course it was.

'No. She doesn't own one. She bought train tickets when she was here a few weeks ago.'

Tom took the names of her friends and promised he would do all he could to track them down.

The mention of Scotland's capital city had set alarm bells ringing in his head. He hadn't paid much attention at the time, but hadn't that been the postmark stamped on the envelope containing Zach's thigh?

'Does the name Zach Willis mean anything to you?' Tom asked.

A look of surprise flashed across her face.

'Yes,' she said. 'Caitlyn had recently started a relationship with him. Ray and I were delighted. You see, she's never managed to hold down a relationship. Because of her disorder, she finds it hard to keep a relationship going.'

'But it seemed different with Zach?'

'I think it did. She brought him for lunch here and, even though it's early days, they seemed smitten with each other. He has a good job and is very good at making her laugh. Caitlyn has had a difficult life. She's entitled to a bit of happiness.'

'Did you try to get in touch with Zach when you couldn't contact Caitlyn?'

'No. I don't have his number.'

Lauren shot a knowing look at Tom, who shook his head slightly. If they mentioned Zach's death now, Linda might shut down, and Tom felt there was a lot more information to be had from the mother.

'You mentioned a disorder. Could you tell us more about that?'

'She has schizophrenia.'

That explained the tablets in Zach's apartment.

'It's a very misunderstood disorder,' Linda continued. 'Everyone thinks about Jekyll and Hyde when they hear schizophrenia, like there are two personalities battling each other, but it's actually very different. It started with small things when she was young, like not finishing a small task like colouring in if she went a millimetre outside the lines, or hating going in the bath. We often had to hold her down in the water, otherwise she would have gone to school stinking. She hated us when she was young.'

Linda paused to wipe a tear from the corner of each eye, before continuing.

'It's really affected her life. She finds it difficult to keep a job or to concentrate for long periods, which means she never passed her driving test. It's taken its toll on my marriage.' She looked at Tom and Lauren with horror etched on her face. 'Sorry! I didn't mean that. I want her back, is all. It's hard, but she's my little girl and I need her. I need her back.'

'We understand,' Lauren said, reassuringly. 'It's difficult.'

'Does she have a job at the moment?' Tom asked, after nodding his own understanding.

'She's working at a Greggs in the city centre. The one near the Central Library.'

Tom made a note, though he didn't really need to. He was planning how to drop the next bombshell on this already distressed mother. He took a deep breath.

'Mrs Hamilton, I'm sorry to be the one to tell you this...'

Linda stiffened.

'... But Zach Willis's body was discovered two days ago. He'd been stabbed to death. Obviously, this is shocking news, and I'm only telling you because it may have something to do with your daughter's disappearance.'

'In what way?' Linda shrieked.

'She may have found out. It may have affected her mental health, and she may simply be using this time to process it. Perhaps she wasn't ready to discuss it with you yet.'

Linda shuddered, and then broke into wracking sobs. Lauren rose from her seat and collected some tissues from a box on the coffee table. She passed them to Linda, and dropped into the seat beside her, placing a comforting hand on the woman's forearm.

'She did it.'

Tom couldn't be sure that he had heard Linda correctly, and shot Lauren a confused look, which she shot right back at him.

'Can you say that again for us?' Lauren said, quietly.

'I said, she did it. Caitlyn killed him.'

30

'WHAT DO YOU MEAN?' said Tom.

'Excuse me for a minute,' Linda said, and stood up. She stepped reverentially from the room, and Lauren followed her, to make sure she wasn't about to do anything stupid. Or illegal.

Linda entered the downstairs bathroom and closed the door. Her cries could easily be heard through the door, as could the sound of her blowing her nose. Some time later, the toilet flushed and she opened the door again.

She re-entered the living room and took her place. Lauren moved back onto the same sofa as Tom. Linda's face was blotchy and her nose rubbed red from the toilet roll. Tear marks had cut little streams through her make-up , but her eyes were ablaze.

'Are you okay?' Tom asked.

'Yes,' she said. 'I'll tell you everything. Just, don't judge her too harshly. Like I've already said, she suffers from schizophrenia. She's been plagued with hallucinations and night terrors for as long as she has lived. It's an awful thing. When she was fourteen, she was admitted to psychiatric care after an... incident.'

She paused, and Tom knew better than to interrupt. She had a story to tell, and any questions he might ask could potentially throw her off track. He'd made that mistake in the past, and his DCI in Manchester had used it as a 'teachable moment': a term Tom thought kind when it had really meant 'an absolute bollocking'.

'I remember she'd had a particularly horrific morning. Lots of defiance. She hadn't slept well, either. Kept calling out random words. We didn't know what it meant, and assumed it was simply another night terror. Anyway, once we got her shipped off to school, late, we thought that was the end of it. I went to work, and so did my husband. At 1:13 p.m. – I'll never forget the time – the school phoned. It was the headmaster, and he was panicking. You could hear it in his voice.'

She paused again, this time to take a sip of her water.

'He said we had to come down to the school right now. That Caitlyn had been involved in an incident. He wouldn't say more. Just that I needed to get there as soon as possible. I remember I couldn't find my keys and *I* was starting to panic. I was shaking, and all I could think was that something awful had happened to Caitlyn. That she'd broken a leg in the gym, or she'd melted her face on a Bunsen burner. Your mind automatically leaps to the worst things, doesn't it? Anyway, I don't even remember the journey. When I got to school, I was taken straight to the headmaster's office. Caitlyn was sitting in a chair opposite him, with a faraway gaze. I thought they'd given her a sedative, or something like that.'

Tears started to fall down Linda's face.

'I went to hold her. To give her a big hug, but she held her hands up to ward me off. Her right hand was covered in blood. And then I saw it all over her shirt, the red stains all over her chest and sleeves. All I could think of, bizarrely, was that it looked like a Jackson Pollock.'

There was a long silence. Tom knew she was back in that headmaster's room, and didn't want to interrupt. After a time, Lauren spoke: 'Was it her blood?'

'No.' Linda shook her head. 'It was the blood of a young girl called Millie. She had been in Caitlyn's group of friends, and had been over to the house a few times, but I hadn't seen her for a while. Turns out they'd had a bit of a falling out.'

She took a breath.

'My Caitlyn stabbed Millie in the neck and in the chest with a pair of scissors during an art lesson. The teacher turned her back to write something on the board, and Caitlyn had grabbed the scissors and sunk them into that little girl who used to be her friend. She stabbed her twice, set the scissors down on the desk, and probably would've carried on listening to the teacher if it wasn't for all the screaming. They evacuated the classroom, locked her in and waited for the police to arrive.'

'Millie?' Lauren said.

Linda nodded. 'Millie Whitlock. As soon as I saw on the news that Millie has been killed, I've thought of nothing else. I kept wondering if Caitlyn was involved. It's ridiculous, but they didn't get on at school. And Caitlyn is very good at keeping a grudge going.'

The emotion that had been straining to get out took hold of Linda, as images from twenty years ago swarmed in front of her eyes. Tom couldn't imagine how he would react if his child had been involved in such an incident, either as the attacker or the victim. He felt sorry for Linda, but her daughter may be out there plotting her next kill. He couldn't let her wallow.

'What happened to your daughter?' he asked.

'She stayed in a secure hospital for a few months and then was released back into our care. It was a horrible time.'

'And what happened to Millie?'

'The wounds were superficial, I was told. There was a lot of blood, but she only needed a couple of stitches on each wound. Her family decided not to press charges, for which my husband and I remain eternally grateful.'

Tom thought Linda's language was carefully chosen. Phrases like 'superficial' and 'only a couple of stitches' made it seem like a stabbing in a classroom was no big deal. The damage to Millie would've been bad enough, but the psychological impact on the other students and on the poor teacher shouldn't be undermined, either.

Tom had a sudden brainwave. He pulled the Christmas list from his pocket and showed it to Linda.

'Does this look familiar?' he asked.

She scanned it for a moment, before shaking her head.

'It's not something I've seen before, no. I recognise some of the items, of course. I'm assuming *No Angel* is the album by...' She trailed off, trying to remember the name of the singer.

'Dido,' Lauren offered.

'That's it. Caitlyn used to sing "Thank You" all the time around the house. It's quite a sweet song, isn't it? Haven't heard it in years.'

With that, she broke down into tears, and pleaded with Tom and Lauren to find her little girl. Lauren moved onto the sofa beside her again, and attempted to reassure her they would be doing all they could.

'We'll need to search Caitlyn's flat,' Tom said, once Linda had been mollified. 'Do you have a key?'

As they left, Tom's phone rang. He waited until he had slammed the car door behind him before answering.

'Hi. Is this DI Stonem?' a voice with a Manc accent asked, booming out of the hands-free system.

'Speaking. What can I do for you?'

'I'm DS Dan Threader. A Mr Golding has handed himself in. It says on HOLMES that we were to get in touch with you should that happen.'

Lauren shot him a look of excitement. Tom cursed the timing of the call and grimaced back. He had a decision to make.

They'd just learned that Caitlyn was in a relationship with the deceased and had a history of violence. On the other hand, Johnny had a definite link to at least one of the murders and had fled from his place of work to avoid any more questions from Tom. Really, Tom needed to speak to both, but there was only so much one person could accomplish in a day.

'I'm going to send someone down to interview him, if that's all right?' Tom said, finally.

'No problem. We'll give him the finest hospitality Stockport has to offer, in that case. Let me know who you're sending and when we should expect him when you get sorted.'

'It seems we're getting somewhere,' Lauren said. 'Alan?'

Tom nodded. 'Alan.'

31

WITH ALAN'S TEMPORARY SECONDMENT to the North West sorted, Tom drove like a maniac on the way to Caitlyn's apartment. Lauren (usually a good passenger, he had noticed) was clinging to the safety handle like her life may depend on it.

While he made his way through the traffic with the flashing blue lights on and sirens blaring, he spoke to Natalie through the hands-free system. He asked her to get a photograph of Caitlyn circulated around the news outlets and the television. She was now the priority, and it was vital that they find her. He also asked her to get Phil onto the Edinburgh friends Caitlyn claimed she had been going to see, to find out whatever he could. To leave no stone unturned.

He had got Henry to check the envelope that had contained the thigh muscle, and Tom had been right. The postmark indicated that the letter had been sent from Scotland's capital. It was a breadcrumb, small as it was, but it meant she had definitely been in a fixed location, and from there they might be able to track her movements.

With those bases covered, he gave his full attention to the road ahead. He could feel his eyelids drooping, and as he battled to keep them open, they began to sting. He cracked the window a couple of inches, allowing a freezing breeze to infiltrate the car.

'Do you want me to drive?' Lauren asked.

'No, you're all right,' Tom said.

They drove in silence for a few more minutes.

'What was up, back in Linda's house?' Tom asked.

'Oh. Nothing really,' Lauren said. 'It's just, Sophie told me a woman with brown hair has been waving and smiling at her on the way to school. I chased a woman down the road the other day. I didn't get a proper look at her, but Caitlyn's picture reminded me of her.'

'Jesus. You don't think you should have mentioned this?'

'Sophie is five,' Lauren said. 'And it's probably bollocks. It's just that the photo gave me a shock, that's all. It's probably just coincidence.'

Tom wasn't convinced, but didn't have time to argue. They'd arrived.

* * *

Caitlyn's flat was very similar to Zach's, though mirrored. Her living room was neat and orderly. The television was small and there was only one sofa and an uncomfortable-looking chair covered in misshapen grey fabric. There was a glass jar with sticks poking out of it. Tom thought it could be some sort of hippy drug system, but Lauren reliably informed him it was called a diffuser, a sort of air freshener thing.

She rolled her eyes at him. Men!

The kitchen was spotless. There was no mess nor crumbs on the surfaces, and in the corner was a bare fridge that had recently been cleaned and a bin that had been emptied and cleansed with bleach.

'It's clean,' Lauren said.

'Maybe too clean,' Tom agreed. 'No one is this on top of things, surely.'

'Maybe she was having a Christmas sort out,' Lauren said. 'Or, maybe she knew she wouldn't be coming back.'

Tom looked in a couple of the cupboards and drawers, but was nothing of note. The place seemed like a movie set; the essentials were here to trick a viewer into believing it was a lived-in space, but to Tom, it felt sterile. Like a sad echo of a life.

Upstairs was much the same. The bathroom had been scrubbed to within an inch of its life. There was no toothbrush, no half-empty bottles of shampoo in the shower.

'Boss,' called Lauren from the bedroom. 'Look at this.'

Tom left the bathroom and joined Lauren in the bedroom. She was standing by a chest of drawers, looking into a jewellery box. There were a couple of gold rings, a jumble of earrings and a ridiculous looking silver necklace. Lauren's face was white.

'What's up?' he said.

'I think Caitlyn might be the smiling woman. The one who keeps waving at Sophie. When I saw the photo earlier in her mam's house, it reminded me of the woman I chased. Dark, curly hair. She was also wearing an oversized necklace, just like this one.' Her words caught in her throat. 'What if she's after Sophie?'

'We won't let her anywhere near Sophie, do you hear me? We'll sort it so that Sophie is only ever with adults she trusts. And we'll make sure those adults know the risk. We will catch Caitlyn before anything bad can happen.'

Lauren nodded, and pointed to a photo frame on top of the drawers. She picked it up in a gloved hand and studied it closely.

'What is it?' he asked.

In response, she handed him the picture. It was a school photo-graph, one of those with an entire year group in it, taken in the assembly hall, children stacked up on benches one behind another. There was a mixture of boys and girls, some of whom had remem-bered it was picture day and had preened accordingly.

Tom noticed Caitlyn on the front row, sandwiched between two boys (class clowns, Tom guessed) who seemed intent on touching each other's legs. She was probably around sixteen or so but hadn't changed much in the intervening years. Her eyes were intense, staring at the lens as if she meant whoever was behind it harm.

His attention was drawn away from Caitlyn and to a girl on the back row. A red X had been drawn over her face, though in highlighter, so her features were not obscured. Her hair hung loose on her shoulders, framing a pretty face, and her tie hung perfectly straight, unlike many of the boys on the same row.

'Jesus,' Tom said. 'She's crossed out Millie Whitlock.'

'Why do you think she's put the X through her like that?' Lauren asked.

'Not sure. Sometimes killers take body parts or some sort of trophy. If Caitlyn is the killer, maybe this is her version: defacing a year-group photo.'

Tom scanned the rest of the picture, but no one else had been marred. He wondered if Caitlyn had stood in this very spot, crossing her off before heading out to kill her, or after the deed had been done. What was she thinking? Was she in one of her manic episodes, or was this cold-blooded and calculated?

'There might be other clues in the flat as to who she planned to kill next,' Lauren said, breaking Tom's reverie.

'Yeah, there could be. Best get forensics over here before we go looking. They'll kill us if we mess anything up.'

They left the flat and called it in. Henry told him it would be a few hours until they were free so Tom may as well head home and get some sleep. He'd phone if anything came up and, if not, Tom was free to explore the flat first thing in the morning.

The pause in action frustrated Tom, but he knew it was the right thing to do: he was running on fumes, and that's when mistakes were made. He called the station and asked for a uniform to come and guard the door, on the off-chance Caitlyn returned or someone chose the lull in action to pay a visit. With one last look back at the locked door, he and Lauren made for the car. They took a more leisurely pace back to the station, where Tom quickly realised that the paperwork related to the investigation was getting out of control. He half thought about turning a blind eye to it, to pretend he'd never walked into his office, but couldn't do it. Reluctantly (after a trip to the vending machine for an armful of the world's most unhealthy foods), he sat down with a pen, and got started.

He awoke some hours later with a Post-it note stuck to his cheek, and drool covering the part of an important document where he should have signed his name.

'Bollocks,' he hissed, as he tried to mop up the mess. Instead, he smeared the ink and made everything worse.

'Time to go home, eh?' said a voice from the door. He looked up to find Natalie looking down at him with an air of exasperation. 'And that's not a suggestion. Henry is at Caitlyn's flat now and will get back to us as soon as he can, but I don't want to see you before eight o'clock tomorrow morning. Got it?'

Tom nodded.

'Good,' she said. 'Now, get going, before I kick you out.'

She smiled kindly and left. Tom gathered his things, pushed the papers he had managed to scatter into a neat pile, ready for tomorrow, and turned the lights off.

The unintended sleep had only made Tom more tired, and exhaustion burned in every fibre of his body. The drive home was difficult. Each streetlight seemed to singe his retinas, and he found himself wishing he could put his sunglasses on, though his innate Englishness prevented it. After what felt like forever, he turned into his street, and he was very pleased to find the spot in front of his house free. He pulled in, grabbed his stuff from the passenger seat, and got out.

The night was cold, though the rain was thankfully taking a break from its seemingly constant existence. A slice of silvery moon hung in the air, fighting a losing battle against a thick blanket of cloud. The lamppost at the front of Tom's house played host to a flickering light. That, coupled with the revelations of the day, set Tom's teeth on edge. He half expected Caitlyn to come bounding round the corner of his privet hedge, knife in hand.

He opened his gate and hurried up the path. He was pulling his keys from his trouser pocket when he sensed movement behind him.

'Hello, Tom,' said a voice.

32

TOM SPUN AND THREW a punch in the general direction of the voice. His balled fist collided with something. A jaw, perhaps? Or a nose, judging by the crunch. The figure stumbled back, and Tom used the moment of confusion to rugby-tackle them to the ground. The wind was knocked out of the figure, and they gave a guttural yelp. The flickering light from outside the gate was no help in determining their identity. Tom rolled the figure over and sat on his (for he now knew it was a he) back, his legs either side of the man's body. He was searching for his handcuffs with one hand when the man spoke.

'It's me, you silly twat.'

Tom recognised the deep Mancunian voice, even though it was muffled by a mouthful of wet grass. Tom slid off and got to his feet, pulling his little brother up.

'What the fuck?' Tom said. 'What are you doing here? Why were you lurking in the garden?'

'I wasn't lurking, was I? I was waiting, that's all,' Seth said. He raised a finger tentatively to his nose and winced as he touched the tip. 'I think you've bloody broken it.'

'Let's get you inside and have a look.'

Tom led him to the door and opened up. He let Seth go first, and had one last look outside, before pulling the door closed behind him. He locked it and slid the heavy-duty door bar into place. He may not have got round to becoming Nina Campbell yet, but he had installed the extra security on the door the first night he'd moved in.

In the kitchen, Tom got his first look at Seth in over a year. He was well-built and tanned. Long, blonde hair spilled from his yellow beanie. Despite the cold, he wore tatty board shorts, a T-shirt advertising some far-flung bar in a language Tom did not understand, and a pair of sandals.

'Not much of a welcome. I thought you'd be pleased to see me,' Seth said with a smile, while blood dripped from his nose. He was managing to catch most of it in his hands, though a couple of drops had found their way onto the carpet. Tom moved past him to the freezer where, luckily, there was a bag of peas. He poured some into a sandwich bag and handed it to Seth, who held it to his nose with a wince.

'Drink?' Tom said.

'Don't suppose you have any maté?'

'What's that when it's at home?'

'A type of tea. South Americans love it.'

Tom hoped his brother wasn't one of those travellers who, when they made it home, looked down on normal things. He'd had friends who'd travelled after university, and had come back with a taste for arepa, some sort of Venezuelan bread. He'd put up with their moaning for as long as he could, before telling them to piss off back to the Southern Hemisphere if a slice of Warburtons wasn't good enough.

'I barely have any English teabags, let alone something from halfway across the world. I could do you some Yorkshire tea?'

'Aye.' Seth nodded. 'That'll do.'

'Go and sit down, and I'll bring it through.'

Seth headed into the living room, while Tom busied himself with the kettle. He wasn't lying when he said he had little in, and he was grateful that Past Tom hadn't scoffed all the Jammy

Dodgers. He cobbled together a plate of biscuits and a cup of tea for Seth, and followed his brother into the living room.

'Sorry for punching you,' Tom said. 'How does it feel?'

'It's sore, but I'll live. When I was in Vietnam, I stood on the exact spot in Saigon where Thich Quang Duc set himself on fire, and—'

'Who?' Tom interrupted.

'Thich Quang Duc. He was a Vietnamese monk who set himself on fire in protest over how Buddhists were being treated.'

'Is that the guy on the front of the Rage Against the Machine album?'

'Yes,' said Seth impatiently, 'but I think he should be remembered for more than that. He stood up to the government. He changed the world.'

'"Killing in the Name" was a Christmas number one. It knocked some *X Factor* numpty off the top spot… I'd say he'd done his bit on this side of the world, too.'

'I only brought him up,' Seth said, pointedly, 'because whenever I experience pain, I simply think of him and my discomfort doesn't seem so bad.'

'Are you a Buddhist now?' Tom asked, thinking of Alan. Maybe the Eastern religion would do wonders for Tom and Seth's relationship.

'I am. Having travelled extensively now, I truly believe it is a pure and unselfish religion.'

'I bet monks wouldn't like you using the word twat,' Tom said.

'Aye, well, I don't think many monks have been punched in the face by their own brother.'

They looked at each other and laughed.

'Is it police policy to punch first and ask questions later?'

'It's my own personal philosophy at the minute, yeah. We're investigating a killer and, for a moment, I thought…'

'You thought they'd come for you.'

'Something like that.'

'Well, when you put it like that, it looks like I got away lightly,' Seth said. 'Now, where's the toilet? I'm dying for a slash.'

Seth disappeared up the stairs. Tom's first thought when he realised it was Seth in his front garden had been a selfish one: that his peaceful, solitary Christmas had probably just gone out the window. He and Seth hadn't always seen eye to eye (the perils of brotherhood), and even though Tom had been ribbing him about the Vietnamese monk, he actually felt glad to see Seth. Maybe a Christmas together was exactly what the doctor ordered. Maybe it would mend some of their broken bridges.

'You look tired, man,' Seth said, when he returned. 'Policing the streets of Newcastle hard work?'

'It's not glamourous, I can tell you that much. It must be nearly thirty-six hours since I last slept,' Tom said, discounting his impromptu desk nap.

'Angela was telling me there was an MP killed or something.'

'Aye, and more besides. It's all a bit of mess, and I could do with my bed.'

'Don't let me keep you up. I can go and find a youth hostel or something, and come back tomorrow.'

'Don't be a dick,' Tom said. 'I'm not going to boot you out and make you stay somewhere. Saying that, I don't have a second bed yet, but the sofa turns into one. You can help me set it up and we'll get you sorted.'

'Thanks, man. I don't want to put you to any trouble.'

Tom couldn't help but notice the change in his brother. Before his world travels, Seth hadn't really known what to do with his life.

The man standing before Tom now was a different one entirely. He had an easy confidence about him, as if the amalgamation of cultures and vistas he had visited had laid a guiding hand upon his shoulder.

'Sorry,' said Tom. 'I don't want you to think I don't want to hang out. It's just, I'm absolutely shattered, but I'd really like to hear all about your travels tomorrow. Do you have one of those projector things that click around and show photos?'

'Not yet, but maybe by this time tomorrow I will, now you've put the idea in my head.' Seth laughed. 'I'd really like to hear about your move up here, too. Maybe we could grab a few beers tomorrow night and catch up?'

He looked at Tom hopefully.

Tom nodded. 'Yeah, that'd be nice.'

'I know we didn't always get on when we were younger. I was closed off, but I feel like I've turned over a new leaf. I feel like a different person, and I'd love it if we could sort of... start again? As corny as that sounds.'

'We're all good, Seth,' said Tom. 'Now, let me get the duvet from upstairs. I know you might be used to sleeping under the stars in Thailand or in some favela in Rio, but you're in the mighty Gateshead now, where the cold is known to invade your very skin cells. Angela would kill me if I let you die from frostbite on your first night here.'

Tom went upstairs and came back with a bundle of sheets and pillows. They worked together, and before long the sofa bed sat in comfortable splendour.

'Teamwork...'

'... Makes the dream work,' Seth finished. 'Thanks for this, bro. Now, get a good night's sleep, and I'll see you in the morning.'

I sleep 'til Christmas

Mum and Dad have been gone for ages, and it's getting really annoying. I went through the cupboards but there isn't anything in them. Same story with the fridge. What *is* in there is starting to stink, but I don't want to throw it out in case Mum goes mental at me when she comes back. I didn't know what to do, so I went to the corner shop and nicked some food. Not loads — I didn't want to get caught and get in trouble. After all, who would look after my little brother and sister then?

I told the shopkeeper, Mr McDonald, that my dad was round the back in the car park and wanted a word. When he left, I stuck a few tins of soup and a small loaf of bread into my backpack, as well as some chocolate.

Miss read us a story a few days ago about a man called Robin Hood who lived in Nottingham ages ago. He took from the rich and gave to the poor, and he was treated like a hero. I'd heard it before, but never thought about the meaning of it. I guess I am a bit like Robin Hood myself, taking from a shop that probably has loads of money, to make sure we don't starve. Mr McDonald who works there is really fat, too, so he's probably not going to notice a couple of bits missing, is he? And if he did, what's he going to do? Chase me? I wouldn't count on it.

When I got back, we had a nice meal. Soup and crusty bread. We all sat around the table, like a real family, and talked about what we're looking forward to about Christmas Day. The little ones were so excited about Santa coming. Obviously, I know that Santa isn't real, but I played along. I really hope that Mum and Dad come back with presents before Christmas Day.

After food, we tried playing a game of Connect 4. It was fun for a while, but then the little ones started messing about and I couldn't take much more. I told them to go to their room and find something nice to do while I cleared up downstairs.

There was a knock on the door shortly after that, and David appeared. He came to tell me about Holly, who was banging on on MSN about how wonderful her decorations were and how the whole house smelt of pine needles and all that crap. There was a group chat, but because I don't have a computer, I've never been invited into it.

I can see her house from mine. Miss showed us a picture of Blackpool Illuminations once, and I swear that Holly's house has more lights on it. They're flickering all night; it must do the neighbours' heads in. I bet UFOs can even see them from space.

Thinking about Holly makes me sad. I didn't let on to David, but as soon as he went, I had a little cry. Why does Holly get to have the perfect family and the perfect Christmas, while I'm stuck in my house with my snotty brother and sister and no mum and dad?

My little sister came downstairs a while later, and as soon as she opened her mouth, I screamed at her to piss off back upstairs. She looked at me for a couple of seconds, and then her eyes filled with tears and she fled back to her room. I felt bad, but I'm just so cross. In R.E., we've been learning about God, who is supposed to be all loving and caring.

If there really was a God, would he give nice boys and girls like me and my family such crap lives? I doubt it. Would he make mums and dads who didn't care about their children? I don't think so. I asked Miss once and she said that God works in mysterious ways. What a cop-out.

The flickering lights of Holly's house that I could see from my front window made me feel angry. Why did she get all the nice things? The nice life?

Right there and then, I came up with a plan to make myself feel better.

Perhaps Holly's Christmas wouldn't be quite as perfect as she thought it was going to be...

33

DESPITE TOM'S LACK OF sleep over the past few days, he couldn't convince his brain to switch off. The clock had just tick-tocked its way past midnight, which meant that it was officially Christmas Eve. The significance of the date was not lost on Tom. If the killer intended to tick off all the items on the Christmas list, it must be assumed they would try to complete it by Christmas Day. Which meant that in the next twenty-four hours, there could be two more murders. It didn't bear thinking about. Tom wanted to get out of bed and do something. Anything. But he knew that was stupid. He needed energy for the day ahead. There were search teams going through every facet of Caitlyn's life to help locate her, and Tom knew that if something was uncovered, he'd be phoned straightaway.

He got his phone from the bedside table and opened up the photos. He scrolled past pictures of Anna and him together, and felt a knot of disappointment and self-loathing in his stomach. He'd been an idiot to not put up more of a fight when she broke up with him. Maybe, after Caitlyn had been caught, he'd go to her house and refuse to leave until she spoke to him. He would convince her that he'd change.

But *would* he be able to?

After all, this was all he knew. Failed relationship after failed relationship. It was usually because of his job, but sometimes it felt like he had a self-destruct button when things were going too well. Maybe he'd been programmed to believe he didn't deserve a happy-ever-after.

Anyway, he didn't have time to dwell on himself now.

He found the picture of the Christmas list, and wracked his brains for what the box of tricks could refer to. His mind immediately leaped to a magician, but was that too easy? Was it some sort of code? Did it link to the other items on the list? Was there even a link to be found aside from the fact the words seemed to have been written by a young girl?

Frustrated, he threw his phone onto the other pillow, and turned over. Once upon a time, at some strange conference about separating police work from your personal life, a sleep expert had taken to the stage and told the assembled officers and detectives that if you are struggling to sleep, you should try and mentally focus on your toes. It had sounded like absolute codswallop at the time, but Tom was desperate, and so he found himself trying to picture his own toes. He gave up after a couple of minutes, as he found it was stressing him out more than calming him down.

He must have drifted off at some point, as he awoke with a start, his head filled with broken dreams of magic wands and his nose with the heavenly scent of bacon. He had a quick shower, dressed and made his way downstairs. In the kitchen, Seth, his long hair tied in a bun and dressed in a patterned kaftan, was standing by the hob with a spatula in his hand.

You didn't go to the corner shop dressed like that? is what Tom wanted to ask. Instead, he said, 'What's all this in aid of?'

'I thought I'd cook you a nice breakfast, to say thank you for putting me up.' Seth smiled. 'There's fresh orange juice in the fridge, and you can choose between toast or a croissant to go with your bacon.'

'Cheers, buddy. I really appreciate it.'

Tom helped himself to a glass of orange juice and sat down at the table.

'I was thinking,' Seth said, 'that I could maybe do us a Christmas dinner. All the trimmings. I know you're busy with the case, but I think it would be nice to sit down and really catch up.'

'I'd like that,' Tom replied. 'I can try and swing by Tesco and—'

'Nope,' Seth interrupted. 'I'll sort it all. Stress-free for you and a way for me to give something back. It's not like I've got loads on my plate or anything. I'm assuming you haven't ordered anything.'

'You assume correctly. That'd be cool, if you're sure,' Tom said. 'But if you need anything, give me a shout.'

'I'll be fine. I'm only hoping there'll be some turkeys left on Christmas Eve. Surely, they'll keep a secret stash for last-minute eejits like you!'

While Tom waited for his breakfast to be plated up, he flicked through the news stories on his phone. Between a story about a spate of London stabbings and one about an aeroplane crash in Asia was a black-and-white picture of Richard Handsworth, shaking hands with some charity workers. The headline read: *MP's widow slams Northumbria Police detective.*

Tom felt his stomach drop and his heart speed up. Reluctantly, he clicked on the story and read from start to finish. It was damning, and Tom's name cropped up a number of times, as Sarah Handsworth cited 'a complete lack of empathy', disgust at the 'ineptitude of the police force' and called the force 'incompetent at protecting the people who pay their wages'. The story also made a big deal of the fact it was Sarah's first Christmas alone. There was a picture of the big house, now devoid of any Christmas decorations. There was a picture of Sarah sitting on the sofa where Tom and Lauren had first interviewed her, stroking her cat and looking suitably morose.

Tom felt his fury in the pit of his stomach. The article was nothing more than a PR piece, trying to garner as much sympathy for Sarah as they could. The piece finished with her saying that, although they were *probably* doing their best, perhaps having a detective who knows how grief feels might be a good starting point in an investigation; that way, he may be less hasty in haranguing a heartbroken widow.

Tom was livid. How dare she presume that he had never suffered loss?

Christmas was always a horrendous time for Tom. A lot of heavy shit had happened around this time of the year. He tried his best to forget about it, to remove himself from any triggering situations. But it was nigh on impossible when Christmas was thrust in your face earlier and earlier every year. It was impossible to ignore, and he had to work really hard not to spiral every single year. He didn't always manage it. And this year, between the killer and the media spotlight, he wasn't coping. His sleep was suffering, and when he did drift off, his dreams turned into nightmares of smoke, fire and broken glass.

He turned back to the article. He found it deeply unfair that Sarah could make proclamations that he and his colleagues hadn't done all they could in solving the case. They'd followed the evidence and found that Sarah had lied to them during the course of the investigation. If that didn't warrant an interview, what did? Of course, there was no mention of *that* in the article. Why would there be? She was stoking the flames of a witch hunt, and Tom didn't much like it.

'Sorry, Seth,' he said to his brother. 'Something has come up.'

'Don't you want…?' Seth said, but Tom was already out of the door.

* * *

On the drive to the station, Tom thought of the accusations made against him. He could do little else. The news came on at eight o'clock, though there was no mention of Sarah Handsworth.

The reason he had joined the police in the first place was to make a difference. To try and stop horrible things from happening, and when they did, to seek justice for the family of the victims. He resented the fact that Sarah's words had painted him in an uncaring light. Yes, she was hurting, but so was he. God knows he was. The killer, despite the force's best efforts, was still at large, and the last thing Tom needed was a distraction today.

By the time he pulled into the station car park, Sarah's words were pushed to the back of his mind.

A knot of reporters, probably around seven or eight of them, stood near the door of the station. As Tom parked his car, they made their way over, cameramen struggling to keep up behind them.

Tom closed his eyes and took three deep breaths. He had been faced with brazen reporters before, reporters who knew nothing about the ins and outs of the case, reporters who simply wanted a soundbite for the news and didn't care how inflammatory their comments became in order to get what they needed.

Be calm, Tom told himself, as he reached for the door handle. *Be calm.*

Instantly, he was mobbed. Furry microphones were shoved in his face, and the squall of reporters' questions made his brain swim. It was like being attacked by a flock of seagulls. He tried to push past, but it was as if the group had pre-planned their ambush. They formed a solid wall; one that he couldn't get around.

'I'm sure you can understand we're doing all we can. There will be a briefing soon to update you and the rest of the country on what is happening,' he heard himself say, as he shouldered firmly through the reporters.

They followed him across the car park, barking their questions and trying to get his attention. As they neared the station door, a tall man with designer stubble and a smart suit grabbed Tom's arm and said: 'Do you agree with the widow, Sarah Handsworth, that you, Tom Stonem, are failing the taxpayers and, perhaps more importantly, the families of the victims? That there is blood on your hands?'

Tom wheeled around, eyes ablaze. He started towards the reporter, who he now recognised as Archie Walker. He'd been a prick at the briefing a couple of days previously, and he was being one now.

Tom took one step, and then another. Any thought of being calm was gone. He pushed Archie against the wall and pinned him there with a forearm across the chest. Tom knew this was all being filmed, maybe even being broadcast live, but he didn't care. The red mist had settled behind his eyes. There was a tipping point for everyone, and the smarmy reporter had just given Tom the last shove he needed.

'You listen to me, you twat,' Tom said quietly in the reporter's ear. 'Don't you dare question what type of person I am. You don't know me. We *will* find the person responsible for all this shit. You keep your fucking nose out of my business and let me get on with the job, all right?'

He released his hold on Archie, who had lost a lot of his swagger, and, with one last raging glare at the rest of the assembled press, walked in the door.

Natalie was waiting for him.

'My office. Now,' she said.

34

Tom sat opposite Natalie. They were like two cowboys waiting for the other to make the first move. Tom had no intention of speaking, in case whatever decided to come out of his mouth was as full of vitriol as he feared. Rain was lashing at the window like death-metal drum fills, and Tom could see that the reporters and their camera operators had scurried to their vans. He imagined Archie furiously typing up his report or playing the victim in front of a hastily filmed breaking news section.

'What was that?' Natalie asked, finally, interrupting Tom's thoughts of revenge on the vultures in the car park.

It was a good question: open-ended. Restorative. Without explicit blame, though Tom knew it was implied.

It was sheer frustration.

It was anger.

It was guilt.

It was an acknowledgement that, maybe, the reporter was right. That Sarah Handsworth was right.

Maybe Tom *was* failing. Maybe he *was* the letdown he thought he was.

'I don't know,' Tom replied, choosing not to voice what he was actually thinking.

'Jesus, Tom.' She sighed. 'I'm trying to help you here. Scum like that lot down there are always going to do or say something to provoke a reaction. You know that. You and I have both been in this game long enough. You gave them exactly what they bloody wanted. And now what? Do you think they are going to can that footage because they feel sorry for the angry police officer, or do you think it's already online and on its way to going viral?'

Tom said nothing.

'Look, we knew what we were getting with you. In Manchester, you had an excellent record of solving serious crimes. You know, and we know, that you are good at your job. But there was the incident with the journalist down there, too. You grabbing Archie by the throat is not the first time you've been in this position, but we chose to overlook that due to your numbers. Perhaps that was a foolish move on my behalf.'

'Look—' Tom started.

'No, I don't want to hear a word. This is going to create a mess for us. I'm going to have to talk to the higher-ups to see what happens next. What I'd suggest is that you go home, and you spend the rest of the day thinking very, very carefully about what you want. Do you want to keep doing this job? Because, if you do, you are going to have to change your attitude.'

'I get that I was a dick just now, but there's a killer on the loose with time running out.' He pulled the laminated photocopy of the Christmas list from his pocket. 'Two more murders. A box of magic tricks, and a surprise. We need to stop this.'

'Agreed. But what we don't need is any more controversy. Look, Tom, I don't know you very well. I don't know what's gone on in the past, but you seem like a decent bloke. You have to understand that every move we make is under the microscope, and what you've just done is completely unacceptable. It was made very clear to me that, when I took you on, it was my responsibility to keep you in line. I'm going to get it in the neck now, because of you.'

Tom could feel tears stippling the side of his eyes.

'Sorry,' he said.

She looked at him kindly now. 'Go home. Have a day to calm down, and by tomorrow, what you've just done will be forgotten about. Or, at least, relegated to page four in the papers. Enough for us to move on. We need you, but not today.'

With nothing left to say, Tom nodded once and left the office. He stalked down the corridors, avoiding eye contact with anyone he met along the way, and went outside. He thought seeking out Archie and apologising might go some way to fixing his reputation, but the proud, wounded part of his personality wouldn't allow it. Instead, he marched across the tarmac, eyes fixed straight in front, and got in his car. Though he wanted to wheelspin and disappear from the scene in a cloud of smoke and burned rubber, he made sure to ease his way out of the car park and join the flow of commuter traffic.

Inside, he was seething. Though the rational side of him knew Natalie was doing what any good boss would do in that situation, he felt betrayed. It felt like she was siding with the media, the very people to blame for stoking up the situation. He thought about turning around and marching straight to Natalie's office and handing in his notice. He didn't need this shit.

Instead, he phoned Alan.

'What's up, boss?' he said.

'How'd you get on with Johnny?'

'I'm just out, actually. He was very apologetic. Said he ran because he couldn't process the news about Millie, and it felt like you were going to arrest him. He has priors, like we knew, and he said he felt that would work against him. He's got alibis, and GMP are checking them now before they let him go, but I can't see that being a problem. Sorry, boss, it's not Johnny. How are things up—'

Tom hung up before Alan could finish. The disappointment that Johnny was innocent, layered with the anger he was already feeling, was almost too much to bear.

He considered swinging into the Sainsbury's and buying a litre bottle of vodka to see him through the day, but it seemed clichéd. Instead, he sped home.

The house was empty when he got there, which he appreciated. He needed time and space to think about his next move. Up and down the living room he strode, negative thoughts circling around his head like a tornado.

What could he do?

He sure as hell wasn't going to sit on his arse all day, considering his next move, like Natalie had suggested. There was a killer out there, and he needed to be active. He'd go through the case again, try to find a different angle. And then he'd go in tomorrow and show the station that he was needed. That would show them.

His phone rang. It was Phil. Tom considered not answering, but thought better of it.

'All right, Tyson Fury?' Phil said.

'I wouldn't, mate. Not today,' Tom said, and Phil immediately took on a more professional manner, perhaps coerced by the venom in Tom's voice.

'I'm ringing to tell you some good news. A copper in Edinburgh has phoned to say there was a burned-out vehicle found on the outskirts of the city. A black Merc. The plates belong to some geezer who lives near the golf course in Gosforth.'

'That's near Caitlyn's mum's house.'

'Aye. That's what I thought. I went back through the CCTV from the night Richard's body was found, and the same car drives past. I phoned the guy who owns it, and he said he reported it stolen on the same day. The way I see it, Caitlyn stole the car, bunged Dicky into the back, dumped him at the Angel and then set off for Edinburgh.'

'Why Edinburgh, though?' Tom asked. 'It's miles away and it would have been horrible on the roads.'

'She's got friends in Edinburgh, doesn't she? Reckon it was worth the trek if she could use them as an alibi. She sets the car on fire when she gets there, gets to her mates' house and tells them she's been in the city all day, seeing the sights and what have you. Her mates are hardly going to question her, are they? Then, she sets off home the next day and pays Millie a little visit.'

Phil had made lots of good points in the last minute. Tom thanked him and hung up before Phil said something to spoil the good work he'd just done. Tom pulled out some documents he had at home and re-read through them. He scribbled in a notebook, jotting down any thoughts that occurred to him.

Richard.

Millie.

Zach.

There was an odd connection between the trio. Richard and Millie were undeniably linked, romantically and professionally. Zach was a strange third wheel but connected by his burgeoning relationship with Caitlyn, who had been at school with Millie. All had been stabbed several times, which seemed to be the killer's favoured means of dispatch.

They *had* to find Caitlyn.

He phoned Henry, but nothing of importance had turned up at her flat. Tom thanked him and hung up before the head of forensics had a chance to bring up Tom's morning scuffle.

So, there was nothing at the flat. That didn't surprise Tom all that much. Clearly, Caitlyn was a planner. The forethought she'd put into posing Richard like an angel, placing the candid picture in Millie's hand and modelling Zach as an alien in the oil tank: it was the work of a crazy person, but an organised one. She was never going to be stupid enough to leave anything incriminating in her flat for the police to find.

All roads seemed to point to Edinburgh. It was a link they hadn't explored fully yet.

Tom pulled out his phone again and called Caitlyn's mother in case her daughter had got in touch. She hadn't, but Tom was undeterred. He asked Linda to send over a photo of Caitlyn's Edinburgh friends, and any details she had about them: names, addresses, places of work, whatever she could get her hands on.

She promised she would try, and hung up.

While Tom was deciding what to do next, the front door opened, and Seth walked in, bringing with him the scent of marijuana. He had a number of Tesco bags grasped in his hands and was still wearing that stupid kaftan. His eyes widened when he saw Tom.

'Ah! Hi mate,' he said, trying for casual but missing spectacularly. 'I thought you were at work all day.'

'I've been sent home. I'm going to pretend that you haven't just walked in smelling like Woodstock, but only this once. Got it?'

'Got it.' Seth nodded, and retreated to the kitchen. Tom could hear him putting stuff away, water running, and then the click of the kettle. He returned moments later with two cups of tea and set one down in front of Tom. 'So, how come you were sent home?'

'I roughed up a reporter. He's a right twat. It's probably going to be all over the news soon, if it isn't already, so the boss sent me home.'

'You can never outgrow your true self,' Seth said, as he sank into the sofa.

'What the hell is that supposed to mean?' Tom growled.

'Do you know that fable of the scorpion and the frog?'

'No, and I don't...'

But it didn't matter what Tom did or didn't want; Seth was already launching himself into the allegory. 'A scorpion wants to get across the wild river, but can't swim. So, a kind frog offers to give him a lift. He's nervous, because he can see the big stinger, but helps anyway. Halfway across, the scorpion stings the frog, paralysing him. He can't swim anymore, and they both start to drown. The frog asks the scorpion why he did it, and the scorpion said it's simply in his nature.'

'And why the fuck are you telling me kiddies' stories?'

'Because,' Seth said, blissfully calm in the face of Tom's ire, 'you are the scorpion. You can go about doling out the law to people, but underneath, you can't change who you are. You're still the angry little boy you once were.'

'I was not angry.'

'You were. We all were. But, unlike you, I have actually managed to change by meditating and expanding my mind. I think you need to talk about it.'

'I can't talk about the case. You know that.'

'Not that case,' Seth said, shaking his head, loose strands of hair falling over his eyes. 'I think we need to talk about the time our Christmas went up in flames when we were kids.'

'And what is that going to achieve?' Tom asked. He really didn't have time for Jeremy Kyle histrionics.

'It might just change your mindset. You might see that forgiveness is healing. I've forgiven myself for my part. I'd love for you to do the same. I think it's something you should really think about.'

'I don't have time for this shit today,' Tom said, rising to his feet. He needed to focus on the investigation, not get bogged down in recriminations from the past. There was a killer stalking the streets right now who needed his attention.

But wasn't that always his problem? He buried his head in the sand, trying to erase that monumental moment when he was just a sad, scared little boy. He turned back to Seth, but then his phone pinged several times, and he grabbed it. A photo of three women in their mid-twenties, one of whom was Caitlyn, appeared in his messages. The other two, according to the accompanying message, were Ellie Thompson and Izzy Baker. Linda also provided a number for Ellie, which Tom saved to his contacts.

He grabbed his coat from where he'd flung it on the sofa, and moved to the door.

'Where are you going?' Seth asked.

'Edinburgh.'

Tom left without another word. He felt bad for losing his rag with Seth, but his little brother knew what buttons to press. He may be coming across as the Buddha reincarnated, but beneath the kaftan and the hippy bullshit, he was still the same Seth as he had always been.

Pushing thoughts of his brother out of his head, he got into the car and started up the engine. Usually, he would line up a playlist that lasted the duration of his journey, but today he wanted silence. He typed an address in the centre of Edinburgh city centre into his sat nav and set off.

The roads were reasonably clear, and Tom made good time. His ETA was just after one o'clock, and he set his eyes on the road and tried to clear his brain. However, Seth's insistence on dredging up the past kept worming its way into his head, and he knew that they *would* have to have that conversation soon.

Tom was not looking forward to it.

35

McGONAGALL'S WAS A FANCY-LOOKING pub, positioned between a greasy spoon (the front painted matte grey and trying very hard to be more than it was) and a Kurdish kebab shop. The windows of the pub were emblazoned with whisky and gin promotions. A menu screwed to the outside wall listed a multitude of award-winning drinks from local distilleries. A trendy man with a pint in his hand and a pork-pie hat on his head sat at one of the small tables that took up some of the pavement outside, an awning overhead sheltering him from the most typical of Scottish weathers.

Inside was a classy affair. The bar was stocked with a horde of bottles, and the beer taps featured drinks only from Edinburgh-based breweries. The lighting was low, and there was a genial hum of conversation from those gathered for their lunches. Tom's stomach rumbled loudly as he perused the food menu; loud enough for the bartender to take it as a sign. He ambled over and gave Tom a knowing smile.

'Might I recommend the burger, sir?' he said.

'I'm here to meet someone,' Tom replied, casting a glance around the bar. 'I don't know if she's eating or not, so...'

'No worries. Sure, let me know what you fancy when you're ready,' the barman said, and sauntered off to a woman who had made her way to the bar.

Tom wandered among the tables, and spotted Ellie sitting near the fireplace. Since the picture that Linda had given him had been taken, Ellie had made some radical changes. Her hair, once long, was now cut short, with a dyed fringe sweeping across her forehead. She wore a pair of stylish glasses, and the light green trouser suit she was dressed in screamed money. A glass bottle of Diet Coke sat before her, half of it poured into a glass with ice, from which she was currently sipping. Her attention was fixed on her phone, which she held in the other hand. Her long, manicured nails tip-tapped on the screen. She looked up as Tom approached.

'Hi, Ellie. Mind if I sit down?'

'Not at all,' she replied, motioning to the empty chair opposite her. She slid the phone in her pocket and smiled at him.

Tom took his jacket off, hung it on the back of the chair and sat down.

'Thanks so much for agreeing to meet me today,' he said.

'No problem. I just want Caitlyn found safe and sound.'

Tom nodded 'Us too, and I'm sure anything you tell us today can help with that. Do you mind if I take notes?'

She shook her head, and Tom took a pen and a notebook from his coat pocket.

'To start with, tell me how you know Caitlyn.'

'Caitlyn and I went to school together. Secondary school. We were in the same class, and hit it off quickly. We were both into heavy metal and discovered bands like Metallica and Megadeth at the same time. We started to dress the same, shared make-up tips, that kind of thing. She was my best friend.'

'Was?'

'She was while we were at school. Linda said she spoke with you, and she told you about the incident with the scissors. Her mam told us that having a trusted circle around her would help her recovery, but it's hard at that age. You don't want to be associated with the whack job, but I did try. She was cold towards me after that, and we inevitably drifted apart. It was probably three years or so after leaving school that she got in touch again. I still have family in Gateshead, so I go down regularly, and we met up. She apologised, and we stayed in touch a bit more after that. She's been up here a few times, too.'

'And she was due to come up recently for a visit, I understand.'

'Yeah, but she never showed. It's happened before. Sometimes she has an episode and no one hears from her for weeks or even longer. Her mam is pretty good at medicating and keeping her on the level, so if she doesn't show, I just assume she's in the middle of something major and try to get in touch later.'

'I assume Caitlyn and Millie didn't get on at school?'

'Understatement of the century,' Ellie said. 'The two of them despised each other. Millie was what we described as a mean girl. She was always dolled up to the nines; hair, make-up, the latest fashion. Do you know what I mean?'

Tom nodded.

'So, obviously, her and us didn't get on. We would turn up to parties in Slayer T-shirts, and she'd be there in her heels and a ballgown. Polar opposites, we were.'

'Are you aware Millie was murdered recently?'

'Yeah, I saw. Awful business. After school, when we grew up a bit, Millie and I became quite good friends, actually. She went to uni in Glasgow, and I came here and never left. We'd meet up every couple of months or so and laugh about what dickheads we'd been. That stopped when she moved back down to the North East, but how she was when she was here changed my opinion of her. You're an idiot when you're in your teens, aren't you?'

Before Tom could concur, the barman approached their table, a battered iPad in hand.

'Are you ready to order?' he asked.

'Aye, I'll have a Coke, please,' Tom said. Ellie held up her glass bottle to indicate that was all right for now. It seemed Tom's empty stomach would have to hold out until after the interview.

'Do you think Caitlyn could have killed her?' Tom asked, once the barman had gone to get his drink.

'I know how it looks, right. She has previous and she has a mental disorder that affects her moods and her actions, so, obviously, it's a possibility. But honestly, I don't see it.'

'Why not?'

'Because the Caitlyn I knew was caring and sensitive and wouldn't hurt a fly.'

'She stabbed someone in the neck.'

'That was her illness, not her.'

Tom could see that Ellie was going to do all she could to protect her friend. She excused herself to go to the toilet, and Tom used the time to check his phone. He had four missed calls from Lauren, and a text message from her asking if he was okay. He didn't want to tell her what he was up to, so pocketed his phone and waited. The log fire beside him was crackling and spitting heat his way, and for a moment he imagined sinking into the chair and having a snooze to allow all the shit of the day to slip from his mind.

He considered what he had learned so far, and thought the probing questions he had planned on asking would probably be met with resistance, so he decided to change tack. Softly-softly catchy monkey, and all that. When Ellie returned, he said: 'Tell me about Caitlyn's life, post-school.'

'She got really into art, and was really good at it. She used it to get her emotions out of her head. As you can imagine, there's a lot of dark imagery involved. She's done a few exhibitions, low key and mainly for friends and family, but, honestly, she's really good. And, obviously, she had a kid...'

'Did she?' Tom asked, surprised. He thought her mum would have mentioned that particular nugget when they spoke to her.

'Yeah, she had a wee girl when she was nineteen. Some bloke she met in a club took advantage of her one night, and got her pregnant. She never saw him again. Her mam is obviously a massive Christian, and saw this child as unholy, conceived the way it was. On top of that, Caitlyn could barely look after herself, let alone this baby, so they put her up for adoption.'

'And someone adopted her?'

'Yeah, but I don't know who.'

Tom's mind was swimming. Surely, despite her Christian sensitivities, Linda would have thought that the complication of a child could be quite important to the investigation. Could Richard Handsworth have been the father? Is that why Caitlyn killed him – a long-held retribution?

And then, something else hit him. According to the timescales, Caitlyn's daughter would be five or thereabouts. The same as Sophie. Could Lauren have adopted Caitlyn's daughter without knowing? Is that why the woman with brown hair was trying to get Sophie's attention on the way to school? Was Caitlyn trying to lure Sophie away from her adoptive mother?

And if so, to what end?

Tom didn't want to think about that. He'd call Lauren as soon as his interview with Ellie was finished.

'Can you think of anywhere Caitlyn might be? We've obviously tried her house and her mum's, but no one can find her.'

'Have you tried her studio?'

'Her studio?'

'Yeah, she has a studio in the centre of Newcastle. It's basically a pokey wee flat, but it's where she goes when she needs a breather. No one knows about it, not even her mam, but I thought the police might have some database or...' Ellie trailed off, waving a hand vaguely as if it might finish the sentence for her.

'Why wouldn't she tell her mum about it?' Tom asked.

'Her mam can be quite overbearing. She can become intense and it's a place Caitlyn can go where her mam won't bother her. It's a safe space away from all the shit that goes on in her life.'

'I get that.'

'Also, she pays for it by modelling on Only Fans.'

Tom hadn't been living under a rock, and so had a passing knowledge of this website. Only Fans allowed subscribers to pay 'models' for cam shows and porn videos. 'So she was worried her mum would ask how she could afford an art studio in the city centre, and she didn't want to tell her she was selling videos of herself online?'

'Exactly,' Ellie said. 'So, she didn't. It was easier that way.'

'Do you have the address?'

'Somewhere.' She reached into her bag and leafed through a leather-bound address book. In the age of mobile phones, it felt like a relic of another time. Ellie's lips mouthed words and names, until she reached the one she needed. She passed the book across the table and Tom took a picture of Caitlyn's alternate address.

'I hope I've been helpful,' Ellie said, as she took the book back. 'Like I said, I know that, on paper, Caitlyn sounds like a wrong 'un, but she actually has a heart of gold. I really hope she hasn't got herself involved in something that doesn't concern her.'

She peered at her watch.

'I'm really sorry, but I've got to get back to work. Merry Christmas,' Ellie said, as she shook his hand. Tom mumbled the same salutation back, but without her warmth. He watched as she disappeared through the front door. She pulled her hood up against the storm, and powered up the street with her head down.

Tom pulled out his phone and called Lauren, but there was no answer. He tried again, but the same thing happened. He'd call again in a while. The whole thing was probably his imagination playing tricks. Of all the hundreds and thousands of people who adopted the world over, what were the chances of Lauren adopting this whack-job killer's baby?

He set his phone on the table and considered his next move. Really, he should call this new information in, but if Natalie knew he had disobeyed her orders and travelled one hundred and seven miles to Scotland's capital, he would be in even more trouble. Turning up tomorrow, grovelling an apology and telling his boss he had unearthed information overnight seemed like the way to go.

Go home and think, Natalie had said, so that's what he would pretend he had done. Perhaps one of the other detectives working the case would happen upon the hidden art studio in his absence. And if they didn't, he might feed Lauren the information and let her take the credit. He reckoned he could trust her to keep her lips zipped.

Decision made, he consulted the menu and settled on the BBQ chicken pizza with chips. When he was done, he walked to his car and started the drive back to the North East.

36

IT WAS JUST AFTER three o'clock, and Lauren was in the office when her phone rang. She clicked save on the document she had been working on and answered.

It was her mam, and she was crying.

'Sophie is gone,' she said, and wailed down the line.

'Mam,' Lauren said, her heart racing and bile rising in her throat. 'What do you mean?'

'I've just been to the childminder's to pick Sophie up. And she's gone.'

37

LAUREN STOOD OUTSIDE THE childminder's house, and tried very hard to listen to what Clare was telling her. The sheer volume of the blood pumping in her ears was making it very difficult to understand anything.

'So,' Lauren said, trying to remain calm in spite of the panic threatening to overwhelm her. 'A woman who was not my mam came and took Sophie?'

Clare wiped tears from her eyes and nodded. 'You said granny would be picking her up today. I assumed you meant the other one.'

'Describe the woman who took her.'

'I... I...'

'Clare,' Lauren said, firmly. 'This is important. What did she look like?'

'She... uh... she had a pink raincoat on, and wellies. She, she had brown hair and dark glasses.'

'You let Sophie go with someone you'd never seen before who was wearing sunglasses?'

'They weren't sunglasses,' Clare squeaked. 'Not really. They were those ones that change shade depending on how much sun there is.'

'Did she look like a granny? Was she really that old?'

'I can't be sure,' Clare said. 'I was in a hurry, and she asked for Sophie by name, so I assumed you'd sent her. I didn't really have a good look at her. I feel awful...'

Lauren stopped listening. Her mind conjured up the photograph of Caitlyn that had been on Linda's mantelpiece.

The brown hair.

The glasses.

And then fragments of crime scenes drifted into her head. The broken bodies. A mud-soaked angel; a blood-stained red dress; an oily alien. She forced the unwanted images away.

'Was she walking or driving?' Lauren asked.

'I'm sorry, Lauren. I didn't see.'

Lauren hurried down the path and out into the street. It had taken her twenty minutes to drive from the station to Clare's. More than enough time for Caitlyn to flee the scene. To where? The train station? A car already bound for the motorway?

Lauren leaned against a low wall and vomited.

She knew Caitlyn was volatile and unstable. She was the main suspect in a multiple murder case. Was kidnapping Sophie the surprise? Had she skipped the box of magic tricks clue, or were the final two combined?

Lauren wiped her mouth and pulled out her phone.

'Natalie,' she said, once the call had connected. 'I think Caitlyn has my daughter.'

Natalie sought to comfort Lauren, but it was useless. The DCI asked for the address of the childminder and told her she'd be in touch as soon as she could. She assured her they would do all in their powers to apprehend Caitlyn, but that was little comfort. They'd been trying to catch the killer for a week now.

For all Lauren knew, Sophie might already be… No. She couldn't bear to finish the sentence. Couldn't bear to even contemplate that something so awful was a possibility. Sophie was innocent in all of this. The sweetest and most important facet of her life. It was unthinkable that she had been dragged into this.

She had to do something. But what?

Drive around the city like a lunatic, hoping to stumble on a clue? Or catch sight of her beautiful daughter at a bus stop sitting alongside the woman who snatched her?

Indecision kept her rooted to the spot, with millions of sinister outcomes running though her mind. When her phone rang five minutes later, she answered it without greeting.

'Lauren?' said Natalie.

'Yes.'

'We've spotted Sophie and a woman matching Caitlyn's description walking west on the street you gave us. There's a CCTV camera at the end. Go that way, and we'll try and track her on cameras along the route. Alan is on it. There's back-up on its way. We'll find her, Lauren. We will.'

Lauren hung up and started up the street on unsteady legs. She reached the end of the road and looked up at the camera that had captured her daughter's last movements. Which way now?

Intuition told her to carry on straight, and before long she was on Lower Moor Road. This is where she had chased the brown-haired woman during the school run the other day. Did Caitlyn own one of these houses? Did she use it as some sort of bolthole? Is this where she had thrust the knife into the stomach of Richard Handsworth before setting off for the Angel?

She knew she should wait for back-up, but every second she lingered was a waste. Instead, she marched up to the first house on the street and hammered on the door. A man with round spectacles answered and assured her there were no children at all in the house. She took his word for it and moved on to the next.

Rain was pouring down now, and Lauren was soaked to the skin. Several brown-haired women answered doors further up the street, but they didn't look like the woman Lauren had pursued. They watched Lauren shiver on their top step, before closing the door in her face.

Losing hope, Lauren ran up the path of number 42 and rang the bell. The door had frosted glass inserts, and Lauren could see there was a light on further down the hall. She rang the bell again and bashed the knocker loudly for good measure.

There were footsteps in the hallway, and the door opened slightly, though the chain was on. A woman with brown hair, glasses and an oversized silver necklace answered. When she saw Lauren, her eyes widened.

'Lauren, I—' She was cut off by Lauren lunging shoulder-first at the door. The chain was knocked loose and the door swung open, smashing off the porch's inner wall. The woman was knocked backwards, stumbling a few steps into the house.

Lauren stormed into the woman's home and tackled her to the floor. She pulled her arm back, balled her hand into a fist and was about to bring it down on the woman's jaw, when Sophie toddled out from the room at the end of the hallway.

'Hi, Mammy,' she said. She had a green paper crown on her head, and a cocktail sausage in her hand. 'What are you doing here?'

For a moment, Lauren didn't move.

This was all too surreal.

And then she rushed to her daughter and gave her the tightest hug she had ever given anyone. Sophie hugged her back, but was more interested in finishing her food. Lauren stroked her hair and wouldn't let go of her. Tears stung her eyes, and she realised that the wolf-like howls were her own. The awful thoughts that had run through her head were gone, and the euphoria of finding her daughter safe and well was like a drug. With Sophie still in her arms, Lauren turned back to the woman. It took her a moment to realise who it was.

Helen Miller, the mother of her good-for-nothing ex-husband, was picking herself up off the floor, readjusting her statement necklace. It must have been a recent purchase, because although

Helen was never a style icon, that thing was a whole new level of monstrous.

'Helen, what the fu—She stopped herself just in time. 'What do you think you're playing at?'

'I… I don't know. I'm sorry. I'm truly sorry. I just…' She broke down, sobbing loudly.

Lauren gave Sophie her phone (something she wasn't in the habit of doing) and told her she could have five minutes of free time while the adults talked. Sophie couldn't believe her luck. She ran into the kitchen, and the opening notes of *Vampirina* began not long after.

Helen ushered Lauren into the living room, where they sat on opposing couches.

'Explain,' Lauren said.

'I'm sorry,' Helen said. 'I know what I did was wrong. I just want a relationship with my granddaughter.'

'Jesus, Helen. You could've gone about it a different way. You scared me to death.'

'I know,' she said, blowing her nose. 'But I couldn't see how. I know you and Greg aren't on speaking terms, and I had no other way to contact you.'

'You could've said hello on the street when you were spying on us.'

'I suppose,' she said. 'But I thought you'd tell me to do one.'

'I probably would've,' Lauren said, though her resolve was crumbling. She had always had a good relationship with Helen, and the inevitable fallout from the divorce meant their connection had ended abruptly. 'Look. It's only natural you want to be in Sophie's life. But what you did was fucking ridiculous. You kidnapped her, on Christmas Eve, for Christ's sake.'

'Don't say it like that.'

'I'll say it exactly how it is. I'm hunting a killer at the moment. Do you know what I thought when—'

'I hear you,' Helen interrupted. 'And I'll be sorry to my dying day. But Ray passed away this year, and I'm at a low ebb. I'm not after sympathy, and it's no excuse for what I did. I only wanted to spend some time with someone who might show me a bit of love.'

In a strange reversal, Lauren found herself in the role of consoler. She had been fond of Ray, her father-in-law, too, and was sorry to learn of his death. Against her better judgement, she agreed that Helen being in Sophie's life would be nice.

They swapped numbers, and then Lauren called Sophie. In the hall, Lauren helped Sophie with her coat and gloves. Helen disappeared for a moment, and returned with a wrapped gift. Sophie wanted to open it straightaway, but Helen convinced her to wait another twelve hours. Lauren hoped to God it wasn't jewellery.

They said goodbye and stepped out onto the street. Snow was falling. Lauren felt Sophie's little hand slip into her own, and for a moment, all was right in the world.

CHRISTMAS DAY

Christmas Day is not postcard pretty, like films and television shows always show it to be.

Instead of snowy pavements, a blue sky and families cycling together on shiny new bicycles, the streets are mostly empty. The pavements are icy and there are mounds of slush in the gutter. Some cars splash past, sending waves of dirty water over me.

I barely notice. My attention is fixed on the house at the end of the road.

Holly's house.

People talk about seeing red when they're angry, but I don't. I sort of feel like I do after a really hard game of football, when you are exhausted but your body tries to get you through it.

My vision is kind of blurry, but the sharp point of the knife in my pocket, which I poke the tip of my finger against gently, is doing a good job of keeping me focussed.

It's the sharpest one in the house; the one Mum always says not to use because we could cut ourselves very easily.

I'm shivering, but it's nothing to do with the cold. I know this because I've put on Dad's big coat. It hangs down to my knees and falls off my shoulders, but it's the most expensive thing he's ever bought, and I assume he's left it behind for a reason.

The morning has come together like a jigsaw, so far.

Coat.

Knife.

Rage.

Of course, it hasn't been perfect. When the little ones came down the stairs, all excited, and were faced with an empty room, the crap hit the fan. I had to explain that maybe Santa had forgotten their presents, and he might discover them at the bottom of his sack when he was almost home.

I couldn't stop them crying. The wailing drove me out into the street, with a knife in my pocket and Holly on my mind.

Holly. Fucking Holly. The girl so Christmassy that even her name is a never-ending reminder of the joyous time of year when Christ was born.

I walk up the street and stop in front of her house. The garden is full of inflatable crap, though Santa seems to have sprung a leak: he has folded in half on the pristine lawn. A jolly reindeer with what looks like a fez resting between its antlers rears over him.

I open the gate and walk up the path. As I get closer, I can hear 'Do They Know It's Christmas?' being sung loudly and out of key by a deep male voice. When he finishes, there is laughter and cheering, and it makes me wonder what my dad is up to. I think about turning around and going home, but then my sadness turns to anger again. I poke my finger with the knife tip and can feel the skin give way. The pain focusses me, and I take the bleeding finger and press it against the doorbell.

It smears over the white button, and I am pleased. The little smudge of red is just what I need to see.

Inside, the music quietens and I can hear footsteps. The door swings open and I'm met by a woman with blonde hair that has been braided at the front. She is wearing a short tartan dress and a pair of black tights. One of her toes has escaped through a small hole on the left foot. In her left hand is a slim glass with orange juice inside.

Her face is pretty. When she sees me, though, her wide smile is replaced with a look of surprise.

'Merry Christmas,' she says. 'Tom, isn't it? Tom Stonem?'

38

I NOD. YES, I AM TOM STONEM and I am here to ruin your daughter's Christmas.

I don't say that, obviously. I simply stand in the doorway and let her look at me. My oversized adult jacket; my jeans that are worn away at the knees and so short they show my mismatched socks. My shoes with their broken soles, allowing cold slush to seep in.

I allow her to pity me, because my own parents don't.

'Why aren't you at home with your family, Tom?' she asks, kneeling to look me in the eye.

'I'm getting under their feet,' I say. 'Thought I'd get out of the house and get a bit of fresh air.'

'Good idea,' she says. 'I kinda wish my two would do the same thing.'

She tips her head back and laughs. I can't remember the last time I heard my own mum laugh, but can't imagine it was ever with the same joy as Holly's mum's.

'I also thought I would apologise to Holly for how I treated her the other day. I wasn't very nice to her at school, and I've felt bad about it since.'

The lie feels wrong as it leaves my mouth. Miss, at school, hates lying. She often says she would prefer to sort out a physical fight than spend time trying to dig through a bunch of untruths. She says lies make a person ugly and unhappy, and always brings up *The Twits* when she says that.

'Well, what a lovely thing to do.' She steps aside and holds out a welcoming hand. I step into the house. Inside, it is warm and the foresty scent of the Christmas tree wafts through the house, mingling with the smell of cooking turkey. My tummy rumbles, and it suddenly dawns on me that I need to sort food for the twins back at home. Best make this quick.

'Between you and me,' Holly's mum says, 'I don't believe Holly is blameless in whatever happened between the two of you. Don't tell her I said this, but she can be a right little madam at times.'

I don't know what to say, so simply smile back at her. She directs me up the stairs and to the last room at the end of the hallway. After that, she turns around and walks towards the kitchen. I can hear someone tell a joke, most likely pulled from a cracker. The laughter that follows is loud and sounds so out of place in a house. Except, that's not true. It would sound so out of place in *my* house. Here, it feels normal. So does the warmth coming from the radiators, and the happiness.

I glance up the stairs and take a few steps. The carpet is thick. Framed family pictures are spaced evenly on the cream walls: Holly's mum and dad nursing a small bundle in one. In another, Holly is standing between her parents, her mouth open in a wide smile that shows missing front teeth. Her parents are barefoot and beaming at her. The final picture shows Holly as I know her now, her fringe cut straight across her eyes. She is wearing a tartan dress similar to the one her mum is wearing now, only black and white instead of red and green.

I stop to try and get my shaking knees under control. I'm breathing fast and my hands are sweaty. This moment weighs heavily, and I know what happens in the next five minutes could be life-changing.

I consider backing down. Running down the stairs, letting myself out and tearing away from the house as fast as I can. But I don't. I've come here for a reason, and I need to follow it through.

I reach the top of the stairs and creep along the hallway. One of the doors is open, revealing a bedroom so big it probably would outsize the whole bottom floor of my house.

As I approach the end door, a noise creeps out from the gap at the bottom. It's a soft whining sound, punctuated by excitable panting and a tinkling bell. As I reach out towards the handle, I'm startled by a quiet bark.

I gather my nerves and open the door as quietly as I can.

Holly is on her bed, with headphones over her ears. She is lying on her side, facing the wall. On the floor, trotting towards me is the cutest puppy I have ever seen. It's a Labrador. Its eyes are huge and brown and its ears are floppy. A little bell tinkles on its collar, onto which a big red bow has been tied. Its tail is wagging as it comes to me and jumps up. Its fur is the softest thing I've ever felt, and I am immediately in love.

I sit down on the floor and let it climb over my legs, all the while stroking it. It's then that Holly turns around and sees me. She jumps out of her skin.

'Tom?' she says, her brow furrowed. 'What are you doing here?'

The truth is, now that I'm here, I know I can't go through with forcing Holly to give me her dog. Looking into the puppy's unbelievably cute eyes and Holly's happy face, I know I can't do it. What sort of life would it have with me, anyway? No – it's far better off here.

'I… I…' I stammer, unsure what to say.

'Did you come to see the puppy?' she asks, and then laughs. 'I know I might have mentioned it once or twice at school. God, I must've been so annoying, going on about it.'

Who is *this* Holly? At school, Holly is confident and a bit of a mean girl. Now that I have her alone, she is being nice to me. She's making fun of herself! I can feel tears forming behind my eyes, and a lump develops in my throat.

'Anyway, I'm glad to see you, Tom,' she says now. 'I wanted to say sorry for the other day at school. I was being a right bitch.' She whispers this and peers at the door. 'I deserved what you did. I'm really going to try and stop being like that from now on.'

'I'm sorry, too,' I say, and feeling awkward, nod at the dog. 'Does she have a name yet?'

'Penny.'

At the mention of her name, Penny looks up at me and a little drip of slobber falls from her shiny tongue onto my hand. I laugh and stroke her head. She lies down contentedly between my outstretched legs.

Holly gets up from her bed and goes over to a small, fake Christmas tree in the corner of the room. Under it are still some unopened presents, one of which she picks up.

'I hope this isn't weird, but Mummy always says it's nicer to give presents than receive them. I'm not sure I exactly believe her' – she looks at the package she is holding – 'but I want you to have this.'

'What is it?' I ask.

'That's the beauty of wrapping paper,' she replies, 'it stops you knowing before you open it.'

She punches my arm playfully, before leaning in for a very short, awkward hug.

'I don't have anything to give you,' I say, when we break apart.

She looks at the dog. 'Penny is all I need.'

'Can I come and visit her again?'

As if the question had been addressed to her, Penny barks and jumps up at me. Holly laughs and I give her a couple more strokes before leaving.

Downstairs, I let myself out as quietly as I can. I really didn't want to meet her mum or dad on the way out and have to tell more lies about why I was there, or worse, have them discover the knife.

The experience has left me flat as a pancake. All the rage I'd felt on the way there has drained away. I'm shaking. I'm not ready to go home.

Instead, I wander. I don't go in any particular direction; I go where my feet carry me. Through the windows of the houses I pass, I watch family after family being families, and I realise I am crying.

I miss Mum and Dad and, even though I know it won't happen, I imagine them sitting on the floor with Seth and Rachel when I get back, arguing over a board game or chomping on chocolate from a selection box.

I'm not sure how much time passes, but by the time I decide to head home, my legs are sore from so much walking and I am soaked to the skin. My hands are frozen and aching from carrying the present Holly gave me. Letting the twins open it might go some way to saving the day for them. At least they'll have one present to share.

As I turn onto my street, I notice how dark it has got. The sky is black, the moon hidden, but there are other lights.

Blue lights.

The street is full of people, and there is thick smoke billowing from one of the houses.

Someone must've burned their turkey, I think, though I quickly realise it is more serious than that.

Two fire engines take up most of the street, and an army of men with hoses are battling a fierce blaze. It's then I realise it's my house that's on fire.

I drop the present and take off running, my sodden shoes slapping hard on the slippery pavement. My lungs are on fire, and, as I get closer, I can hear my name being called by my neighbours.

As I reach the cordon set up by the firefighters, I'm squeezed round the midriff by a muscly arm. I fight against it. My brother and sister are in there, I scream, but the human barrier remains in place.

I lash out at the man holding me, but he clings onto me. I turn to look at him. He's a big man, with tattooed arms and a kind smile. He's got a cut on his chin, maybe from shaving, and there's a bruise on his cheek. Despite his rough and ready appearance, when he speaks, his voice is soft. His words cut through the confusion. He tells me it's all going to be all right.

There's been an accident, but I'm going to be looked after.

'What about my brother?' I shout. 'What about my sister?'

He looks to the woman standing beside him, a question in his eyes. She's plump, and her hair has gone frizzy from the rain. She is wearing a lanyard around her neck with the words 'Social Services' on it, and her photo is on a card attached to the end. Instead of an answer, I'm led towards a black car.

I begin to cry in earnest as the car pulls away from the kerb with a sharp squeal. As we set off, I realise that the present Holly gave me is lying in the street where I dropped it.

39

When Tom's alarm went off on Christmas morning, he turned it off and rolled over. He had already been awake for some time; sleep hadn't come easy in the night. He was pleased to see there weren't any missed calls or messages from the station. The killer had obviously had a quiet night. He had a feeling in the pit of his stomach that, whatever direction the case was going to take, it was going to end today.

He felt uneasy. Firstly, he was going to have to explain to his boss how he had come by the information linking Caitlyn and her city-centre studio. Natalie hadn't got to be DCI by chance: she'd be able to smell his bullshit from a mile away. So he reckoned the best thing was to be straight up with her. He had to tell her about the trip to Scotland.

Secondly, he was going to have to swallow some of his pride and apologise for his stupidity yesterday. Natalie was probably cursing the day she hired him, and he needed to make sure she knew he was being sincere and that she could trust him in the future.

Before all of that, though, he had to face Seth.

Remembering Christmas Day all those years ago was painful.

Holly.

The knife.

The puppy.

The fire.

Rachel.

After the social workers had taken him to a safe space for the night, the worst years of Tom's life had begun.

On the first night, he had barely slept. He had smashed the room to pieces: thrown lamps, kicked the walls until his feet decimated the plaster, and scratched at the locked door until his fingers bled. The social workers had visited him often, and when they did, he screamed at them. All he wanted to know was if his brother and sister were safe. His captors genuinely didn't know and apologised for the lack of clarity, but their soothing voices and calm demeanour only enraged Tom further. He didn't want sympathy; he wanted fire and brimstone and blood and fucking answers.

Dawn arrived with revelations.

Seth had made it. Rachel hadn't.

The bluntness of the delivery had shocked Tom into silence. He hadn't cried. He hadn't done anything except try to comprehend the enormity of those few words.

His sister, his flesh and blood, the little girl who was only a couple of years younger than he, was no longer a part of this world. How could that be fair? Had she died knowing her big brother had abandoned her in search of petty revenge? Tom didn't think he could bear the shame.

When the social workers had given him what they thought was enough time to process that information, they gave him some more. Apparently, Seth, hungry and determined, had attempted to cook something for himself and Rachel. Somehow, the house had been set ablaze.

That's when Tom had reappeared on the street, but Seth had already been taken away to a hospital.

In the aftermath, the police had organised a search team and had found his parents' bodies in no time at all. Both had been face down in a well-known drug den. The dealer who supplied the smack had abandoned ship and was never found.

Tom and Seth had stayed apart for a few years. Tom bounced from one foster family to the next; the anger and guilt in his heart too raw for anyone to endure for more than twelve months at a time. His grief tested the strongest of sibling relationships and frayed the knot of the strongest marriages. That is, until he met Angela and Nigel. They were experienced in grief and, over time, broke down his red walls. They eventually fostered Seth, too, though by that time, Tom was ready to leave for university and only made sporadic visits home. Because of this, and the spectre of Rachel Stonem, the two brothers had never been close.

From downstairs he could hear Seth pottering about the place.

Best get up and face the music.

40

SETH WAS SITTING ON the floor when Tom went downstairs, his legs folded like a pretzel beneath him. His eyes were closed, his brow furrowed in concentration. His lips moved, but no sound came out. Tom tiptoed past him and made a cup of tea, assuming his brother would be finishing whatever cosmic yoga thing he was doing soon.

Sure enough, his eyes opened not long after Tom had plonked a mug on the fireplace next to him.

'Thanks for the tea, mate,' he said, picking it up and taking a sip. 'Where did you get off to in such a hurry yesterday?'

'Edinburgh,' Tom said. 'I had to interview one of the main suspect's friends. Sorry for running out, only, it was a priority.'

'I get it. You gotta do your job, eh?'

'And where were you last night, you dirty stop-out?'

Seth laughed. 'Strangely, I met a girl in Cambodia who lives near St James' Park, so we decided to meet up for a couple of drinks.'

'You stay over?'

'Nah. I got back here just after one o'clock, I think. The memory is a little hazy.' He smiled, and then looked at Tom with those piercing eyes of his. 'I think we should talk about it, don't you?'

Reluctantly, Tom nodded. He really did have to get to work, and he reckoned that if Seth got whatever it was he needed to off his chest, he would be more inclined to let Tom go. Seth began what quickly became apparent as a rehearsed speech.

'During my travels around Asia, I became interested in the idea of Nirvana...'

Tom inevitably thought of the American grunge band.

'... It's the idea that one can achieve a spiritual awakening, a practical solution to the existential problem of human anguish. I've always believed what happened to Rachel was my fault. You cannot begin to understand the torment I've been carrying around for twenty years. I stayed in Asia longer than I intended, keen to soak up as much of the teaching and healing as I could. Rachel's spirit has never left me, but I felt her particularly keenly in those temples. I could feel her, and heard her voice more than once, whispering that none of what happened was my fault.'

Tom wondered how much weed Seth had smoked on the other side of the world. Of course, the thought of a loved one speaking to you from beyond the grave was a pleasant one, but Tom was too engrained with the English burden of rationality.

He wondered, too, why it had taken them over two decades to discuss this. Tom hadn't been a great big brother. Seth had lived with the knowledge that his actions had killed his own twin sister. Obviously, he was not the only one to blame. Tom had left two bored, hungry eight-year-olds alone in a house on Christmas Day. Tom's parents had left three children under twelve alone for days. Everyone had played their part in the run-up to the disaster. Yet, Tom had never told Seth this. He had never felt the need to help Seth through the horrific ordeal. He'd simply retreated into his own life and put shutters up in an attempt to conceal the trauma. Tom knew the conversation, and his admittance to a part in the disaster, was needed, but it was not going to be easy.

'Mate,' Tom said. 'You know this is not on you, right? Rachel's death was not your fault at all.'

'You really believe that?'

'Of course.' Tom struggled to order his thoughts in the right way. He wanted to tell Seth how sorry he was, to show him that he had been hurting, too. But the words wouldn't come freely. He took a moment to compose himself, and said, 'I should never have left the two of you alone. It was such a stupid thing to do, but I was upset about Mum and Dad leaving me in charge. I needed a bit of time to myself.'

Tom looked down at Seth, still folded in on himself. Tears ran down his face, and fresh ones glistened in his eyes.

'You have no idea how much it means to hear you say that,' he said, reaching for Tom's hand. 'You have no idea.'

Tom pulled him to his feet, and the two brothers hugged. Despite his scepticism about Seth's Far Eastern philosophies, Tom had to admit it felt like they were on the cusp of something. They'd never really been *brothers*; more like two people who happened to be related but had never been invested in each other's lives. It felt like that was about to change.

'This Christmas can be different,' Seth said, once they'd broken apart. 'This Christmas, we can start to make new memories; really get to know each other.'

'I'd love that, mate,' Tom said. 'I really would. How about you get yourself into the kitchen and get some music on. Did you manage to get the ingredients for dinner?'

'I sure did. I might try something a bit different with the turkey, something I picked up in Mexico.'

'Sounds good to me, as long as it's not too spicy.' Tom shrugged. 'I trust you, and I'm really looking forward to hearing all about your travels. Now, I shouldn't be too long...' He took one step towards the door.

'What do you mean?' Seth said.

'I have to go to work.'

Anger bloomed on Seth's face. 'Are you fucking kidding me? After what we've just spoken about? After that Christmas Day where everything got fucked up in the first place because you left, you're leaving me again?'

'Seth, you're not eight years old anymore. You're a grown man, for Christ's sake.'

Seth looked disappointed, and Tom felt bad. He really did need to go to work. Even if he hadn't, he still might've made an excuse to leave for a while. To go for a walk on his own or a quick jog around the block, to help him process everything. The conversation they'd just had had exhausted him emotionally. He needed a bit of time, and work was the convenient excuse.

'Look, mate, the killer we've been tracking is in our sights. We have an address, a name, and a team standing by to take her in. I just need to go and grovel so that I don't lose my job, sort the arrest, and I'll be back in time to help you with the last bits, and then I promise we'll spend some quality time together. How do you feel about Monopoly?'

'It's a game specifically designed to promote consumerism and greed.'

'Everything you're against,' Tom said, 'so I see an easy win in my future.'

Seth grinned at him.

'Go on, then, hero brother. Go and make the arrest, clean up the streets of Newcastle, but dinner is being served at three o'clock whether you're here or not. Got it?'

'Got it,' Tom said.

'Oh, and I get to be the race car,' Seth said.

Tom pulled Seth in for one more hug before grabbing his coat and making his way out onto the frozen streets.

41

Tom stood at the front of the briefing room, fresh from a bollocking from Natalie. Apparently, in the past twenty-four hours, his decision-making had been poor. Poor enough that, at the end of this case, he might find himself unemployed. It was a decision she couldn't make now – not with the investigation hanging in the balance. She'd told him to put all of his nonsense to one side and focus on the task at hand.

So, here he was, in front of the pull-down screen. Gathered in front of him were Natalie, Phil, Alan, and a host of uniformed officers. There was a strange atmosphere in the room: a mixture of excitement at the prospect of the case being over, and a sadness at being pulled away from families on Christmas Day.

Natalie took to the front, and informed them of Lauren's absence. She spoke of the ordeal involving Sophie the day before, and the need for Lauren to spend some quality time with her family.

Tom felt heartbroken for her. He knew how much she loved her little girl, and how she must've felt when she thought she might never see her again.

Natalie handed the floor to him. He told the team about how he came by the information and took some stick for 'going Jack Bauer on their asses' – Phil's words. Natalie, in turn, told Phil to shut up.

Tom pressed a button on the remote he was holding, and a picture of a block of flats appeared on the screen.

The flats were horrible grey blocks, rising twenty stories into the sky. One of the windows was circled in red, and it was to this window that Tom pointed.

Before he could speak, the door opened and Lauren burst in. Her heavy winter coat was frosted with snow.

'Lauren,' Natalie said. 'I told you to stay at home today.'

'And miss the excitement? I don't think so,' Lauren said. 'You said you had a plan when we spoke. I don't want to miss out on looking into her eyes as we make the arrest.'

'If you're sure,' Natalie said.

Lauren took a seat and stared at the screen. Tom gave her a warm smile, before continuing his briefing.

'This flat is currently being rented by Caitlyn, under a different name. Her friend told me she uses money she earns from OnlyFans to pay for it. She uses it as an art studio, but since her house was clear of them, I'm wondering if we're going to find her killing supplies.'

'Makes sense that she'd store them in a place no one knows she has any affiliation to,' Lauren said.

'Agreed.' Tom nodded. 'I'm not trying to paint her as some sort of Batman villain, but I do think it's worth being wary of how clever she is. She's evaded us for so long, she's taunted us, she's led us on a merry chase to that Christmas card, and we know she has a violent past...'

'And present,' Phil added.

'So it's worth bearing in mind that there may be some sort of booby trap in the flat. Our entrance will need to be thought out, as will each step of the plan that follows.'

Tom clicked through the rest of the slideshow. The flat's letting agency had obviously not picked up their phones on Christmas Day, and the only other point of contact was an e-mail address that would likely go unchecked until some point in the new year, so Tom was making do with pictures advertising one of the adjoining flats. After some careful checking, he was reasonably sure that Caitlyn's flat would have the same layout.

He and the team discussed each facet of the operation. The entry. The multitude of scenarios that could follow. Where each person would be stationed, and their reaction to what may occur.

The trouble with the human mind was, no one, not even the most eminent psychologists in the world, could predict what was likely to happen. Every eventuality could be considered, and yet, something seemingly outside the realms of possibility was the thing that was most likely to occur.

It keeps you on your toes, was Angela's rather English-country-garden way of putting it.

With plans in place, the assembled got to their feet and made for the door. It was time to go and find their Christmas Killer.

42

BING CROSBY MAY HAVE dreamed of a white Christmas, but Tom certainly hadn't. In fact, he could have done without the icy roads and the thick curtain of snow that seemed to be falling with ever-increasing urgency. Combined, the elements caused the convoy of police vehicles to slow to a snail's pace as they made their way from the station in Gateshead across the bridge to the south-west of Newcastle city centre. On the way, Lauren filled Tom in on Sophie's abduction and subsequent finding. Though it had been a happy outcome, Lauren still seemed on edge. With good reason, Tom thought, as he indicated and turned into the car park.

The pristine, undisturbed snow, coupled with the falling tufts from the sky, should have made the scene postcard-perfect. But the towers from Tom's PowerPoint were even more ghastly in real life. They rose into the pregnant sky, the tops disappearing into low clouds. Despite a recent coat of paint, and new windows and frames, the towers remained stuck in the 1960s, when they had first been erected. After the tragedy of Grenfell, the side of one of the towers was being used as a screen, with a message damning the cladding and asking the question: Are we next?

Tom considered the down-at-heel flats for a moment and contemplated what lay behind the door of the studio rented by Caitlyn. He knew all the frustrations and pain of the case were almost over, but he worried she might go out with a bang. Hopefully not in the literal sense.

Tom and Lauren got out of the car and followed two burly officers across the car park and into the building. The lobby of the tower block was large and rectangular, cold and unwelcoming. A black orb hung from the ceiling, an old CCTV camera with its wires frayed and exposed. There was a reception area, but no one was staffing it. The place smelt like weed and piss, and the stench only got worse as they scaled a stairwell covered in faded graffiti.

They climbed to the fourth floor and tiptoed up the corridor. Their wet boots squeaked occasionally on the tattered linoleum, though the mixture of different music drifting through the flimsy doors either side of the corridor hid their approach.

The best-case scenario, of course, was that they would knock and Caitlyn would answer. They would arrest her straight off the bat, and afterwards the forensic team would uncover damning evidence within her studio. With any luck, Tom would be able to keep his promise to Seth that he'd be back home for Christmas dinner at the arranged time. No fuss, no muss, no upset brother.

The officers let Tom past. He knocked smartly on the door and took a step back. The door did not open, so he knocked again. This time he did not step back; instead, he put his ear to the door and tried to listen for any movement. The music and merriment drifting from the adjoining flats didn't help, and he couldn't tell if any of the noise was coming from Caitlyn's.

'I think we should force entry,' he said, and Lauren nodded.

Tom moved out of the way as one of the officers moved into position. In his hands was a manual battering ram made of solid steel. The man wielding it took a few practice swings, the action and the look of sheer concentration reminiscent of Tiger Woods before approaching his golf ball. It was almost laughable.

What happened next was not.

Confidently, the battering ram was swung at the area of the door immediately below the handle. On impact, the wooden door exploded inwards. The meagre hinges were torn from the wall and flecks of paint and concrete dust confettied through the air.

Entry had taken less than the time it took to blink, but the sight that greeted them took a few seconds longer to comprehend.

The hallway was dark, with the only light coming from a window in the room at the end of it, presumably the kitchen. In their way was a silhouette, framed by the light. The body hung from the ceiling, and for a split-second, Tom couldn't make sense of what he was seeing.

And then the penny dropped.

Caitlyn was trying to hang herself.

A rickety chair, presumably what she had been standing on before she wasn't, lay tipped over on the floor, on its side.

All that mattered was getting Caitlyn down before she succeeded in killing herself. The four of them rushed to her. Lauren pushed up against the soles of her bare feet, to take the strain of the rope off her neck. When the tension had been loosened, Tom and the other two officers worked to remove her head from the noose.

When she had been freed, they lowered her gently to the floor. A vicious red welt crisscrossed her throat, impressions of the rope branded on her skin. A horrible rasping noise was escaping from her open mouth. She'd wet herself and her bowels had loosened, presumably as the rope tightened around her neck. Her trousers were filthy, as was the floor around her. She was unconscious, her eyelids fluttering, and Tom and the others moved back, creating space for one of the officers to administer first aid. While he battled with the forces of death, Tom phoned for an ambulance. Assured that medical aid was only minutes away, Tom left the first responder to it and took the chance to explore the flat.

The hallway, now lit by the same type of cheap-looking chandelier as in Linda's house, was narrow and oppressive. Framed prints of dark figures cowering in the cavernous tunnels of the

London Underground filled the walls. Tom recognised them as Henry Moore's work – he had learned about him in primary school and had been mesmerised by the mix of human fragility and hope.

The kitchen at the end of the hallway was nondescript. It looked like it could've been taken straight from an IKEA catalogue. A small, circular glass table stood in the corner, with only one wooden chair tucked underneath. Its missing partner was currently an active part of the crime scene in the corridor. A small fridge hummed tunelessly against one wall. The worktops were clear, aside from a wine glass by the sink, the rim stained pink by a particularly vibrant lipstick. The smell of last night's microwaved dinner lingered slightly, though not powerfully enough to allow Tom to know what it had been.

Now, two paramedics made their way down the hallway, bringing with them a host of equipment. Tom hoped it would be enough to save Caitlyn's life. Though he had never yet been involved in one, he hated hearing about cases where the perpetrators evaded justice by taking their own lives. It was a selfish act, destroying any chance of closure for the victims' families that an arrest and trial may have brought.

As they barrelled through the door, Lauren began filling them in on the situation. The officer who had been administering first aid quickly stepped back; relief obvious on his face that he could now give up the role.

Tom let himself into the remaining room. In any other flat, the room would've been filled with a sofa, television and the other fittings of a sitting room. Here, in Caitlyn's, the room was like something from the mind of Pablo Picasso.

King-size bed sheets were gaffer-taped to the floor. A mannequin with a David Bowie lightning bolt painted down its torso was lying on top of the sheets, its top and bottom halves separated and placed side by side. It was impossible to know whether this was an art installation, a work in progress or part of a scrap pile. A variety of different-sized easels were folded against one wall, and dozens of canvases littered the floor. Some looked like they had been left to dry; others were definitely discarded. These had either been stamped on, set on fire, or torn to shreds with a very sharp blade.

The thing that stopped Tom in his tracks was what was set up in the centre of the room. A canvas sat on an easel, illuminated by a floor lamp. The lamp was classy. The tripod looked like it had been made from salvaged wood, and the bulb atop it was encased in a brass cylinder. The painting was a landscape scene of the Angel of the North site. The monument loomed large, as if the painting had been done from the perspective of someone hovering just behind its left wing. Snow had fallen and covered the ground, but in the foreground there was a small smudge.

Tom got closer, making sure not to touch anything. In roughly the same area as Richard's body had been buried, there was a small cross, like a makeshift gravestone. It was painted in a deep crimson colour, and at once Tom was sure it had been daubed in blood.

It was only then that he noticed the little trestle table behind the easel. It was made from cheap wood and had wobbly metal legs, like one of those tables that was pulled out of storage in an emergency at a village fete. It was splatted in paint, and on it sat a wooden box.

The box was made from cheap pine. It had a gold clasp and looked like it had been bought recently. It certainly showed no sign that it had been distressed like every other piece of furniture in the room. In fact, it was unremarkable, aside from one thing. On the top of the box, Caitlyn had gouged a picture into the wood.

It was the unmistakeable outline of a magic wand.

43

'LAUREN,' TOM SHOUTED, LOUDER than he meant to. His partner appeared in the doorway. She walked across to where he was standing, and Tom saw her eyes widen when she saw what he was looking at.

'A box of magic tricks,' she whispered. 'The fourth item on the Christmas list.'

'Can you call down to Mike and tell him there's a suspected bomb?'

'Will do,' she said.

Tom was glad they'd floated the theory of a bomb during previous briefings. It meant they had come prepared, and didn't have to wait half a day to get the bomb squad here. He would owe Mike a decent bottle of Scotch for dragging him here on Christmas Day.

A couple of minutes later, Mike appeared. He waited until the paramedics could manoeuvre Caitlyn – who was now breathing more easily – onto a stretcher, then made everyone leave the flat and had a look at the box. Protocol would usually suggest that the building be evacuated, but Mike was reasonably sure, after some careful inspection, there was no bomb inside the box of magic tricks. Tom and Lauren loitered in the car park for a few minutes, trying to ward off the cold, waiting for Mike to make his call. Eventually, Tom's radio came to life in a burst of static, and they were allowed back in. The box was safe.

As they passed Mike in the hallway, he said, 'Since it was a quick job, a bottle of Bushmills will suffice.'

Tom thanked him and told him the whiskey would be on his desk as soon as Mike returned from his leave.

Back in the room, faced with the box, Tom said: 'Henry will kill me if I open it before him. But I need to see what's in there. Will you film me while I open it, so that we can show him we didn't tamper with anything?'

Lauren pulled her phone from her pocket and pointed the camera in his direction. The torch lit up as she pressed record, and Tom found that, as he reached towards the box, his hands were shaking and his mouth was dry.

This was make or break. He swallowed, trying to encourage some saliva into his mouth. For the sake of the video, he said the time, date and their location aloud, and gave a brief description of what he was about to do. He opened the clasp carefully, and then lifted the box's lid.

Inside was a treasure trove of death. A knife took up most of the length of the box, its black plastic handle melding with the jagged length of metal. The blade was coated in dried blood, and Tom wondered if the same knife had been used on Richard, Millie and Zach. Nestled beside the knife, inside a length of plastic packaging, were approximately fifty cable ties. Beside them was a crumpled box of tablets, bearing the name flunitrazepam.

'Rohypnol,' Tom said. He opened the flap of the tablet box and saw there was only one sheet of tablets inside. There were six blisters, and four had been used. Was there a victim out there who had been drugged by Caitlyn and had managed to escape? Or, had she taken one herself before slipping the noose around her neck?

He set the tablet box back into the bigger box and closed the lid, keen to preserve as much of the evidence as possible. He'd seen what he needed to see.

'Tom, look,' Lauren said, and stooped down. Trapped under one of the legs of the easel was a piece of paper. Gently, she tugged it free and turned it over.

It was another copy of the Christmas list. The childish scrawl of the letters still got to Tom every time he saw it: even more so now that he had a theory.

He reckoned the list belonged to Caitlyn's daughter; the one she had to give up for adoption. Maybe Caitlyn was mad at the world for forcing her to part with her baby, and this Christmas list was all that remained of their time together. Of course, the baby would have been just that, a baby, and therefore unable to write the list. But perhaps they still had some contact, and this had been sent via the adoptive parent to show Caitlyn what her little girl had asked for. Maybe that was the driving force behind her killing spree. Or perhaps Caitlyn – in a regressive state – had written the list herself. Either for her younger self, or for the daughter she had never really known.

Looking at it more closely, Tom saw that, on this copy of the list, the first four items had been crossed off. *No Angel*. The red party dress. The alien egg toy. And now the box of magic tricks.

Beside the final item – surprise – was a little smiley face and a one-word promise: soon.

Maybe her attempted suicide had been the surprise, and the police had ruined it. Maybe the list would not be completed after all.

'Let's get out of here,' Tom said. 'Forensics will have a field day, but I think we've got what we need.'

Lauren followed him out of the flat and down the stairs. The ambulance was waiting in the car park, by the door. When Tom walked past the open back doors, he saw that Caitlyn was still on the stretcher, though she was sitting up. Perhaps it was the fact she hadn't achieved what she had set out to, or maybe it was because she knew she had been caught red-handed. Whatever it was, mania burned in her eyes. When she saw Tom, she bucked her hips and strained with every sinew in her body to get free from her captors. The paramedics, alongside the two uniformed officers, were doing all they could to subdue her.

One of the medics stroked her hair gently and whispered in her ear. It was like watching a mother try to console an upset child, and for a moment, Tom found the scene very moving. Caitlyn was obviously unwell, and seeing her in this state was tough.

She let out a frustrated roar, and then threw herself backwards, smashing her head onto the stretcher. Quickly, the other medic positioned her fleece jacket under her head, providing a soft landing pad. When Caitlyn realised she had been thwarted in her plan to bash her head in, she stopped.

When she noticed Tom still peering into the ambulance from outside, instead of trying to injure herself further, she smiled. Her gums had receded, clear evidence of drug use, and her teeth looked like oversized gravestones crammed into a small plot of land. She ran her tongue over her cracked lips and cleared her throat. She pushed herself up, so that she was resting on her elbows.

'Stonem,' she said, in a splintered voice. Tom nodded, and she broke into hysterical laughter. Tom looked to Lauren, who shrugged.

'How do you know who I am?' Tom asked, which only made her laugh more.

'Your... brother,' she said, between each roar. 'He's... he's in danger. Surprise!'

With her message delivered, she collapsed backwards onto the stretcher and laughed until she vomited over herself. Tom was already sprinting across the carpark, barking down the phone. He demanded that any available officers get to his house and make sure his brother was all right. When he had been reassured that two officers were on the way, he hung up and dialled Seth's number.

It went straight to answerphone. Tom hung up.

'Fuck!' he screamed. Seth might be lying dead on the kitchen floor, killed by whatever surprise Caitlyn had planted. It was all too much to take in.

The car park was busier than when he had arrived. A family, arms laden with wrapped gifts, were getting out of their Volvo estate. They greeted him with a 'Merry Christmas', but it barely registered. They walked away towards the tower block, muttering about the lack of cheer in their police officers.

Tom could only think about getting home before something bad happened to Seth.

Surprise.

That was the remaining item on the list. He couldn't make sense of it. How could Caitlyn have got to Seth? What had she planned for him? None of the pieces fitted together, but all Tom knew was he needed to get home.

When he got to the squad car currently occupied by Phil, he slipped into the passenger side.

'Take me home,' he said.

'Part-timer.' Phil smiled. 'Has the boss said you can knock off early?'

'That bitch,' Tom said, pointing at the ambulance, 'has just issued a threat against my brother. I need to get home to make sure she hasn't fucking killed him already, so fucking drive!'

Phil did as instructed. With shaking hands, Tom keyed in his details into the sat nav, and let the computerised voice lead them home. He took his phone out and tried Seth over and over again, but it only went to his answerphone message.

'Seth, bloody phone me back when you get this. I need to know you're all right. I love you.'

He felt sick. After their talk this morning, he'd let Seth down by running off after a killer. He could've let his team handle it. He could've passed the information on and requested that he spend time with his brother. But, no. Tom had felt the need to be the hero.

He took some calming breaths, knowing he needed to keep a clear head. He could punish himself later if anything happened to Seth. He checked his phone was not on silent, before placing it between his legs. Phil wisely chose not to make conversation, instead focussing all his concentration on what was happening on the other side of the windscreen. Tom silently cursed every single car and tumbling fleck of snow that were slowing them.

He checked the time on the dashboard clock. It had been seven minutes since he'd phoned for back-up. Surely the officers, who'd claimed they were close by, would have reached his home by now. Why hadn't they phoned him? Were they administering vital first aid in an attempt to save Seth's life? Had his life already been ended, and instead of phoning Tom they were securing the scene of a murder?

'Can't you go any faster?' Tom spat at Phil. Despite the ice on the road and the poor visibility, Phil increased his speed, keen to please his DI. But, as they came to a junction and he tried to brake, the car began to fishtail across the road. The tyres churned but couldn't find any friction. Instead of stopping, they drifted helplessly towards the main road, and spun sideways onto it. Tom grabbed the handle above the door and braced for impact.

Luckily, the A road *had* been gritted, and the vehicles already on it were able to come to a stop to avoid a collision with the police car.

Phil took several deep breaths and gave a thankful wave to the stopped cars. Hands shaking, he steered into the right lane, and took off again. Slower this time. Tom's breathing had increased in speed, too, though he passed no further comment.

Instead, he grabbed his phone to try Seth again. Before he could dial, the screen flashed into life with a number he didn't know.

'Stonem,' he answered.

'Hi, mate. Just letting you know that your brother is alive and well.'

'He's okay?' Tom said.

'He's absolutely fine. Aside from being deeply confused as to why two police officers were hammering on the door. He's in the middle of making your dinner, and he seems to be doing a bloody good job of it, judging by the smell. I've just asked him for whatever recipe he's using so I can pass it on to the wife.'

'Will you stay with him until I get there?'

'Absolutely, especially if there's the chance of a bit of turkey.'

Tom thanked him and hung up. He shoved his phone into his pocket and started to cry tears of utter relief. He couldn't imagine losing another sibling, especially on Christmas Day of all days. He thought of Rachel, and the feeling of guilt almost ripped his heart in two.

He was going to make sure Seth knew he was loved.

'Sorry for the way I spoke to you,' he said to Phil, when he'd managed to get his emotions under control.

'No bother, boss,' Phil replied, chirpy as ever. 'Let's just make sure my part in the heroic rescue of your brother is properly documented when this is sold to television.'

'I'll make sure you're in charge of casting, to sweeten the deal. Who's playing us?'

'Reece Shearsmith from *Inside No. 9* would be perfect for you. I always thought I had a touch of the Richard Madden about me.'

'You fucking wish!' said Tom, and a bark of laughter escaped his lips. The release of tension was joyous. Phil joined in and, for the first time that day, hell, that week, Tom felt like the weight of the world had been lifted from his shoulders. For the first time in what felt like an age, Tom didn't have to think about death.

They'd found their killer.

They'd won.

44

One of the two officers who had responded to his call for back-up was standing by the gate, acting as a sentry should anyone of criminal persuasion decide to make an appearance.

Tom thanked Phil as he pulled into the side of the road, and then got out. He pulled his ID from his pocket and showed it to the officer, who stood to the side with a smile and permitted Tom access to his own house. He jogged up the path and practically vaulted the three steps to the front door.

The first thing to hit Tom was the smell. Home-cooked meals were a rare luxury for him. The life of a cop consisted of grabbing whatever you could, whenever you could, and often comprised of repetitive meal deals or greasy fast food. The mix of aromas that swirled through his house was already setting his saliva glands to overdrive, and he had to swallow back a mouthful of drool when the officer he had spoken to on the phone appeared around the living room door.

Tom introduced himself, and the officer did too. His name was Jamie, and he looked like a fairly new recruit. His hair was cut short, and his muscular body suggested he spent plenty of hours in the gym.

'Thanks for getting here so quickly,' Tom said.

'It's no bother, Tom,' Jamie replied, in a thick Scottish accent.

'Is he all right?' Tom said, nodding towards the kitchen.

'Aye, grand. Cooking up a storm. I stayed with him while poor old Elliot outside did a sweep of the garden and the street. As far as we can see, there's nothing doing.'

'I appreciate it.' They walked towards the front door, where they parted ways with a hearty handshake. Elliot waved goodbye as Tom shut the door.

In the kitchen, Tom was greeted by a whirlwind. Every available inch of kitchen worktop was taken up by pots, pans and ceramic dishes Tom didn't know he owned. From Alexa, Coldplay were singing about Christmas lights, and Seth was in the middle of it all, a whirling dervish, appearing to possess more limbs than he actually had.

'Did you get her?' he shouted over Chris Martin's warbling, as he transferred a dish of stuffing from the kitchen island into the glowing oven.

'We got her,' Tom said. 'I'm all yours...'

'Great to hear.'

'... As soon as I've done a debrief with my boss and had a shower.'

'You just want to get out of plating up, don't you?' Seth laughed. 'Well, you best go and ring her now. The food will be on the table in about forty minutes.'

'Thanks, mate,' Tom called, as he hotfooted it upstairs. He went into his bedroom and sat on the edge of his unmade bed, pulling his phone from his pocket as he did so. He dialled Natalie's number and was unsurprised when she picked up after a solitary ring.

'Congratulations, Detective Inspector Stonem. We have our killer in custody.'

'Team effort, boss. I'm just pleased it's all over.'

'Everything went to plan. Once you left and the paramedics were happy there was no longer any risk to life, the rest of the team moved in. Lauren made the arrest. Caitlyn didn't put up too much more of a fight. I think she could see that the writing was very much on the wall.'

'Are you interviewing today?'

'That's the plan. She's saying she doesn't want a lawyer, but we're going to call her mother to make sure. The evidence recovered from the art studio is conclusive. I'm 100 per cent convinced that knife is the weapon used in the murders of Richard Handsworth, Millie Whitlock, and Zach Willis, and that the other bits and pieces in the box played their part. Obviously, we'll need a bit of time for forensics to match the blood and what have you. I've been talking to Lauren, and we might have a pre-interview chat with Caitlyn, to let her know how much shit she's in and advise her that having a lawyer might be the best course of action.'

'Good idea.'

'I wanted to say well done for sticking to your guns with the Christmas list. We believe it may have belonged to someone close to her back in the day. Maybe her kid, but the items are a bit too old for that. Could be her own from when she was young. Again, it's something we'll have to check with her.'

'Did Lauren explain how we found her?' Tom asked.

'Hanging by the neck,' Natalie confirmed. 'The working theory is that she knew we were coming and she wanted to escape justice by killing herself before we could arrest her.'

Tom reckoned that was probably pretty close to the truth. That, or, as a killer with a touch of the theatrics about her, she wanted to put on a show just as the police entered her flat.

'Do you need me back in the station today?' Tom asked, hoping against hope that the answer would be a resounding...

'No,' Natalie said. 'Lauren explained about your prodigal brother cooking for you, so you enjoy your day with your family, and we'll see you tomorrow. As soon as we've interviewed Caitlyn, we'll let you know the bullet points. Once it's all wrapped up, we will have to seriously discuss the measures you took in the past few days and decide on the best course of action to take.'

'Yes, Ma'am. Make sure Lauren gets away as soon as possible, too,' Tom said. 'She needs to see her daughter.'

'Of course.'

With that, she hung up. Tom threw his phone onto the bed, took his clothes off and got in the shower, where he let the water wash away the frustrations of the past month. Afterwards, he quickly got dried, gelled his hair and pulled on an ancient Christmas jumper he'd found in a black bin bag before moving. He looked at himself in the mirror, decided he was suitably festive, and made his way downstairs. Waiting for him was a cold tin of beer and the promise that dinner was almost ready. Tom felt a smile creep onto his face.

45

PLATTERS OF FOOD COVERED the table, save for the spaces left for Tom and Seth to sit. Chunks of succulent white turkey meat lay on one plate, surrounded by fatty roast potatoes, aromatic carrots and parsnips, and a whole array of other deliciousness.

'Cheers for this,' Tom said as he pulled out a chair and sat down facing his brother.

'No worries at all,' Seth replied. 'I always thought cooking was boring, but I actually took a load of classes on my travels. In Mexico, I learned how to make this blue corn quesadilla from scratch and, honestly, I fell in love with it. The chef there also taught me the recipe for the glaze on the turkey. What do you think?'

Tom ate a mouthful, the flavours exploding on his tongue. He nodded appreciatively as he shoved another chunk of meat into his gob.

'Tell me about the places you went,' he said.

For a while, Seth told him all about his travels across the planet. Scuba diving in the Great Blue Hole in Belize, trekking up Machu Picchu with a girl he temporarily fell in love with, trying to get over the inevitable heartbreak by gambling in Las Vegas, and everything in between. Eventually, he had made it to Asia and found Buddhism.

They ate in companionable silence for a while. Once or twice, Seth got up to grab another beer. The food was delicious, cooked to absolute perfection. Tom ate more than he knew he should and decided the ensuing stomach ache would be worth it. Seth seemed pleased Tom was enjoying the feast he'd laboured over. Finally, with bulging bellies, they set their cutlery onto their plates and leaned back, mirroring one another, before letting out a laugh.

'We're more alike than we thought.' Seth smiled.

Tom smiled back. 'Look, mate,' he said, 'what you have done today is above and beyond. I've been a shit big brother. I'm sorry it's taken me so long to arrive at that realisation, and I'm sorry for all the pain I've caused you. It's not been on purpose, but I recognise now that I have not been the role model for you that I should have been, particularly with the parents we were lumbered with.'

Seth started to say something, but Tom held his hand up.

'I just want to say I'm unbelievably humbled that you decided to come up to Newcastle and give me a second chance. It's been belting hanging out again, and I really hope you can accept my apology and we can be... friends.'

'We can be more than that, you big softie,' Seth said, before becoming more serious. 'I appreciate your kind words. Karma is very important to my religion. Are you familiar with the concept?'

Tom nodded.

'Good. I'm so pleased you opened your home to me, because it's enabled us to get back on track as family. Even if you did batter me before inviting me in.' He laughed, before jumping up and going to the living room. He returned a minute later, carrying a Christmas stocking with Tom's name sewn onto the fluffy white top part.

Guilt pooled in Tom's stomach, as he thought back to his unsuccessful (and unenthusiastic) shopping trip to the Metrocentre. Part of him wished he had simply plumped for the boring black socks in Next. At least he would have had *something* to give.

'Ah, Seth, you didn't have to. I'm just waiting for yours to be delivered...'

'And I'll look forward to it arriving,' Seth said, sitting down at the table again. 'But, until then, you can open yours. We should not give simply to receive.'

He handed the laden stocking across the table, careful not to let it touch any of the leftover food. Tom took it and felt the contents before dipping his hand inside and swishing them around, like he was about to start an FA Cup draw.

'Should I open them in any particular order?' he asked.

'Any order is fine,' Seth replied.

Tom pulled out the top present. It was curved, wrapped in paper covered in a repeated pattern of Santa's face, sunburnt and wearing sunglasses. He weighed the small rugby-ball shaped item in his hand, before finding the sellotaped edge and pulling the paper off carefully.

Tom's jaw dropped, and he looked at Seth, who was smiling at him.

In Tom's hand was a transparent egg. Inside, a vibrant blue goo filled most of the container, and resting inside the sticky gunk was a little grey figure with a thin body, long legs and an oversized head. Two almond-shaped eyes looked out at the world from the transparent prison, as Tom gasped in horror.

'Do you remember these things?' Seth asked. 'Everyone had them at school. Well, everyone except for us. I remember my friend letting me stick my fingers in the goo and feeling repulsed. Rachel was desperate for one. Do you remember? She kept going on to Dad, anytime we went to the corner shop, that was one of the things she really wanted for Christmas. I don't think she would have been happy with a blue one, mind, but that was all the website had.'

He motioned to the stocking. 'There are more in there.'

'Seth…' Tom started.

'Don't be ungrateful.' Seth smiled. 'Open the rest of your gifts.'

Tom didn't know what to think. The alien egg could be coincidence. But he knew deep down that wasn't true. The look in Seth's eyes contradicted the playfulness of his voice. And he'd mentioned Rachel. Tom knew exactly what was going to come out of the stocking next and could think of no way to stop what was about to happen.

Reluctantly, he plunged a hand into the sack and withdrew the next present. It was soft and squashy, and Tom thought he knew what was inside. With shaking fingers, he undid the Sellotape and let the square of material fall onto the table. He lifted it between his thumbs and forefingers, and let the fabric fall into shape.

It was a little girl's dress made from a chintzy red fabric, with a fancy collar and circular gems sewn into the bodice. Tom could see from the label that it was designed for a girl aged eight.

'Pretty, isn't it?' Seth asked, sounding genuinely excited. 'The woman beside me in the shop told me my little girl was going to be very happy on Christmas morning when she unwrapped the dress. I explained it was actually for my sister who would be eight forever more. Don't you think she would have looked beautiful in this? She would have absolutely loved it. Anyway, what's next?'

Tom had no idea the list he'd been carrying around with him the past week was his own sister's. When they were young, he'd never bothered looking at Seth's or Rachel's Christmas lists. There was no point – he knew there was no way they'd get even one gift off their lists, never mind all of them.

'Tom! You're staring into space,' Seth shouted, banging on the table. 'Hurry up and open something else.'

Next was a Dido CD.

'I thought we could put that on later,' Seth said. 'I only ever knew the singles that Rachel played, and that song she did with the rapper. She's quite mournful, isn't she? I imagine her music will be a fitting soundtrack for what's about to happen.'

After that, at Seth's encouragement, Tom opened the final present from the stocking. It was the largest and the heaviest and, when Tom pulled the wrapping paper from it, a box of magic tricks was unveiled.

Merlin's Box of Magic boasted over two hundred parts. On the lid of the brightly decorated box, there were white rabbits appearing from bowler hats; red and yellow cups with the promise of concealed balls within them; playing cards cascading like they used to at the end of a winning game of solitaire.

'She used to love Paul Daniels. Do you remember how she would sit transfixed in front of the telly when he was on? Or when she came back from one of her friend's birthday parties, and there'd been a magician? She couldn't wait to get this. It was going to be her main present. She thought she could use it to get out of the shit life we had. To get on telly like Paul.'

'Look, Seth, I know—'

Seth zipped an imaginary line across his own mouth. 'Rachel didn't ever get to receive the gifts from her Christmas list because someone did not keep her safe. It seems only fair you should have them, being her big brother and all, but it feels like you aren't totally pleased with what I've got you. Well, you *will* be pleased to know that we're not done – there's one more gift for you.'

He pulled an envelope from the front pocket of his hoodie. It was red, the type of red you associate with happy, festive times. Tom knew that, if he survived the day, he'd never look the same way at a simple Christmas card again. They would be forever tainted by the sheer lunacy of whatever was happening right now.

Seth handed the card across the table and, for a moment, Tom hesitated. What would happen if he refused to take it? Would Seth accept his refusal? Would it put a stop to his plan, or would it simply escalate whatever he had in mind? Was it better to keep his brother sweet; to go along with the fantasy that was being broadcast inside his head?

Tom's eyes scanned the room, taking in a million details. He could use something from the cluttered table (a ceramic dish, a serving spoon, cutlery) to take his brother down. He could make a break for the door and hope that Seth's Buddhist beliefs would prevent him from throwing a knife or something else sharp and deadly in his direction.

'Tom, there's no point in trying to escape. You won't be able to, and you'll come across as even more thankless than you already are. Now, take the fucking card and open it. That's all I ask. There's a surprise in there.'

Despite the frenzy in his eyes, Seth's voice was flat and monotonous. His hand never wavered, and eventually Tom reached across and took the envelope from him. His name had been scrawled on the front of it with a blue biro. He tore the triangular flap at the back and slid the card out. On the front was a traditional scene: three wise men adorned with crowns and jewels, dressed in robes of primary colours, trekking across a golden desert at night. In the distance, a hut was visible, with two silhouetted figures hunched over a manger. Above it, in the midnight blue sky, floated an eight-pointed star from which light fell in a column towards the shelter's roof.

Despite the danger he was in, or maybe because of it, Tom's thoughts drifted to the similar beam of light on the film poster for *Independence Day*. With further encouragement from Seth, he opened the card and read the surprise message inside.

For my final trick, you will decide.
This Christmas Day, will you or I survive?

46

'You see,' Seth said, 'I've been doing a lot of work on myself recently. I wasn't lying when I said I'd discovered Buddhism. It helped me see I had been carrying around all this extra weight, that should never have been mine to carry in the first place.'

'Seth—'

'I hated myself for what I'd done. I was the one who turned the oven on. I was the one who left it on. I forgot about it and, in the end, that's what killed her. I spent my formative years unable to let myself enjoy life, because all I could think about was that Rachel wasn't there to enjoy it with me. Did you know that, even at eight years old, we had made plans? We were going to travel the world together. She was going to move to a city and become a wedding planner because she wanted to make people happy. She never got to do any of the stuff she planned to, and do you know why?'

Tom started to answer, but his mouth did not want to play ball. There was a slight tingling on his tongue – he'd never felt anything like it before. Was it nerves? Or was it a subliminal message from his brain to hold back? Seth obviously had a spiel he needed to get out. Maybe interrupting him would make things worse. Tom waited.

'Because of you,' Seth said, finally. 'You said it yourself this morning. And because of you, I never got to do what I wanted to do either. The guilt ate me up. Any time I made headway with a girl, or got offered a promotion at whatever dead-end job

I was working at the time, no part of me could enjoy it. I felt bad for still being on this earth. Can you imagine how that feels?'

Again, Tom waited. He didn't want to stoke Seth's ire further. And, anyway, he didn't know what to say. The news that his twin siblings had made plans for when they were older was heart-breaking. Big plans, too. Travelling the world and getting well-paid jobs. All Seth and Rachel had wanted to do was escape the life they'd been born into. Anything Tom might say now was pointless. He deserved Seth's anger. In a way, he welcomed it.

'Of course you can't,' Seth continued. 'While the black dog wandered through my head, you were out there saving everyone else. You cared more about other families than your own. Angela and Nigel were so fucking proud. They kept every newspaper clipping and recorded the news any time you got a mention. It made me feel sick, and that's why I needed to get away. I booked a one-way plane ticket to Venezuela and went with no plan at all. Part of me thought about simply wandering into the sea and leaving everything behind, but the image of you collecting another commendation saved me. Because I wanted you to fucking pay for what you'd done.'

Seth stood up and began to pace. His hair had come loose from the bun he had tied it in. Tom instinctively knew he was going to raise the stakes, and cursed himself for leaving his phone upstairs on the bed. He was considering escaping again, when Seth stopping striding up and down the room and fixed his manic eyes on Tom once more.

'You left a pair of already abandoned, hungry children alone. On Christmas Day, you fucking scumbag. What the fuck did you expect us to do? You were supposed to look after us, man, and instead you went off galivanting with your mates.'

'I wasn't galivanting.' Tom put air quotes around the word. 'You're making it sound like Mum and Dad leaving and putting me in charge was a piece of cake for me. I was ten years old. What the hell did I know about looking after a couple of kids?'

'We weren't just a couple of kids. We were your family. You should have put us first.'

'And I tried. I did. We were alone for days. I just needed space.'

'Oh, and you bloody well got it, didn't you. The big house in Manchester with the huge garden and the football nets. Nice new foster parents fawning over you.'

'You got that, too!' Tom shouted. 'You got the exact same treatment as me.'

'Did I fuck. They loved you. They tolerated me. Damaged goods. But that doesn't matter. It was Rachel who deserved the loving home and the doting parents. She was the one who didn't get it...' Seth broke off, his voice strained. 'And that's why we're here.'

Silence fell between them like a physical thing. The tingling in Tom's mouth was intensifying. Seth stood, bent over slightly, with his two palms resting on the table.

'Do you know why I came back?' Seth asked. Tom shrugged, and let his brother continue. 'Because I wanted to show everyone that you weren't who you said you were. You were in the press as this hero cop, and I wanted everyone to see you for what you really are. A big fat phoney. So, I left my travels earlier than I'd intended to, and came here. I picked someone who I thought would make front-page headlines. Richard Handsworth was a dickhead who said lots of stupid shit that made a lot of people angry, so he seemed like the perfect victim. There was no doubt in my mind he would make front-page news and you would be assigned to the case.'

He barked a wild laugh, causing long strands of hair to fall onto his face. He swept them away with a frantic hand and continued.

'I kept the social media posts going. I scheduled photos of those bright and sunny skies of Ho Chi Minh and Da Nang.

They were my cover story. Of course, I never thought you'd suspect me. Why would I be killing people in the North East of England? But I covered all my bases, just in case.'

'And you did all this to teach me a lesson?' Tom asked.

'Exactly,' Seth replied, pointing at him. 'You finally get it. I talked about karma earlier, and I meant it. Actions have consequences. I wanted to show the world that you are not who you say you are. You aren't some hero cop who can solve every crime served up to him. No, you're a regular guy who killed his family. So, I led you on a wild goose chase. I loved when you accused the poor widow and dragged her over the coals. The come-back from that was wonderful to watch.'

'The Christmas card fiasco was a nice touch,' Tom said. He thought, maybe, if he kept Seth chatting, Caitlyn might start talking, too. He assumed she had been another part of Seth's collateral damage. If he was right, maybe her testimony would clear her, and his team would get here once they knew the truth.

'Yes, I liked that, too. That one took a bit of preparation, but I had time on my hands. What I didn't like was you forcing me into this.'

'Into what?'

'Today,' he said, gesturing around him at the table and the decorations. 'After our little chat this morning when you finally seemed to get it, I thought none of this was going to have to happen. If you hadn't run off, your police mates would have found Caitlyn in a compromising position with all the evidence they needed nicely packaged up for them, and you and I would have spent a lovely Christmas morning together, where I would have given you the other stocking, filled with stuff I thought you'd actually like.'

Seth pushed himself upright again. His blonde hair spilled onto his shoulders, and he reached for the knife he'd used to carve the turkey. He ran a careful finger along the plastic handle, before picking it up and turning it in his hands. It was theatrical, designed to stretch the moment and test Tom.

'I didn't even bother wrapping that shit, though, because I knew exactly what you would do. At the first chance of being the leading man, you'd fuck your little brother off once more and go running. And I was right. I pleaded with you to stay, and you told me I was a big boy now, you patronising prick. If you'd just stayed here, you and me would be on a different page now, a new leaf. Because of your actions, I need to give you the surprise. And here it is...'

Slowly, Seth raised his hand so that the tip of the knife came to rest against the soft flesh of his own throat. Tom could see the little indent in the skin that proved what Seth was doing was real.

'It's your choice now,' Seth said. 'Who dies: you or me?'

47

THE MOOD IN THE station was buoyant. The killer who had darkened the North East's door had been brought to justice, and not a moment too soon: it meant most of the officers who had shown up today could probably get off home in time for a sit-down with the family.

This, of course, appealed to some and horrified others. The thought of having to return home to a house full of in-laws was awful to some, and a surprising number of officers suddenly seemed to discover the joys that paperwork could bring.

Lauren was not one of them. She had been eager to get home, to see Sophie, but now she had an opportunity to get some answers. Natalie had asked her if she would sit in the interview with Caitlyn, but promised she could get off as soon as they were done. Lauren felt pleased to be picked; pleased that she got to be there as the final nail in the coffin of this case was hammered in.

She had just finished wolfing down a Mars bar when the DCI appeared.

'Ready?' she asked.

'As I'll ever be.' Lauren nodded, and got to her feet. They walked down to the interview suite and entered the room.

Caitlyn was sitting behind the desk, her head resting on her hands on the table. She had tied her hair back, exposing the marks on her neck where the rope had recently bitten into it. When she heard the door opening, she looked up. Gone was the crazy giggling maniac they'd encountered at the flat. In her place was a scared girl; one who knew she was probably going to spend a large portion of the rest of her life behind bars.

'Caitlyn,' said Natalie, as she slid into a seat opposite her. Lauren followed suit. 'I know you've made it very clear you don't want a lawyer, but I'm here to urge you to reconsider. You are going to be questioned in relation to serious offences, and it might do you good to seek legal representation.'

'I don't want any,' Caitlyn said, quiet as a mouse.

'Are you sure?'

This time, she didn't answer.

'In that case,' Natalie said, 'I am going to request that a doctor examine your injuries, and a psychiatrist will do an evaluation before questioning to make sure you are of sound mind before we begin. We'll be back soon.'

Natalie began to get up, but before she could rise fully, Caitlyn spoke: 'I can tell you exactly what happened now.'

'I don't think that's—'

'I promise I'm all right. I'll take the test from the doctor when I'm done, but I think you might need to hear what I have to say.'

Quickly, Natalie started the recording. 'Beginning interview with Caitlyn Hamilton. It's twenty-fifth of December, 4:47 p.m. Present are DCI Natalie Freeman and DS Lauren Rae. Caitlyn has refused legal representation.' When she was done, she asked Caitlyn to tell her what she could. She was expecting a confession. They could record this now, then check the psych evaluation, and re-interview once they were sure she had been cleared as fit.

'I didn't do any of the killings,' she said.

'But there was a box in your art room with a knife in it. The knife was covered in blood. The knife is with forensics now, and I can all but guarantee that we will find the blood of the three victims on it. You have to admit, that looks pretty bad.'

'I'm being framed,' Caitlyn said. She spoke calmly, and Lauren was already certain the validity of the interview was gone. 'Seth and me met at a bar earlier this month, and we went home together. He's been staying at my place and not letting me leave. He took my phone off me, and my keys, and he's been giving me tablets that make me feel all woozy.'

'Seth?' Lauren said. She thought of Tom's brother's recent and unexpected appearance in the North East. 'Seth who?'

'Stonem.'

Icicles formed in Lauren's stomach. 'Did he make you do things you didn't want to do?'

'No. He went out a lot, but never told me where he'd been. He came back covered in blood a couple of times. I told him he should go to hospital if he was hurt, but he told me to shut up. He told me if I tried to escape, or mentioned his name to anyone, he would kill me slowly and then do the same to my mam.'

At the mention of her mother, Caitlyn burst into tears. They gave her a few moments to recover.

'Caitlyn, this is awful,' Lauren said, placatingly. 'But I need you to focus on Seth. This morning, you tried to hang yourself and, when you saw DI Stonem, you giggled and told him Seth was in danger.'

'Seth knew they were going to find me. He left me in that position a lot over the last few days, standing on a chair, neck in a noose. When the police didn't come he would come back at night and allow me to get down. He showed me photos of Tom and said he was going to Tom's house, to make pretend friends. He told me, if the police ever showed up, I was to act crazy and tell them Tom's brother was in danger. He knew I wouldn't actually die. That the police would rescue me in time. He told me he had rigged up cameras in my flat and he would know if I hadn't played my part. I had to act crazy to sell it that I was the killer.'

'Is Tom in trouble now?' Lauren said, her breath ragged and uneven.

'Seth said he had a score to settle with his brother,' Caitlyn said, nodding. 'He was really pissed off with him. Tom might be dead already.'

Lauren pushed herself out of her seat and was gone.

48

Tom glanced at the clock on the kitchen wall. It was just after half past five. He silently urged time to slow to allow his team's rescue mission longer to get here.

He looked across the table at Seth. This man was not his brother. This man with the manic eyes and the knife to his own throat was surely no blood relative of the trustworthy police detective.

But Tom thought back to the times when *he* had been the one with the metaphorical knife to his throat: threatening the reporter a few days ago; punching a different reporter in Manchester just over a year ago; shoving a particularly rowdy and violent drunk through the front window of a bar in the Northern Quarter; and, of course, walking to Holly's that day with malevolence running through his bloodstream.

He could try and convince himself that he and Seth were different, but maybe they were more alike than Tom cared to admit.

No.

Tom was not a murderer. Tom hadn't killed three people for the hell of it; to prove a point. Tom had worked his arse off for over a decade to prevent that kind of thing happening; it was the reason they were in this predicament now.

'Seth, you need help,' Tom said.

'No, Tom, I *needed* help. Years ago. You ran out. You killed your sister. My twin. And now the choice is simple. Who dies today?'

Tom raised his hands to show he was not a threat. Gently, he pushed his chair back, the legs scraping on the parquet flooring. The sudden squeal made Seth flinch, and he pointed the knife at Tom, spittle flying from his mouth as he shouted.

'Fucking move again, and I'll slit my throat, right here, right now.'

'All right, all right,' Tom placated. The words felt funny in his mouth, like they were oddly shaped and foreign. Like his tongue was not his own. He pushed himself up a few inches, partly to alleviate the stress on his knees and partly to test Seth.

In a controlled sweep, Seth brought the knife to his throat again and pushed the tip in. Blood immediately dribbled from the cut, which was not deep enough to do real damage, but it did serve as a warning.

Seth meant it.

'I told you. One more movement, and you've chosen me to die.'

'Come on, Seth. I meant what I said this morning. We're brothers. We need to put all this behind us. We need to look out for each other. Mum and Dad sure didn't give a shit about us, but we found people who did. What would Nigel and Angela say if they could see this?'

Tom could see it in Seth's eyes. Some of the insanity had receded at the mention of their foster parents: the ones who had rescued them. The ones who had given them a modicum of hope. Tom decided to press the advantage.

'All they ever wanted for us was happiness. They wanted us to be brothers. Brothers who looked out for each other, and…'

Tom's eyes began to sting, and the tingling in his mouth intensified, spreading up the side of his face.

What was happening?

'… and… look, Seth, what I'm trying to say is I love you.'

Seth pulled the tip of the knife from his neck, wincing as he did so. More blood spewed from the wound, though it was superficial. It ran down his neck and stained the collar of his hoodie.

'It's too late, isn't it?' Seth said. 'You know what I've done. Jesus; you know I've murdered people! I'll be thrown in jail for the rest of my life, won't I?'

'No,' Tom whispered. 'I know how to play the system. We'll plead insanity, and a good lawyer will take care of the rest. I'll look after you, like I should have done all those years ago. Let me make it up to you.'

Tears welled in Seth's eyes, and he set the knife onto the table with a loud clatter. He wiped his eyes with his sleeve and smiled at Tom, snot bubbling in his nose. Outside, a car drove past, its engine revving. The exhaust backfired, making a noise like a gunshot, and Seth's head snapped in the direction of the blast.

Tom took a breath and took his chance: he launched himself across the table.

He collided with his brother with such force that Seth was thrown backwards off his feet, his elbow connecting painfully with the wall. The table had tipped, and they landed in a mess of bowls and food and solid silver cutlery. China smashed on the floor, shards splintering in all directions. Somewhere in the distance, Andy Williams was singing about the most wonderful time of the year.

Tom managed to scrabble on top of Seth and pin him to the floor. Seth flailed and rocked from side to side, trying to get free. His body was sinewy and tough, and Tom could feel the muscles straining in their extreme to get him off.

'Stop, Seth. It's over!' he shouted.

Dazed, but not quite confused, Seth managed to free a hand, and began blindly searching the floor for sharp pieces of stoneware. Before he could grasp one, Tom raised his fist and drove it into his brother's jaw. The hurt look in Seth's eyes was heartbreaking, but Tom extended his arm again and brought another punch down. Seth closed his eyes, expecting another blow to the face, but this time Tom aimed for Seth's stomach. Seth pitched forward; the breath knocked out of him. Tom pressed his advantage, turning him onto his front to negate the threat. But in the middle of trying to flip him over, something strange happened.

The tingling that had started in Tom's mouth and face was now spreading into his torso. When he tried to move his arms, it felt like they were working at half-speed, as if the air had somehow become laden with treacle. He blinked his eyes in rapid succession, and shook his head, trying to clear the feeling of nausea that had crept into his stomach.

Unable to hold himself up, he collapsed on the floor next to Seth, who was twitching and bleeding from the mouth.

'What have you done?' Tom managed to get out.

Seth smiled at him. 'I went a little more Heston than Nigella with the glaze. I added a little arsenic to season our meal.'

'Why?' Tom asked. 'Why would you do this?'

'Security,' smiled Seth. 'It's fast-acting. All of this will be over soon. You can't really have thought I'd let you get away with this. We were always going to die together, you and me.'

Tom's vision began to swim, and darkness descended. As he blacked out, he faintly noticed two things.

One, Seth had reached out for his hand and grasped it as tightly as the poison would allow.

Two, there was a loud hammering somewhere nearby...

49

Very slowly, Tom opened an eye and groaned.

The room was very white, and the harsh light streaming in through curtainless windows only served to highlight the whiteness of it all. He closed his eye again and tried to piece together what he knew.

He was either in Heaven, Hell, or a hospital ward. Judging by the constricting sheets, the thin mattress and the mingled stink of urine, disinfectant and worse, he plumped for the latter.

He cast his mind back to how he'd ended up here. Hazy, ghost-like images of a table loaded with Christmas food, a knife, a sound like a gunshot, and a fight drifted across his eyelids, *Generation Game*-style.

Summoning the courage to sit up, he hoisted his body inch by inch until he was slightly more upright than before. He felt like he might vomit, so stayed in the half-sitting position for a few minutes until his insides had righted themselves. When he opened his eyes again, bit by bit, he realised he was not alone.

'How you doing, boss?' Lauren asked.

'I've been better,' Tom rasped. 'Could you hand me the water?'

Lauren stood and poured from a jug into a small, plastic cup. She handed it to Tom, who gulped it down like a man lost in a desert. She refilled it, and this time he took small sips, appreciating the coolness in his ragged throat.

'What the hell happened to me?' Tom asked.

'You were poisoned,' Lauren said. 'By Seth.'

New spectres swam in Tom's eyes: Seth's smile, collapsing on the floor, holding hands with his murderous brother as they drifted out of consciousness together.

'Is he dead?'

Lauren shook her head. 'No, the paramedics managed to save both of you. It was touch and go, mind, but he's in custody.'

His brother. In custody. The pieces of their showdown would come back to him in days to come, but it would take years for Tom to come to terms with this, if ever. The trail of destruction Seth left in his wake, how he had used people as pawns in his deadly game, was sickening. Tom hated that the same blood ran through both their veins. Part of him wanted to see Seth, to get answers. But a bigger part of him wanted to forget that he ever had a brother.

Tom was aware that he'd been quiet for a few moments, but Lauren didn't seem to mind.

'How did you know I was in trouble?' he asked.

Lauren explained about the interview with Caitlyn, and when she'd finished, Tom burst into tears. If it hadn't been for his partner, he would've died. Her quick thinking had saved his life.

'Is there enough evidence to charge Seth? He confessed everything to me, but I didn't record it or anything.'

'There's enough. He wasn't nearly as clever as he thought. His blood was on the knife, in the recessed part where the blade joins the handle. All three victims' blood was on it, too, so we have more than enough to get it through the court.'

Tiredness fell on Tom like a veil, and a swirl of emotions raced through his brain. Was he partly responsible for the deaths? Seth had made it clear that he had held him responsible for a long time, but was he? Did he have to go on living a life tainted by his fucked-up family?

He breathed deeply, and turned to Lauren, who was standing up and retrieving her bag from the end of the bed.

'I'll leave you to it – I can't imagine what you must be feeling,' she said. 'The doctors thought you might wake up today, and I wanted to be here if you did.'

'What date is it?' he asked.

'Boxing Day. You haven't been out too long.'

'Lauren, what happened to Sophie? I only know what Natalie told us.'

'How much time do you have?' she said. 'You know about the kidnapping, and the fact it was my ex-mother-in-law. Part of me suspected that Caitlyn was Sophie's birth mother, but I've spoken to her this morning. She doesn't know the names of the adoptive parents, but she does know they were from somewhere near London.'

'What a mess,' Tom said. 'I'm so glad everyone is safe. If you ever need help with babysitting, or whatever…'

He didn't really know what he was saying, and he felt his eyelids drooping. His head grew heavy, and the sentence went unfinished. Lauren said goodbye, but he was already asleep.

Epilogue

THE NEW YEAR BROUGHT with it the promise of change.

The morning sky was streaked with pink and orange, casting an ethereal glow over the graveyard. It was calm and quiet, aside from a family of birds stationed in one of the trees doing all they could to disturb the peace.

But, to Tom, the trills and tweets were beautiful. They were the sounds of life and love, things he was glad to be alive to hear. He walked among the headstones, searching for the one that belonged to his sister. He'd realised, while lying in his hospital bed, that he had never been to see her resting place, and had vowed to correct that as soon as he was fit enough.

It had been two weeks since he was discharged from hospital. In that time, he'd been put on gardening leave pending an investigation into his performance during the Christmas Killer case.

The old, angry Tom would've nipped the investigation in the bud by telling his superiors exactly where they could get off. But, since leaving the hospital, he had worked on himself. Two weeks was hardly enough time to fundamentally change a personality, but he found quiet meditation was helping him through situations he would normally have lost the plot over.

He liked his team, and he liked Newcastle. His house in Kibblesworth was taking shape, and he was starting to like that, too. It would take some time to get over the trauma of what had unfolded in the kitchen, but he was working on it. He hoped that those in charge of his future would see the good work he had done as overriding the not so good.

He had also got in touch with Anna and extended an olive branch. He apologised for how he had treated her and promised to do better. She had accepted his apology, but made it clear that any romance between them was gone. Tom had accepted that and was simply pleased he'd had the chance to right a wrong.

At last, Tom found the plot he was looking for. The headstone was a simple affair. Black marble, with the names and dates of those buried beneath the soil engraved on it in gold lettering. It annoyed him that Rachel was buried beside his mum and dad. They hadn't given a shit about their children when they were alive, so why should they be allowed to lie forever beside one of them? Tom made a mental note to look into the legalities of moving a loved one from one grave to another.

The grass around the grave was overgrown and thickets of weeds had spread unchallenged. Tom had expected as much and had come prepared. For a while, he chopped at the jumble of roots and thorns with a pair of hedge trimmers, taking care in his work.

When it was in better shape, he knelt at the foot of the grave. He laid a bouquet of flowers at the headstone's base, and uttered apologies that were over twenty years too late. Tears fell from his eyes onto the soil.

He stayed a while, trying to remember everything about the short time he had spent with his sister. When he left, he did so with a promise that he would visit more regularly.

As he got in his car, his phone rang.

It was Natalie.

He took a deep breath, and vowed that, whatever decision had been made, he would accept it. Even if it meant the end of his career.

He answered and placed the phone against his ear.

'Tom,' Natalie said. 'I've got some news...'

Acknowledgements

I ALWAYS FIND THIS very hard to do, as there are countless people that I am sure I will miss. If you were expecting to be mentioned here, but aren't, know that it was a moment of brain fog, and not deliberate! Thank you to the following:

Firstly, to the HarperNorth team. From the moment Daisy and I discussed the idea of *The Killer's Christmas List*, I knew we were onto a winner. Daisy's excitement and passion for the book shone through. The book has been such a joy to work on, and made immeasurably better by her edits and incisive suggestions. Thank you to the rest of the team: Gen for her enthusiasm, Megan for putting up with my emails, and particularly Alice, who I worked alongside closely on the publicity side of things. It has been an absolute joy.

To agent extraordinaire David Headley. I sent him a speculative email about representation, laughing at the mere prospect of a reply. Reply he did, and the rest is history. David has been a wonderful sounding board: chock full of advice, and a huge support during the entire process. I am very excited for what is to come in the future, and look forward to a long and successful partnership. Thanks also to the rest of the DHH team, for making me feel very welcome (and for plying me with unbelievably good books, Harry Illingworth!).

To Sean Coleman, who made my dreams come true in 2020. He took a chance on my debut *A Wash of Black*, and believed in me enough to publish nine more books. I am so proud of what we achieved together – Sean changed my life, and I will never forget that. Thanks also to Rob Parker. Rob is such an incredible support, not just to me, but to crime writers nationwide. During the pandemic, the three of us started a podcast called The Blood Brothers Podcast. Through it, we talked to the biggest names in the world of crime writing, kept each other sane, and had a whale of a time doing it. The three of us shall be brothers forevermore. Thanks to all the guests who gave up their time to chat to us. I walked away every week renewed and inspired to meet the blank page.

To Steven Kedie and Jonathan Whitelaw. I probably talk to these two more than anyone else, including my family, and it's mostly a load of nonsense about football. But, you are both legends and I wouldn't be without you. Thank you for the writing chat, the conversations about craft, movie talk (I finally watched *Heat*!) and everything else. Just a shame you support the wrong teams, but nobody is perfect.

To the birthday cake of faithfulness – you guys are the best! Thanks for the years of friendship, encouragement and support.

To Graham Bartlett for the policing advice. There were bits of procedure I was unsure on, and Graham was great at offering advice on how it would be done in real life. If you are a writer, and need some of his sage advice, do look him up and get in touch. Any policing mistakes left in there are my own.

To Benjamin Amos, for letting me use his wonderfully fitting lyrics at the front of the book. I've known Ben since my teens, and have always been a fan of the bands he was in – from Delayed (which I was a member of very briefly), to The Good Fight, Sullivan and Gold, and now his solo career. His latest album, *Letters*, is such a beautiful, heart-felt set of songs, and well worth your time.

To those who have read what I've written in the past, thank you. A special thank you to Andy Wormald who has been unbelievably supportive, right from the start of my writing career. We do it for people like you! And, to you, reading this now, thanks for taking a chance. There are so many books out there, and it means the world that you've taken a chance on mine. I hope you have / have had a lovely Christmas!

Finally, to Sarah, Emma and Sophie. My beautiful family – thank you for everything! I love you all – you mean the world to me.

Chris Frost – 23.9.23

Harper North

would like to thank the following staff and contributors for their involvement in making this book a reality:

Fionnuala Barrett
Samuel Birkett
Peter Borcsok
Ciara Briggs
Sarah Burke
Alan Cracknell
Jonathan de Peyer
Anna Derkacz
Tom Dunstan
Kate Elton
Sarah Emsley
Dom Forbes
Simon Gerratt
Monica Green
Natassa Hadjinicolaou
CJ Harter
Megan Jones

Jean-Marie Kelly
Taslima Khatun
Sammy Luton
Rachel McCarron
Molly McNevin
Ben McConnell
Petra Moll
Alice Murphy-Pyle
Adam Murray
Genevieve Pegg
Agnes Rigou
Florence Shepherd
Eleanor Slater
Angela Snowden
Emma Sullivan
Katrina Troy
Daisy Watt

For more unmissable reads,
sign up to the HarperNorth newsletter at
www.harpernorth.co.uk

or find us on Twitter at
@HarperNorthUK

**Harper
North**